Advance Praise for *Vin...*

"Smart. Sexy. Unputdownable. *Vintage & Vogue* hooked me on page one."—Tessa Layne, USA Today best-selling romance author

Visit us at www.boldstrokesbooks.com

VINTAGE & VOGUE

by

Kelly & Tana Fireside

2023

VINTAGE & VOGUE

ISBN 13: 978-1-63679-448-8

This Trade Paperback Original Is Published By
Bold Strokes Books, Inc.
P.O. Box 249
Valley Falls, NY 12185

First Edition: June 2023

CREDITS
Editor: Cindy Cresap
Production Design: Susan Ramundo
Cover Design By Ink Spiral Design

Acknowledgments

We've written this book at least six times. Seriously. Each time there were the same characters, same basic plot, same small town. But, when we started it, we had no idea what we were doing. So we can't publish this final version without first thanking the people who helped us figure it out.

Our first readers—BM, DC, EW, KLH, KK, MM—cheered us on, but also gave us (in some cases copious) editorial notes that made us think and challenged us to do better, not just in how we told the story but in how we handled the important issues this story addresses. This little group of readers was made up of very big brains, open hearts, and diverse perspectives—just like the heroines of Owen Station. We appreciate and admire you all.

Likewise, the folks at Bold Strokes—Radclyffe, Sandy, Ruth, and especially our editor, Cindy—have provided exactly the kind of coaching we hoped they would when we decided to join the team. Thanks for seeing what this story could be, and giving us the tools and opportunity to make it happen.

And, Jennifer—you challenged us to write this book and coached us all along the way. But, most of all, you helped us see how important it is to tell stories like these—about strong women who have agency and control over our own bodies—especially now, at a time when our rights are increasingly under attack. And you reminded us about the power of happy endings—because without joy, love, and hope we cannot act to make things better.

We also want to acknowledge the importance of Arizona—and the beautiful mountain town we once called home—for inspiring us with its quirky characters, complicated history, and rich cultural diversity. All of the characters in this book are fictional. But the landscape, architecture, climate, social and political issues, and even many of the historical details are real. We love this part of the country. Out here, life is as wide open as the vast, majestic sunsets. It fills us with awe. Sometimes, it also makes us cry. We hope that our love, care for, and belief in this place and the people who live here comes through.

Finally, to our kids—Emma, Kirsten, Ethan. No matter what wild idea we dream up and do next, you're there for it. We're so thankful to be your moms.

Dedication

To all the writers out there—keep going.

Prologue

1905

Celestina's hands trembled as she tore open the envelope Felipe had smashed into her hand through her bedroom window just after midnight.

"Hurry, cousin," he whispered, looking over his shoulder to be certain no one had followed. "Do not delay. I will be waiting for you at the stable."

By the light of her candle, she recognized the handwriting at once. It was as loose and reckless and free as the redheaded author. Everything Celestina was not.

My dearest C.

There is not much time. My father insists on this marriage, though my heart is breaking at the thought of our impending separation. I fear that just one hope remains. I have arranged for us to meet Señor Verduzco tonight. He is here in Nogales from Oro Blanco, preaching a new faith, one divorced from the cruel constraints of Mother Church. They say that he wields the power to make tables move and bean pots talk, that in his presence chairs write the wonders of a new world and a new creed, that he stands in the gap between what we see and what is yet to be. We will ask him to join us together in the next world, even if it cannot be in this one. Your cousin will bring you to me. Come quickly. Come now.

My heart is forever yours.

H.

Celestina slid her hand beneath the feather pillow on her bed, feeling for the silky cotton pouch that held a silver brooch with a simple pearl inset. A reminder that beauty can be born of pain. She tucked the pouch into the pocket she had sewn inside her riding skirt. Then she pulled on her leather gauntlets and boots and slipped quietly through the window. After making haste down the dusty road to her family's stable, she found Felipe sitting astride his mount. He had already saddled her favorite mare. Shadows from the moonlight deepened the ragged creases in his brow.

"Do not look so worried, cousin." She hoisted herself up onto the saddle and took the reins. She spoke with a confidence she did not feel.

Forever was a dangerous promise to make.

CHAPTER ONE

HEAT WAVE

Hazel stepped into Banter & Brew, took a deep breath, and squeezed her eyes shut for a second to let the aroma of Knox's freshly ground coffee transport her back to Grandma's kitchen. She was eight or nine years old. *The Princess Diaries* was in her lap. Bacon sizzling. Percolator on the stove. Sunday's paper spread across the table. Frank Sinatra, Grandma's favorite, crooned on the antique turntable in the living room. Grandpa in that raggedy flannel shirt—the one that smelled like WD-40, which he used for everything, including the time Hazel got Bubble Yum stuck in her long red hair and went *berserk* thinking it would all have to get cut off. Dad doing a clumsy Moonwalk, trying to get Mom to dance with him. Everyone together. Healthy. Happy. Alive.

Those were the days.

Which was why Hazel would have done almost anything to hang on to them.

She had scurried into the coffee shop, Owen Station's first and only micro roaster, just as the lunch crowd was straggling back out into the brutal July heat. She set her own hours so technically she could have lunch whenever she wanted, but she liked being open during the traditional lunch hour just in case somebody needed to drop off an overdue book or pick up a new paperback. Plus, she looked forward to having Knox more or less to herself.

He tossed an easy smile from behind the enormous, gleaming espresso machine, wiping his hands on the edge of his apron. "Afternoon, Hazel. How's my favorite librarian?"

"And your oldest friend." She slapped the vintage copper counter as she hopped up onto her stool.

"Hazel, how on earth could I ever forget?" He reached across to ruffle her hair.

"Hey now!" She ducked and swatted his hand away. His boyish smile was annoyingly irresistible.

Once in a while, somebody new in town—like a guest renting her little casita for the weekend—would make the mistake of assuming she and Knox were a couple. It never bothered her. She made that mistake herself once upon a time, for about five minutes junior year. Then she realized she'd rather date his sister. It took a few years before she was ready to share that with anyone else. But Knox? Nobody knew more of her secrets than he did. Oh, Delaney knew a lot, sure. But they had only been close friends since Hazel came back to Owen Station after college, about a decade ago, when Mom got sick. Besides, with so many people sitting in her chair at the salon, Delaney had become the town's biggest busybody. Even though she kept some of Hazel's darkest secrets—and Hazel loved her for that—it was Knox she trusted to know them all.

He handed her a towel to wipe her brow and poured a tall glass of water, which she downed before it even had time to sweat. Then he tipped the pitcher and filled it again. "Still hot as hell out there?"

"Well, it feels a lot like Phoenix."

"Same difference."

She snickered. Phoenix *was* hell. Too full of people. Too full of traffic. Altogether too full of itself. Just about everybody in her little town, three hours south of the city, would have agreed.

Knox took a swipe at the counter with a wet rag.

"What'll it be, Hazel? The usual?"

She pretend-flipped her hair back and sniffed. "Do you *even* have to ask?"

The corner of his mouth ticked upward as he pulled out the chicken Caesar wrap he had all ready for her and slid it across the counter. "Oh, I don't know, Hazel dear. I keep hoping one of these Tuesdays you'll go wild and ask for my grilled cheese panini."

"Not likely. *Mondays* are grilled cheese. And, by the way, I am *very* happy you agreed to add it to your menu." She arched an eyebrow to remind him of how he argued with her even after she searched high and low for that Edicraft sandwich maker, circa 1930, and bought it for him at an estate sale outside of Patagonia from people who had no idea what they were selling.

"Yeah, yeah, I know." His eyes rolled but his dimples deepened. "Wednesdays are quiche, Thursdays turkey subs, Fridays tuna fish. There's nothing my Hazel likes better than a routine of historical proportions."

So what if he was making fun. Her reflection in his twinkling eyes grinned back at her. Plus, he had a point. Life had become predictable. Maybe even a little boring. At least that's what Delaney was always saying.

It didn't used to be this way. Hazel had always been on the lookout for adventure. The exact opposite of that mousy little Mia Thermopolis. Hazel never would have run away from the challenge of being a princess. She would have filled *her* diary with tales of exploration and adventure. Like that night after a junior high dance, when she convinced everyone to sneak into the shuttered Mile High Mine, which everyone knew was haunted.

Knox pried off the boards and in they went, just deep enough to spook themselves silly. When he screamed because he thought he saw Headless Sam, the 1912 miner who stood a little too close to a blast, they spilled outside, tripping over each other in the moonlight like jackrabbits, laughing until their sides hurt. When Hazel went off to the U of A to get an English degree—with a minor in library science because, although she was daring, she was practical—she was secretly hoping to have crazy sex with as many sorority girls as possible. She begged Knox to come with her. Instead, he surprised everyone and married Lace, his senior prom date, and got a job bussing tables at the truck stop out near the highway.

But that was all long ago, before responsibility and freedom had a fight to the death over who would get to finish her story. Freedom lost.

Now, Fridays meant tuna.

Somewhere between coming home to take care of Mom after the diagnosis and that soul-crushing day a few years later, when Father Mike sprayed holy water all over everywhere and Mom's casket disappeared into the ground, something happened. Knox said she was haunted by memories. Delaney said she was stuck in the past.

Whatever.

What's wrong with loving where you came from, anyway?

Nothing. Unless it keeps you from figuring out where you're supposed to be.

Oh my God. This is stupid.

Hazel shook her head trying to scatter the uncomfortable questions piling up around her.

She loved Knox and his grilled paninis and her library and her routine and going out for girls' night once a month with Delaney and Lace and the little house she inherited and this town. That didn't sound like being stuck, did it?

She couldn't deny it, though. The weeks and months were starting to bleed into each other with the monotony of endless, long days under a blazing desert sun. She was past ready for a personal monsoon. Or at least some cloud cover and a few sprinkles. Something to break the building heat. Anything. Sometimes Hazel felt almost combustible. A marshmallow inside a microwave. But that wasn't something she was ready to admit out loud, even to Knox. She could hardly admit it to herself.

Hazel took off her heavy, black-rimmed glasses and used a corner of her white cotton tee to clean them. "Seriously, Knox, I can't remember it ever being this hot out there. I told Delaney I was ready to take my lunch to go and eat in her break room at the salon if your old swamp cooler wasn't up to snuff."

He winced. "I've been worried about that myself. It's 105 out there today. They're predicting triple digits for the next week and still no sign of rain."

She pushed her glasses back on and twirled around on the stool to look at the empty sidewalk on the flip side of the café's window.

It hadn't looked like this since the year the world shut down. But things were getting back to normal. And it was unusual to see so few people on Main Street, even during low season.

That was mostly due to Dad, thank you very much.

Hazel's mom always sat a little taller when she told the story, and Hazel knew it by heart.

After the last mine closed in 1978, Owen Station nearly died. There had been more than eight hundred students in Mom's junior year class that year. At graduation, the following year, there were three hundred and forty-two. They picked "Stairway to Heaven" as their senior class song, an ode to disappearing hopes and dreams. But Dad had seen the future. He knew he needed a different plan than working the mines, and he'd already gone off to college three years before. When he came back with a degree in business, he proposed marriage, and went to work saving the town. He rallied everyone together. Got the few families with money, who hadn't moved away, to invest. And almost single-handedly he ensured the preservation of those magnificent historic buildings on Main Street. By the time Hazel was born, Main Street was alive again, more or less, with tourists strolling through art galleries, boutiques, and gift shops. At night, they trailed through town on one of half a dozen ghost tours. Because, what's an old mining town without ghosts? Dad never got to see the rest of his vision realized. His heart gave out when Hazel was just thirteen. Everybody said he literally died saving Owen Station. And there was no one like him to fill his shoes.

But Dad's dream of preserving their beloved town didn't die. Hazel wouldn't let it.

She spun back around toward Knox. "I was going through boxes of old periodicals yesterday, and I ran across a copy of that travel magazine that put us on the cover a few years ago. Remember that?"

"Of course I do," he beamed.

Knox opened the coffee shop not long after Hazel moved back after college and got his real estate license not long after that. Both businesses took off after that article came out, and the increased traffic helped him finally pay off the renovations at Banter &

Brew. That's when Hazel started doing short-term rentals of her guesthouse, too. All those tourists needed places to stay, and she sure needed the money.

"I had forgotten that article was called 'Owen Station: Small Town with the Best Year-Round Weather.'" Hazel picked up her chicken Caesar wrap. "That seems ridiculous on a day like today."

"To be fair, it's usually eighty degrees at this time of year and glorious." Knox leaned lazily against the counter. "I think this heat is making everybody in town a little extra. Yesterday the Murphy boys were in here planning a sidewalk egg frying contest. I guess there's some town outside of Yuma, where it's always a hundred plus degrees, that's been doing it for years. And, this morning, Alabama Joe and his posse from the encampment up at Gulch Haven were in the park, shaking their booties and singing 'Purple Rain,' trying to get the sky to open."

Hazel snorted, glad she had already swallowed that first bite, and wiped her mouth with a napkin. "I hope the Prince of Rain heard them." Sometimes she cracked herself up.

"Yeah, me too."

Then Knox's smile disappeared. "Less funny, though. And speaking of *extra*. This morning Sirus and some members of your Save Owen Station group were in here. It sounds like they might be planning some kind of protest."

Hazel took a deep breath. "Seriously?"

Knox nodded, shrugged, and shoved his hands into his pockets, like he was trying to keep them clean.

Hazel dropped the wrap on her plate and squinted at him.

"You know perfectly well, Knox, that I agreed to help Sirus start SOS because his family helped my dad save Main Street. And we *needed* a historical preservation society in this town."

She spread her hands open like she had nothing to be ashamed of.

Knox studied her face, squinting back, silent.

She blinked and pushed her glasses up, which were slipping down her suddenly clammy face. "I know Sirus can be a little hard to take…"

Knox's eyebrows shot up to the top of his forehead. "Sirus is a bully. And he thinks just because he owns this block, his voice is more important than anyone else's. It's gotten even worse over the past few years. I think he's been spending too much time listening to the crazies out there—the other day I told him to unplug his TV. Anyway, Sirus couldn't care less about our buildings—he just wants to make sure nothing in this town ever changes. Because the more it changes, the less important he becomes. But some of us—including people like me, who are trying to grow our businesses—actually think change is good for Owen Station."

"Change for the sake of change is never good, Knox. Remember all those city people who swooped into town during the pandemic, thinking they wanted small town life? All they did was buy up land, knock down historic buildings, and build those ugly homes. Then, once it was over, they got bored, went back to the city, and turned their houses into short-term rentals. How is *that* good for Owen Station? They've driven real estate prices up so high that real Owenites can hardly afford to—"

"*Real* Owenites?" Knox tilted his head sideways and looked at her like she just sprouted prickly pear on the tip of her nose.

"You know what I mean." Hazel's ears tingled and the muscles in her shoulders stretched rubber band tight.

Knox kept staring, his unspoken words shooting upward and then nose-diving in her direction. Even though he had lived in Owen Station since he was seven, he was still considered a newcomer by the old-timers who ran things. And he hated it.

"I'm just saying there is a right way to change and a wrong way." Hazel sat up straight, like her mom would have. "When my dad—"

"Okay, that's enough, Hazel. I know all about it. Your dad was a hero. Rallied the town. Saved these old buildings. Did it without needing outside help."

Knox's face softened. "But that was a long time ago. And, except for my little coffee shop, Lace's toy store, the tequila tasting room next door, and a handful of other businesses, nothing much new has happened here since then. In fact, I think things are getting worse. If a town's not growing, it's dying. And we're not growing. Remember when the Millers wanted to retire last year? They couldn't find anyone to buy their antique shop. Just boarded it up, sold their house, and bought an RV. It's all they could afford. Last I heard they were Boondocking outside of Quartzite. At least tourists buy things and drink my coffee. At the moment, that's the only thing keeping Owen Station alive. I understand your concerns, but I haven't heard any better ideas coming from you or your SOS friends for giving this town the boost it needs."

Knox dropped his eyes and leaned forward to pick up a towel, which he used to start rubbing circles into the counter. It sucked when they would get into fights. She knew he thought so, too.

"I just love this town so much."

"I do, too," he said. But when his normally warm brown eyes met hers again, they were cool as augite.

"I think the work my dad started here is worth continuing. Don't you?"

"Your dad didn't *preserve* Owen Station, Hazel. He did everything he could to help this town *survive*."

Then he took his rag and shifted over to clear some dishes off the counter a few stools down.

This was an old argument. Usually, it ended in a draw. But lately, she was starting to wonder if maybe Knox had a point.

Silently chewing her bottom lip, she thought about last night's SOS meeting. It was business-as-usual at first. They approved the minutes from last month and reviewed the very simple financial statements. Then they looked at the agenda for the upcoming town council meeting and made a list of those properties they wanted to research, in order to be ready for the call-to-audience part of the meeting when they would get to state their objections. But then, right before they were ready to adjourn, Sirus said Doc Adams had something to say. Doc was the large animal vet who stopped in the library for a new mystery often enough to make Hazel think she might have a crush on her. Doc looked a little sheepish, but Sirus sort of pushed her shoulder to get her out of her seat and nodded his head.

"Go on, Doc," he said. "Tell 'em."

Doc finally stood up and cleared her throat. She looked nervously down at Sirus and then at the rest of group. "As you all know, I was born and raised here. But then I left for school and never looked back. I've lived on both coasts and three cities in between, and I'm here to testify that there is no place as special as this town of ours. It's more than those beautiful buildings on Main Street—which we have Hazel's dad to thank for preserving. It's our culture...our way of life. In Owen Station, everybody knows everybody, and we take care of each other. I see all the problems and crime out there, and it makes me thankful for the town we've built together. We need to make sure we don't lose the things that make Owen Station special."

It made all the little hairs on the back of Hazel's neck wave, trying to get her attention. Partly it was what Doc said. Hazel loved Owen Station. But it wasn't perfect.

Mostly what bothered her, though, was Sirus.

He was manipulating people. And, according to Knox, he was making plans she wasn't part of. Instead of bringing the town together, like Dad had done, it felt like Sirus was pulling it apart. Hazel knew she should have talked to him right after the meeting instead of being in such a hurry to get home.

Home to *what,* anyway? A crossword puzzle and a glass of stale boxed wine?

It was super hard with Mr. Serious a few feet away, but she scrunched up her face and tried to shake the feeling that she'd started something she'd end up regretting. What could she do about it right in that moment, anyway? Not a thing.

The guy on the stool next to her looked like he was getting ready to pay up. He definitely wasn't a tourist. Big hands. Cheap jeans. A lingering smell of gasoline. Probably a trucker carrying a load of vegetables up from the border.

Hazel leaned in his direction. "This little town has quite a history, you know."

Lucky fellow couldn't have known he was sitting next to Owen Station's resident expert on everything old—and someone in serious need of a distraction.

His unintelligible grunt gave her permission to keep going. She turned her head to catch his reaction to one of her favorite facts. "We used to be the largest town west of the Mississippi."

His disbelieving side-eye was a shot of lighter fluid on a tiny flame. "I know! It's hard to believe, but it's true. Back in the early 1900s, this place was booming thanks to the copper mines. Big department stores. A stock exchange. Oh, there were plenty of bars and the brothels, but there was culture, too. Theater! Architecture... the first Otis elevator in the state was installed right here on—"

Knox's eyes darted toward the door, an uncharacteristic grimace stretched across his face, just as a blast of heat hit Hazel in the back. Like someone opened the door on a 450-degree oven and couldn't decide whether or not to pull out the pie. She interrupted her story, which made the trucker look very relieved, and spun around on her stool, following Knox's eyes as he roared.

"Close the door, already! My swamp cooler isn't big enough to take on Main Street, too."

A woman behind fancy dark sunglasses was standing in the open doorway, slowly looking around like she knew she was in the right place, but it was all wrong.

Knox's face twisted as his voice rose two octaves. "Please?"

Looking like she belonged on a red carpet, the woman finally closed the door and stepped all the way inside, pausing dramatically, shoulders as straight as a saguaro, chin high. Hazel stopped breathing as the newcomer shoved her sunglasses up onto the top of her head and *for real* flipped her lusciously long, jet-black hair over her shoulder.

L.U.S.C.I.O.U.S. Having a delicious taste or smell. Richly luxurious. Sexually attractive. LUSCIOUS.

Reciting dictionary definitions to herself usually helped Hazel focus when she was uncomfortable. It helped her stay grounded.

This time it wasn't working.

She glanced at Knox to see if he saw what she was seeing.

With a shaky smile, he reached over and patted her hand, looking a shade paler than he did just seconds before. "Whoa there, old friend. I don't think she's your type."

"I'm not so sure about that," Hazel whispered. Her gaydar was ding, ding, dinging. She gave his hand a squeeze and then patted him back. "You don't exactly have a good track record when it comes to knowing the difference." She was referring of course to his marriage to Lace. "But she is *definitely* out of my league."

Hazel had never seen anything—or anyone—like this woman before. A tight royal blue dress hugged every curve. Legs too long to be for real. And that attitude. Seriously? Like she owned the ground she walked on.

Hazel licked her lips. She was pretty sure she didn't like anything about this woman, but her body wasn't getting the memo. Hazel's heart thumped against her breastbone and heat rose in her cheeks. A warm tingling sensation crawled slowly from her thighs down to her toes, then shot back up, lighting her middle on fire.

"Knox..." Her voice was raspy. And, although she was talking to him, her eyes never left the terrifying stranger in the doorway. "Get me another glass of water, would you please? It's freaking hot in here."

Knox pulled the top of his Banter & Brew apron up over his face to wipe the sweat from his brow. "It most certainly is."

There weren't many customers left inside the coffee shop, but those who lingered were mesmerized. Every eye was on the stranger as she slowly surveyed the room. She grazed past each one and skimmed right over Knox until her eyes finally—and what felt like inevitably—pinged Hazel.

Hazel swallowed hard. Pinned to the stool, she couldn't move. But she should have. She should have gotten up right then and there and gone running in the opposite direction. As fast and far away as possible. Every red flag was waving, every warning bell blared, the microwave beeped wildly, and all the smoke detectors were screaming. This stranger wasn't just a spring shower or even a summer monsoon. She was a once-in-a-century hurricane plowing up through Baja and across California to hammer the thirsty Arizona desert with flash flooding and winds that snatched you up into its irresistible, swirling vortex and wouldn't let you go. She was trouble.

T.R.O.U.B.L.E. Disturbance. Disorder. Turbulence. Tumult. TROUBLE.

The exact opposite of what Owen Station's most responsible, routine-loving librarian needed.

CHAPTER TWO

POWER LINES

S ena glared at her phone and read the email again to make
sure she was seeing the address right.

Owen Station?

Check.

Main Street?

She held a hand over her eyes to block the sun and studied the
faded street sign at the corner for the tenth time.

Check.

Five hundred and forty-seven?

Oh, for God's sake. Check!

The number was right there in front of her, but the name on the
heavy glass door, right *below* the number 547, said Banter & Brew.
What it definitely did *not* say was Reynolds Real Estate Agency,
"Voted #1 for friendliest service five years in a row!" according to
her Realtor's email signature.

What the absolute fuck.

Directing your client to the wrong address wasn't just unfriendly.
It was stupid. Like hitting "reply all" in an email scorching your
boss when it was clearly only meant for the one person you knew
would agree with you. Sena hadn't met *Mr. Reynolds* in person
yet, but in the transactions she'd had with him up to this point—
all electronically, of course, because nothing was a bigger waste of

time than talking on the phone—he had seemed like someone she could do business with. She bought a house from him sight unseen, hadn't she? Sena was figuring he'd be her first stop when she started making moves. She had big plans. And she planned to move fast.

Your loss, Reynolds.

Sena shoved the phone deep into her sleek Prada bag, right next to her ten-inch tablet and noise-canceling ear buds, and turned around to survey her new town. Or at least the three or four blocks of it she could see.

Just what she expected.

This was the main drag. Owen Station's historic district. And it was all that was left of a town that used to be known for its hustle. A couple of old saloons with greasy food and rooms for rent. A string of antique stores, art galleries, and souvenir shops selling Owen Station swag stamped with sayings like "Ghosts don't believe in you either." All squeezed into the street-level storefronts of impressive but half-empty buildings from the early 1900s. They must have cost a fortune to restore. But that clearly happened decades ago.

Sena put her hands on her hips and scrunched her nose, like she was afraid she might catch something. For the first time, a nanoparticle of doubt zinged through her head. It started in her taste buds. Shopping, she could do online. Entertainment? She'd be too busy to notice there wasn't any. But where in the hell did people in this town *eat*? She dug back into her bag for the phone and pulled up her task list to add *Look for a personal chef* and marked it *Important*. For the past decade, anything she wanted was a quick Uber away. Ethiopian meets Bolivian. Japanese meets Italian. The best seafood on the planet. There were more three-star Michelins in the Bay Area than New York City. And she'd eaten at the chef's table of a dozen James Beard nominees. She sure as hell wasn't going to live on fried mushrooms and cheese fries. A shiver went through her body just thinking about it, even though it was a hundred and fuck degrees.

Sena leaned forward and took another long look up and down the street. No sign of a real estate office anywhere. Across the street, she looked up at the crown jewel of the historic district. The public library. Three massive stories high. Huge wooden doors at the entrance were at the top of a wide stone staircase on the second floor. Obviously, it was built before accessibility was an issue. Not that anyone was clamoring to get in. The place looked abandoned. So did the whole town, for that matter. Not a tourist or even a local in sight. Well, no wonder. It was too damn hot to be walking around outside. It was time to make a move.

The coffee shop.

Maybe somebody inside would know where to find her missing Realtor.

Sena checked her reflection in the glass door and ran her hands down the front of her dress-to-kill, mid-thigh, *very* expensive bodycon. Going easy on the jewelry was a good call. She wanted all eyes on those curves. Genetically, they came to her from her mother. But Sena knew how to use them. Nothing was more exhilarating than the panic on someone's face when they realized her mind was even deadlier than her hips. Using her fingertips, she swept her hair back away from her face, threw her chin up in the air, pushed her shoulders back, and thrust open the door of Banter & Brew.

She gave her eyes a minute to adjust after the blinding sun. And, then. Wow.

Wow. Wow. Wow.

That woman. Perched on a stool at the counter. Skin the color of her mother's homemade crema. Fiery red hair, all mussed up, like she'd spent the day running her hands through it. She had a kind of retro chic thing going on. A simple tee, penny loafers, a pencil skirt. Like she stepped right out of a vintage *I Love Lucy* episode. Sena's eyes widened behind her dark glasses and she moistened her lips with the tip of her tongue.

Well, hello there, beautiful. I wouldn't mind being your Ricky Ricardo.

The black-rimmed glasses on the bridge of Little Lucy's nose did make her look a bit like one of the coders who scampered around Silicon Valley. Or a librarian. Hopefully, a naughty one.

Maybe this old town was going to end up being more fun than she thought.

Sena tore her eyes away for a moment to scan the room. Not much—and no one else interesting—to see. Exposed brick walls. A few Banter & Brew logo tees and mugs for sale. No ghost souvenirs—that was something, anyway. Mismatched tables and chairs. A small kitchen in the back that smelled more like pastries than cheese fries, thank God. Some board games and a rickety bookshelf with a sign on it. Take one—Leave one. And, oh. A tall white guy in an apron yelling…at her.

Are you kidding me right now?

Sena didn't even bother flicking an eye in his direction. She slid her Givenchy aviators to the top of her head like a boss, straightened her back, tossed her hair over her shoulder, and let the door close behind her. The sharp sound of clicking heels ricocheted through the shop as she strode across the refurbished wooden floor.

Sena Abrigo had arrived in Owen Station.

"I'm looking for the Reynolds Real Estate Agency," she demanded, inserting herself between a man at the counter wearing a trucker hat and sexy Lucille Ball, whose mouth was in the shape of an O. As in, *Oh my God.* Sena was used to this reaction but still had a hard time not laughing.

Thankfully, the guy behind the counter had stopped yelling. Instead, he was beaming at her like a fifth grader crushing for the first time.

"You found me. I—I mean, you found it. The real estate agency. Oh, for God's sake!" The guy steadied himself against the counter and took a deep breath. "Let's try this again. I'm Knox Reynolds, owner of this fine establishment *and* your friendly neighborhood Realtor. This is my oldest friend and our town librarian, Hazel Butler."

Sena stole a sideways glance at the redhead.

No shit, a librarian. Totally called it.

"And…" Knox paused dramatically, opening his arms as wide as the goofy smile on his face. "I bet you're Sena."

She slowly shifted her focus back to Knox and dropped her bag on the counter with a thud. "It's not *See*-na, Mr. Reynolds. It's *Seh*-na. My father named me after a powerful ancient empire. It means *bringing heaven to earth.*" She felt the thrill of having every eye in the place glued to her. "You're *welcome.*"

The poor guy's ears turned bright red as her pronouncement reverberated. She knew they'd be talking about Sena Abrigo's grand entrance for years to come.

"Uh...um—" he finally managed to mumble. "It's good to meet you in person *Seh*-na. Welcome to Owen Station. And, please, call me Knox."

Sena kept her gaze fixed on the Realtor-slash-barista as he stammered, but she shifted her weight just enough to allow her to graze Hazel's bare arm with her own. It was so subtle that no one else would even notice, but a bolt of electricity arched between them. Like power lines blown together in a dust storm. A surge of energy exploded within Sena's groin, blasting heat up into her belly and down her legs. Beside her, Hazel shivered, and a gasp, barely audible, escaped her lips. Sena almost felt sorry for her. But not sorry enough to pull away.

As if nothing unusual was happening between her and the redhead—or between her legs—Sena slapped an open hand on the counter, expecting it to be filled.

"I'm here to pick up my keys."

Knox tittered nervously. "Well, I have good news and bad news. Which would you like first?"

He had managed to put a crooked grin on his face, but Sena was careful to remain expressionless. The jury was out on this guy. If she had to guess, she'd say just another example of predictable mediocrity. She'd seen plenty of that in Silicon Valley. There was no reason to make this easy for him.

"The bad news."

"Okay." He took a deep swallow. "The workers aren't quite finished with your new home. Houses here in Owen Station are all a little wonky. You would be, too, if you were a century old."

That's doubtful.

But, please, go on.

Knox chuckled nervously and cleared his throat. He was sweating so badly wet spots started to form under his arms. "Well.

Anyway. They ran into a problem with the copper pipes under your main bathroom. It's not a big deal, but it is going to take them a week or so before it's ready." He paused, flinching, clearly prepared to be eaten alive.

Instead, Sena remained calm. She knew that would be even more terrifying. "And what's the *good* news?"

Her tone would have frightened a lesser man. It always did. Instead, unexpectedly, Knox's face exploded in boyish enthusiasm.

"Oh! That! I am proud to inform you that I have the best rhubarb pie in the state right here in this shop. And I'm giving you one on the house."

Dammit. The guy may or may not have been an idiot, but he made it hard to maintain a scowl. "Oh, what the hell. I'll take a piece now. But what am I going to do for the next week or so while I'm waiting for my house?"

Emphasis on *week*. Now that she was in town, she would project-manage the shit out of things.

"Good question," he said, a playful smile on his face. "You *could* stay with me…"

Sena shot him a look that had wilted dicks in three states. He didn't need to be told twice.

"I'm just kidding, Sena," he said sheepishly. "Don't worry. We'll figure something out."

Sena had been ignoring trucker hat, who had been ogling her while watching the exchange, like all he needed was a bowl of popcorn. But it was time for him to go. Sena snapped her head in his direction. "Do you *need* something?"

He winced like she'd just crushed his balls, threw twelve bucks on the counter, and fast-tracked it out of there. Knox laughed, probably relieved it wasn't him on the receiving end, then scooped up the cash and headed down the counter to make the deposit.

Sena and Hazel were alone.

Sena shimmied up onto the trucker's vacated stool and spun around to face Hazel, who responded by appearing to study what was left of her lunch. So, Sena clasped her fingers across her stomach, leaned an elbow on the counter, and let herself appreciate the view.

She slowly traced the profile of Hazel's heart-shaped face, skipping across the freckles on her rosy cheeks and off the end of her tiny, kissable nose.

How long can she pretend not to notice she's being stared at?
A long-ass time, apparently.

Sena's gaze traveled lower, down Hazel's slender neck, across her shoulders, to her chest, where very perky nipples poked through a soft cotton tee.

Still, Hazel didn't move. She hunched over her plate, as if frozen in place, staring at her half-eaten wrap through wide, unblinking eyes—that mouth of hers apparently stuck in a permanent O shape. Beads of sweat dotted her upper lip. Heavy framed glasses slipped down her nose.

Sena stifled a laugh, leaned in close enough to smell Hazel's lavender soap, and purred just loudly enough for Hazel…and no one else…to hear.

"*Come* here much?"

Hazel's breath burst out of her lungs, as if she'd been holding it for the past ten minutes, which she actually might have been. She covered her mouth with her hands, trying to stifle a coughing fit of giggles as her cheeks turned as red as the hair on her head.

Sena leaned forward and picked up Hazel's glass. It was hard not to feel a little sympathetic. "Here, have some water."

Hazel's sparkling blue eyes peered at Sena over the top of the glass as she took a few slow sips. Then she placed it gingerly back on the counter and turned to meet Sena's gaze head-on with a cheeky smile and a slow, playful drawl.

"Sorry, *Seh*-na. Just an itchy throat. It's pretty dry up here in the mountains, before the monsoons start. But, yes, as a matter of fact, I do *come* here often."

So, okay. Maybe she had underestimated the librarian. Hazel was a flirt. Game on.

"It seems nice here," Sena observed coolly, pretending to look around. She'd already determined that nothing in the place was more interesting than the woman sitting next to her.

Hazel seemed ready to play. She crossed her arms and matched Sena's practiced monotone. "So, you're new in town?"

"Yes, I'm new in town." Sena cocked her chin and peered down her nose at Hazel. "What gave me away? Asking Señor Tall, Dark, and Handsome for my new house key?"

Mischief flickered in Hazel's bright blue eyes. "Actually, it's the shoes."

Sena sat back on her stool, impressed. "Really? You don't say."

"Christian Louboutins. Black leather, probably from Italy, impossibly expensive. Yeah, you're not from around here." One eyebrow raised triumphantly, a tiny smile frolicked across Hazel's face, and she winked. The woman was full of surprises.

"You got the shoes right. But the rest of it's wrong."

Now Hazel looked surprised. "Do tell."

"Okay…" Sena crossed her arms again. "I actually *am* from around here. I grew up in Nogales."

"No way!" Knox was back. He leaned against the bar and shoved his hands in his pockets. "It sure looks like you took the long way around to get to Owen Station."

You have no idea.

Sena had spent the past decade-plus about as far away as anyone could be from her hometown of 20,000, just a few hours away from Owen Station, where you could literally walk across the border to Mexico.

"You're not wrong about that," she said to Knox, while crossing one leg over the other, her red-soled right foot dangling intentionally in Hazel's direction. "I *have* taken the long way. But it's also true that my family has been in this region for nine generations, since before there was a border. My family invested in the railroad and we've been in transportation ever since. We move thousands of tons of veggies north across the border every year. Maybe you've heard of Abrigo Enterprises," she said proudly. "That's us."

"No kidding." Knox whistled softly. "You're one of *those* Abrigos, huh? I don't know how I missed that. What's bringing you to Owen Station, of all places?"

Sena took a deep breath and exhaled slowly through her nose. "Fair question." She paused, thinking about how to tell this story.

"It all started because I'm a math geek."

She paused again. That little factoid was always way more surprising to people than it should have been. Half the time, when she said it to people, they'd snicker. Like it couldn't possibly be true.

But neither Knox nor Hazel responded that way. They waited for Sena to continue. Knox looked like he had all the time in the world. Hazel leaned in a bit, her lunch forgotten, like she was really interested in Sena and her story. It was so unexpected, Sena almost forgot what story she was telling.

"So, yeah." She cleared her throat. "After high school, my parents wanted me to stay close to home, but I was dead set on an IT degree from USC. I know they hoped I'd come back home and take my place as CIO or COO. But my father had already decided that one of my younger brothers would eventually replace him as CEO—even though he knows I'm the most qualified by far. So, you know what? *Screw* that."

"Yeah, screw that," Hazel echoed.

"Language!" Knox gave Hazel a look of mock horror and then turned to Sena, laughing. "My old friend here never uses bad language. You've got her all worked up."

Hazel's cheeks turned three shades of red as she smiled apologetically. "Seriously though…how *unfair* is that?"

It was adorable. The freckles. The pink cheeks. The squeaky clean language. The way Hazel looked at her, as if there was nothing to be afraid of. Adorable. And distracting. Sena shifted on her stool, trying to tamp down the tingling between her legs—and the tug on her heart. She couldn't remember the last time someone bothered to listen, much less empathize with her. She was Sena Abrigo. Someone to be feared. Not protected. Challenged. Not defended. Admired and desired. Not *seen*.

Wait a minute.

Actually, Sena *did* remember the last time she felt seen.

She looked down at her hands and spun the ring on the middle finger of her right one. Her grandfather's silver wedding band. Neither of her brothers had wanted it—it was too plain and, besides, they both had wedding rings of their own. But she loved it and never went a day without wearing it. Abuelo—her mother's father—was the only one in the family who ever really seemed to *get* Sena and, even though he'd been gone for more than twenty years, she knew he was never far away.

She sighed and looked back up at Hazel and Knox, who were still there. Waiting.

"Okay, where was I? After graduation, I took a job in Silicon Valley. It was everything I wanted. Or should have been. It took me about five minutes to realize the guys in the room—and they're ninety-nine percent guys—couldn't deal with the fact that I was smarter than all of them. I'm a woman *and* I'm brown." She rolled her eyes. "How embarrassing for them, right?"

Hazel shifted on the stool across from her and dropped her eyes to the floor.

"Pretty shitty, right?" Sena shrugged. "Just imagine what it's been like to live it."

It sucked, that's what.

Sena had been on a shopping spree in New York City the year Michelle Obama was plugging her new bio, and Sena managed to snag tickets to hear her speak. The crowd went nuts when the former First Lady said what Sena had been thinking for years about "lean in" feminism: *That shit doesn't work all the time.*

Sena had the receipts to prove it.

She stayed in Silicon Valley for a decade. Way longer than she should have. The money was great and, even though she didn't need to—she was an Abrigo, after all—it felt fucking awesome to be making it on her own. Also, what was she supposed to do? Run home crying to Dad? Let him think he was right? That she's *not* CEO material? That he was *justified* in leaping right over her, tapping her brothers to lead the company? And then what? Squeeze back into her mother's kitchen? Her mother's life? No way in hell.

But one day she just had enough. Enough watching the white dudes in the C-suite snag CNN interviews where they'd take credit for her work. Enough mediocre men talking over her in meetings. Enough slobbering attempts by tech bros, trying to pick her up at offsite social events. Enough bro everything. So she got online and started looking for someplace to settle, anywhere but NorCal. An online search turned up Owen Station. Apparently, it was the small town with the best year-round weather in the country. And it had available real estate. Lots of it. It was a place she could get a big bang for her bucks. Plus, it was familiar territory—surrounded by a landscape and close enough to the culture she loved—but "home" was far enough away that she wouldn't feel like she was in her family's backyard. In fact, they didn't even know she was coming. So, she settled on Owen Station. And started making a plan.

"That sounds terrible, Sena. I can't imagine how frustrating it must have been to be treated that way. Or how painful." Hazel was looking at her again, head at an angle, her freckled brow knotted, as if Sena's trauma had literally hit her right between the eyes. And those eyes. Clear blue. Like a cloudless Sonoran sky. Sena wanted to lie back and float in them.

Did Sena feel tempted to slip those heavy glasses off and kiss her right on that soft little mouth of hers. Yes. Yes, she did. Because Hazel was right. It *was* terrible. It had been fucking awful. And she'd done it all on her own. With no one to confide in. Commiserate with. Not even someone to meet her at the door at the end of the day with a glass of wine, who would tell her she was a rock star just for showing up every day.

"So…what's next?" Hazel gently prompted her. "What's your plan? I know you have one."

Damn, if Hazel's tender smile didn't tear open a little hole in Sena's heart. Yes, Sena had a plan. Of course she did. But how could someone, who didn't even know her, see that? See *her*. So clearly. And so quickly.

"Yes, come on," Knox said excitedly. "What's your plan? What's bringing you to Owen Station?"

Sena's heartbeat quickened and she took a deep breath. She had been working on this next move for months. And things were about to get very exciting.

KELLY & TANA FIRESIDE

"Oh my God, you're going to love this. I'm done answering to anyone. Fuck their glass ceiling. This town sits in one of the most beautiful places on earth, but it's been struggling to recover for decades. Now, it looks like it has all kinds of affordable real estate and lots of potential. It is a prime location for the right kind of development."

She used her fingers to create a frame and held them up dramatically. "Picture this: the next Silicon Valley, where women are in charge and it isn't so blindingly white, nestled right in the middle of these magnificent mountains."

Hazel's hands flew to her mouth and she gasped.

"I know, right?" Sena's heart was racing now. "It's brilliant!"

Sena lowered her hands, dissolving the imaginary frame, and spun her grandfather's ring.

"To tell you the truth, I can't think of a better place to build the next Abrigo empire…except this time, this one will be mine."

Chapter Three

Color Me Crazy

H azel couldn't get out of there fast enough. *A Silicon Valley where women call the shots? Great idea. Go for it. But build an empire in my town? You've got to be kidding me. I don't care how beautiful or brilliant or irresistibly magnetic you are.*

Luckily, she had that appointment with Delaney she was trying to squeeze in during her lunch hour, so she snarfed down the rest of her wrap, said good-bye, and hustled out of Banter & Brew.

Delaney was waiting for her at Color Me Crazy, the hair salon right around the corner. It wasn't Delaney's yet. She was still working out the details with the Johnsons, who were in the middle of retiring to their fishing lodge not far from Vancouver. But she had managed it for them for years and it looked like her. White walls and bright cherry trim. Retro, teal-colored vinyl chairs. Zebra print cushions. A bank of bright purple nail stations. Large, playful drawings of women, in all shapes, sizes, and colors, hanging in ornate gold frames on the walls. Bottled water, juice, and soda in a vintage Coke cooler, free for the taking. A plate of homemade cookies on the counter. The music varied, depending on who was DJing at KBIS-FM, Owen Station's very own radio station. That afternoon, Walt was on the mic. He managed the station and got paid so little to do it he might as well have been a volunteer. He must have been in a good mood—or a very bad one—because why else would anyone play a whole set of old songs by the Jonas Brothers?

"It's like Camp Rock in here." Scowling, Hazel dropped into the chair at Delaney's station.

"Well, it's always a party when I get to see you, my friend." Delaney's face was bright in the mirror. Good old, always bouncy Delaney.

She was a fourth-generation Owenite—her people had come from Wales to work the mines. Hazel had known her since kindergarten but they didn't become close friends until after Hazel moved back home. Delaney's bleach-blonde exuberance was just the elixir Hazel needed as she became her mother's caretaker, drafted into service and immediately promoted to general in that losing battle with cancer twelve years ago.

It was Delaney who convinced Hazel to chop off her long red hair after her mother died. The week after the funeral, Delaney opened up the salon after hours, pulled out a bottle of Jameson, hooked up her old iPod, and blasted the most eclectic playlist ever made, including songs by dozens of artists, all singing about change with a capital C. Ziggy Marley. Tracy Chapman. 2Pac. Michael Jackson. Taylor Swift. The Head and the Heart. Even a classic by Bruce—it was old-school but it worked. Delaney put it together herself, just for that moment, just for Hazel. It must have taken her forever.

That night, as tears streamed down her face, Delaney snipped and trimmed and helped give birth to a new Hazel. Well, a new *looking* Hazel, anyway.

"What'll it be today, my friend?" Delaney asked cheerfully after a quick shampoo, scissors at the ready.

Hazel studied herself in the mirror. She loved the asymmetrical pixie Delaney had given her. It felt like the most playful thing about her these days. But she'd had this same cut for years now. And where did those wrinkles between her brows come from, anyway? Too much time frowning, no doubt.

She shot her friend as much of a smile as she had in her. "Just a trim, Delaney. Nothing new."

Delaney snapped a cape around Hazel's shoulders. "Nothing new? Why, Hazel Butler…what a surprise!"

Her mood eased a bit at Delancy's teasing. She twisted her neck, trying to stretch out the stress, and took a deep breath.

Shake it off, Hazel.

Shake HER off, you mean.

Yeah, that.

She looked up again at Delaney through the mirror and forced a wider smile.

"Speaking of new, I've got a bit of town gossip for you."

Delaney's eyes crinkled and she clapped her hands together. "You've got a bit of whaaat? Spill the tea, girl! You know how I love gossip."

"And I love knowing something before you do. It doesn't happen very often."

Delaney shook her head, proudly. "No, it doesn't. Now, what *is* it?"

"It looks like we're getting a new neighbor. Knox sold another house and the owner stopped by to pick up her keys this afternoon."

Delaney's eyebrows popped. "*Her* keys? Yes! Who is she? What's she like? Where's she from?" She gave Hazel a playful poke. "Is she cute?"

Hazel scrunched her nose. "She's rich. Filthy rich."

"Well now, that's exciting!" Delaney stopped snipping and probed Hazel's face in the mirror. "Is she a doctor? A lawyer? More importantly," she lifted an eyebrow, leaning forward eagerly, "is she single?"

"She's an Abrigo."

Boom.

"An Ah-breee-go?" Delaney's eyes widened and she stared at Hazel slack-jawed. "As in *the* Abrigos?"

"I knew this juicy bit of news would make your day. Yep, *those* Abrigos."

"Wow!" Delaney's voice trailed off. "What the heck is she doing in Owen Station?"

"Good question. She came here via Silicon Valley. You'd never know it to look at her, though. She doesn't look anything like a programmer. No pocket protector. No khakis. Actually, it looked like she just waltzed off the cover of *Vogue* magazine. You should've seen that dress."

"*Girrrl*, you sound *interested*!" Delaney's eyes gleamed.

"Not even a little." Hazel shrugged and pretended to smooth her skirt, one of her favorites from Grandma's closet.

"Oh, come on. You can't lie to me." Delaney grabbed a strand of Hazel's hair in one hand and suspended the scissors over her head in the other. "Give me the whole truth and nothing but the truth…or else. You *are* interested, aren't you?"

"Okay, maybe a little." Hazel couldn't hold back a second longer. "I mean, she is *hot*, Delaney. Oh my gosh. Is she hot. And I don't know for sure, but my gaydar was definitely off the chart." She dropped her voice to a whisper even though no one else was in the shop. "I think she was *flirting* with me."

"No way." Delaney leaned in toward Hazel's reflection. "Did you flirt back? Please tell me you flirted back!"

Hazel watched a silly grin stretch slowly across her own face in the mirror.

"You did!" Delaney started swinging her hips around in a circle, excitedly pumping her arms, singing, "You did it, you did it, you really, really did it!"

Hazel laughed hard. "Actually, I do feel pretty proud of myself." She tilted her head back over her shoulder to look at Delaney. "I don't think I did a very good job…but, to be honest, I wasn't sure I still knew how to do it at *all*."

"I'm sure you were amazing," Delaney said, softly tugging on Hazel's ear. "Now, *please* tell me you're going to ask her out!"

Hazel sighed heavily and swung her head back around toward the mirror.

Delaney stopped dancing. "Wait, why do you look so salty all of a sudden? You should be happy."

That's a good question. What is wrong with me?

A hard shiver shot through Hazel as she remembered the sparks when Sena's bare skin brushed against her own. The way

Sena explored her body with those deep brown eyes. The hot energy between them as they sparred. And…

Bingo. That's what's wrong. Too much. Too fast. Too hot. Too… scary.

"Hazel?"

She met Delaney's eyes in the mirror.

"You should have seen her, Delaney. Prancing into Banter & Brew in a pair of Louboutins that cost more than my paycheck. It was like watching someone from an alternative universe…who could snap her fingers and have anything she wants. *Do* whatever she wants. It was unreal and not in a good way."

"I don't get it." Delaney gave a shrug. "What's wrong with being rich? Isn't that a good thing?"

A hard shell snapped around Hazel's heart. "She actually said she's here to buy up all the real estate in Owen Station and turn us into the next Silicon Valley."

Delaney looked skeptical.

"I'm serious, Delaney. That's exactly what she said. So, I don't care how beautiful she is, she represents everything I've been fighting against."

After Mom died, making Hazel the last remaining member of the Owen Station Butlers, she threw herself into carrying on her father's legacy. Honestly, what else did she have left?

She joined the board of the local museum and co-chaired the Copper King Festival, which celebrated the history of their funky little town with old-fashioned games, local live music, and fried food. The highlight was the Annual Donkey Race. They used real donkeys until 1993, when the local PETA group chained themselves across Main Street, but ever since, Owenites lined the streets the third Saturday in April to cheer on their favorite person-dressed-like-a-donkey, while tourists drank beer out of plastic cups and sent pictures to their friends. The winner's name was added to the official register, which dated back to 1952. Hazel loved every second of it.

She had become sort of a hero to Owen Station old-timers, showing up at town council meetings armed with books and notepads crammed with meticulous research, to protest a new building project or renovations that didn't meet exacting historical standards. When Sirus asked her to become a co-founder of an historical preservation society and host their meetings at the library, she didn't hesitate.

Hazel slumped a little in her chair. "You have to understand, Delaney. I've been doing everything I can to protect this place from out-of-town developers who don't know or appreciate our history, don't care about our town, and only want to make a quick buck. My dad showed us that we can save ourselves. In fact, you know as well as I do. He *died* saving Owen Station the first time. The last thing I'm going to do is let some developer in fancy shoes come in and turn us into another McTown, full of McMansions and big box stores, pricing us all out of our family homes and bulldozing our history. That's what SOS is all about, Delaney. That's what I've committed myself to. And, as far as I'm concerned, the Sena Abrigos of the world are our worst nightmare."

Delaney's scissors paused in midair and she looked through the mirror at Hazel, who braced herself for one of Delaney's infamous lectures. Instead, after a long minute, Delaney bust out laughing.

"Girl, you are too dang serious. You need to get laid!"

Delaney spun Hazel around in the chair, a full circle, and then stopped her short, right in front of the mirror. "Look at that beautiful face…and you're about to get a great cut. I do fantastic work, Hazel Butler. Don't waste it this month!"

Before Hazel could respond, the phone rang and Delaney shot over to the front desk to pick it up. "Color Me Crazy! How can we help you go wild?"

A pause.

"Oh, hi, Knox. How's it going? Hazel was just telling me about your latest sale." She shot Hazel a big wink. "Congrats!"

Another pause.

"Of course, she's right here. Hang on a minute."

Delaney held the phone out toward Hazel, one eyebrow arched disapprovingly. "He says he tried calling your cell. You really ought to keep that old thing turned on."

Hazel just shrugged. Technology might be a fact of life, but she wasn't about to let it run hers. She rarely bothered to make sure her phone was even charged.

She shot an exaggerated air kiss at Delaney and took the phone. "What's up, Knox?"

"I have an idea about where Sena can stay for the next few days."

"Oh really? Where? Not that I care." She looked at Delaney and rolled her eyes.

"Your place."

"Knox, no!"

"Why not? I know your little bed-and-breakfast is totally empty right now."

"It's *not* a bed-and-breakfast, Knox." She was annoyed now on several fronts.

Dad had built the little casita behind the main house for Grandma after Grandpa died. Hazel absolutely hated strangers staying in it. But she was a millennial—part of the generation that basically invented the gig economy—living in a small town, six thousand feet above sea level, where ghosts outnumbered jobs about two-to-one. Without that extra income she would never have been able to make it on the pittance she got paid as a county librarian. Make that a *part-time* county librarian and, since the budget cuts, the *only* librarian. During high season she could get sixty-nine bucks a night for that guesthouse from the weekend tourists who came from Phoenix and Tucson, looking for art galleries during the day and drunken, stupid nights in the entertainment district, a strip of about seven dive bars just off Main Street, some of which had been in business for more than a hundred years.

This was not the high season.

"Right, right, I know that, Hazel. I only meant that you do short-term rentals. And I know this time of year is slow."

Hazel chewed her lip silently. Sena was trouble in high heels. *Double* trouble. A menace to her town...*and* a threat to her orderly, predictable life. She should put a stop to this right now. Tell Knox to stuff it. Sena was his problem, not hers.

But, to be honest, Hazel's heart raced at the possibility of another close encounter. At the thought of Sena sleeping just steps away. She also thought maybe she had seen something beneath all the sizzle and pop. Vulnerability, yes. But strength, too. Resiliency. Hazel couldn't even imagine what it must have been like for Sena to deal with Silicon Valley's bro culture. The stories of sexual harassment were legend.

And there was no question. Hazel did need the money.

"Come on, Hazel," Knox cajoled her, laying on his boyish charm. "What do you say?"

A lock of hair fell into her face. She tucked it around her ear and pushed up her glasses, weighing her options. Finally, a brainstorm.

"You're right, Knox," she said. "I shouldn't be so inhospitable. That's not the Owen Station we know and love. Sena is *more* than welcome to stay at my place as long as she needs to."

Delaney, who had been hanging on Hazel's every word, looking confused, started jumping up and down across the room, silently clapping her hands.

"Rent's just a hundred and forty bucks a night."

"A hundred and—?" Knox started to object—he knew darn well that was twice the off-season rate—but Hazel cut him off.

"Don't even start," she said. "What's a hundred and forty dollars to someone wearing those shoes?" She didn't feel the least bit bad.

Knox didn't respond. Instead, she heard him dutifully convey her offer to Sena. The Abrigo didn't even hesitate.

"I'll take it," Hazel heard her say.

Hazel didn't wait for Knox to relay the message. "Give her my address and tell her to meet me there at five thirty." She stuck her tongue out at the phone and hung up.

"Girl, get over here." Delaney's face must have hurt from smiling so big. "I need to finish making you beautiful for your big date."

"It's not a date, Delaney." Hazel's brow furrowed. "It's business."

"Uh-huh, sure," Delaney chortled as Hazel took her seat again. "Frisky business, I hope. And, speaking of which, I cannot *wait* to tell Lace. Ooo, *girl!*"

As if on cue, the door to Color Me Crazy blew open and in walked Lace Reynolds, Knox's ex, in her usual weekday outfit.

Jeans, colorful high-tops and a crisp short-sleeve button-down with a logo for Frisky Business, the adult toy shop she opened after the divorce. She was Delaney's next appointment—and one of her favorites. Delaney loved cutting Lace's thick, wavy hair—a gift from her Italian grandparents—especially since she had convinced Lace to wear a pompadour. And Delaney wasn't wrong—Lace did look fabulous.

"Can't wait to tell me *what?*" Lace rubbed her hands gleefully.

Hazel's cheeks suddenly felt like they were on fire. "Come on, Delaney. Is *nothing* private?"

"Private?" Lace bellowed as she plopped herself down in the chair next to Hazel. "What kind of secret would you tell *Delaney* and not me? You know I'm way better at keeping them than she is."

"There are no *secrets*, Lace. It's nothing." Hazel glowered at Delaney through the mirror. "Delaney, you are exasperating. Can we talk about something else? Please?"

Delancy laughed. "All right, honey. Sure. Lace, here's the short version. Hazel's hot for a new girl in town, one of the Abrigos if you can believe that."

Hazel dropped her head into her hand and moaned.

Delaney ignored her. "The big news is that this new girl— what's her name again, Hazel—?"

"Sena," Hazel said, rolling her head back in defeat.

"*Sena* is moving into Hazel's guesthouse. So, you know. Forced closeness and all that. I expect them to be visiting your shop together within the month and married before Christmas."

"Delaney!" Hazel snapped. "Can you please just finish me up so I can get back to work?"

Lace and Delaney looked at each other and laughed. Hazel just shook her head. But when they finally calmed down, Lace saved the day. She was good like that—she'd do anything for you. It wasn't hard to see why Knox had fallen for her or why he still loved her, even after she switched teams on him.

"Okay, Hazel. New topic. Did you get your car back from the shop yet?"

Hazel's eyes lit up. That fifty-seven Chevy was the only good thing to come out of her mother's death. Hazel had been the executor of the will, of course. There was no one else. And Hazel found all kinds of things she never knew existed, including a storage unit with her grandfather's long forgotten car in pretty decent condition. Selling her mom's sensible sedan and reintroducing that Chevy to the road was the easiest decision Hazel made in those painful months. It was the star of the annual Owen Station car show, which raised money every year for the animal shelter.

"Yep! Picked it up yesterday. Runs like new."

"I very much doubt that," Delaney interjected. "You oughta retire that antique and buy yourself a cute little sumpthin-sumpthin. What's your beautiful new housemate gonna think, anyway, when you come rolling up in that old piece of junk?"

"Dammit, Delaney!" Hazel's sharp tone and atypical use of the D-word made her blabbermouth friend stand down. For a hot minute, anyway.

"First of all, I am done talking about *Ms. Abrigo*. Second, she is my new renter, *not* housemate. And third," she smiled, "you know I love that car. When I get behind the wheel, I swear, it's like they're all right there with me, Dad and Mom, all the grands. I have co-pilots everywhere I go."

"Ghost co-pilots, you mean." Lace laughed.

Hazel joined her. "Yes, but they're friendly ghosts!"

"Whatever. It's not natural, Hazel." Delaney frowned. "You shouldn't be hanging out with ghosts, whoever they are. And that car attracts them! I know, I know. You *say* you like driving around in the past. And I know it's just because you miss them all, especially your mom."

"She was one-of-a-kind," Lace offered helpfully. "I don't blame Hazel for missing her. We all do."

"I know, I know." Delaney chattered away as she snipped and clipped. How could she even focus with that incessant talking? "But it's not healthy, Hazel."

Hazel sighed heavily and closed her eyes.

B.E.S.E.T. Embattled. Hemmed in. BESET.

"Hazel, are you even listening to me?" Delaney wouldn't let it go. "You need to get out there and live again, girl!"

Lace leaned forward and put her hand on Hazel's arm. Her voice was as soft as Delaney's was loud. "You know we're just worried about you, right, Hazel? You've done your job. You took care of your mom. You've always put everyone else first. We want it to be *your* turn for a change."

"It's time for you to glow up, Hazel!" Delaney squawked. "Have fun! Have sex! Fall in love! Quit curving every woman who hits on you. And, for God's sake, Hazel, sell that car and buy something that looks like it belongs to a hot thirty-something, not your grandpa. Your mother would agree with me and you know it."

Lace dropped her head and ran her fingers through her short hair. Even she thought Delaney was too much sometimes. Her eyes were round and soft when she looked up at Hazel.

"I don't know how to say this exactly, Hazel, and the last thing I want to do is hurt you. But sometimes it does seem like you spend so much time in the past, you don't think you even deserve a future."

Tears welled up behind Hazel's eyes.

In the background, Walt was reading a list of public service announcements. The animal shelter needed volunteers. Someone had found a broken but clearly repairable umbrella in the park and was trying to find the owner—the first monsoon of the season was finally in the forecast. The following week's pickleball tournament was postponed because the line judges were going to be visiting their newly divorced daughter in Santa Fe.

Hazel was barely listening.

Delaney and Lace, plus Knox, had been Hazel's rock since she moved back home for Mom. No one knew Hazel better than they did. And no one cared more. They only wanted the best for her. That's why they could get away with saying the things they did. But that didn't make it any easier to hear.

"Oh, sweetie, I'm sorry." Delaney looked through the mirror into Hazel's teary eyes. "We don't mean to be so hard on you. We just love you so much, Hazel. We want you to be happy. You deserve a happy ever after more than anyone…and so much more."

"Apology accepted."

The sting didn't go away, though. In fact, she was still thinking about it three and a half hours later as she parked her old Chevy under the carport beside her house. Maybe her friends were right. Everyone else seemed to have happy endings. Well, a lot of people, anyway.

Why not me?

That thought was interrupted when Sena's Audi pulled in behind her.

As still as a desert cottontail who knows she's being tracked, Hazel watched wide-eyed through her side-view mirror as one red-soled shoe and then the other emerged from the sports car and stepped out onto the bricks. For the second time that day, Hazel stopped breathing as Sena's curvaceous frame unfolded out of the car and she stood up to take in the scene. There was no mistaking it. As Delaney would say, Sena was *lit.* Hazel closed her eyes and tried to push down the brew of anticipation and dread bubbling within her.

CHAPTER FOUR

A FRIENDLY PUSSY

S ena stepped out of her car and looked around, taking in Hazel's cute little bungalow and xeriscaped yard, full of beautiful drought-resistant plants, and the classic car in the drive. She hadn't known what to expect, but she'd been thinking about this moment all day, even as she pored over real estate listings with Knox.

The guy was growing on her, in spite of her early concerns. He was working hard to make up for the crossed wires earlier. Unlike the men she was used to working with, he didn't take himself too seriously, but he did take *her* seriously. And that was going to be necessary if they were going to work together. She was on a mission that was going to change everything for a whole subset of the tech world—the people who looked like her. She didn't plan to waste a single moment.

But she was also intrigued by the town's librarian.

Seeing Hazel perched on that stool at Banter & Brew, with that blazing red hair and skin the color of fresh milk, made her cream. There was no question about what Sena wanted. And, God knows, if they were back in NorCal, Sena wouldn't have thought twice about taking it.

But there was something different about Hazel. She seemed so comfortable with her place in the world—so at ease in her own skin. After all those years in California, Sena had more than enough of plastic-souled, Botox-filled, dressed-to-kill babes. For one thing, they were boring as fuck in bed. And, once you committed to a life of faking it, it was hard to turn that shit off.

It was almost impossible to imagine Hazel faking anything. She seemed smart, with a good sense of humor. She clearly wasn't afraid of a friendly duel. She was so obviously hot for Sena, it was hysterical. But she seemed to genuinely *care*. Like she actually wanted to hear Sena's story, to get to know her. As a person.

Sena had forgotten what that was like. Her memories of growing up on the ranch were mostly of being suffocated, unable to be herself, except with her grandfather. When he died, he left an enormous hole that no one else was able to fill. So, Sena fled, trying to find a place where she could be herself. What she found, instead, was a place where *nobody* was honest about who they were. And nobody cared who she really was at all.

She jumped at the chance to rent Hazel's casita and would have paid twice as much or more. Yes, of course she was hoping the electricity between them would lead to great sex. But she was hoping for something more, too.

Even if she didn't quite know what that was, yet.

Sena adjusted her dress, pulled her bag up onto her shoulder, and swaggered up the driveway toward Hazel, who was waiting at the gate.

"Nice house," she said. Then she threw a thumb back toward the Chevy. "And that is one sweet ride."

"I can't tell if you're serious or poking fun." Hazel squinted into the late afternoon sun, faint lines between her brows.

"That's good."

"Why is that good?"

"It'll be fun to keep you guessing."

"I'd rather not have to guess." The lines deepened and Hazel tipped her chin up with just a touch of defiance. "Besides, I'm not that interested."

"In guessing? Or in me?"

Hazel looked a little flustered. "Both. I mean neither. I'm not interested in guessing and I'm not interested in…"

"In me?"

"No. I mean—I mean, *yes.* I'm not interested in you."

"Really?"

"Really."

"Okay. If you say so."

"Why? Do you think I am interested? I mean, why would you think I am?"

Hazel's cheeks pinked up. God, she was cute when she was flustered.

"What do you mean, *why would you think I'm interested?* Just look at me." Sena swept her hands down both sides of her body. "Who wouldn't be?"

Sena hoped Hazel saw the humor and cocked an eyebrow just to be sure. It took a few clicks but, finally, there it was. Hazel burst out laughing. Sena joined in.

"You're unbelievable Ms. Abrigo."

"Why thank you, Ms. Butler. I try."

Sena shifted their attention to the orange tabby crouched at Hazel's feet. "And who is this, may I ask?"

Hazel appeared to hesitate, glancing down at the cat and then back at Sena. Like she was afraid to introduce the two. Suppressing another laugh, Sena dropped her chin to peer at Hazel over the top of her Givenchys. "She doesn't exactly look like a friendly pussy."

Hazel's eyes popped open and, for a second, it looked like her mouth was going to get stuck in that O position again. This was too easy. But after a moment Hazel blinked. Twice. Three times. And then threw her head back in an explosion of laughter, tiny tears squeezing out of those crystal blue eyes.

Sena took her glasses off and dropped them in their case. She was glad to see Hazel was tougher than she looked.

Hazel wiped the tears from the corners of her eyes, a huge grin on her face. "Well, you certainly nailed it, Sena. She's *not* a friendly pussy."

Hazel squatted down to give the cat a scratch under the chin. "Mango showed up the night of my mother's funeral and never left. She gobbles up the kibble I give her but never comes inside, no matter what kind of weather we're having. Usually she's perched up on the adobe wall back here or in the branches of the desert willow out front."

Hazel stood back up, put her hands on her hips, and sent what felt like a warning. A gentle one, but a warning nonetheless. "I think of her as a guard cat, sent by Mom to look out for me. And she does *not* like strangers."

"Well…" Sena grinned. "I'll have to make sure I'm not a stranger for long."

Hazel chuckled and swept her hands toward the gate. "All right then, Madam Abrigo, let me show you to your new home."

As soon as the words slipped out, Hazel looked like she wanted to scoop them up and shove them right back in. Through puckered lips, she clarified, "*Temporary* home, that is."

Being a redhead must have been so hard. Her face always seemed to betray what she was thinking. Pink-cheeked, Hazel cleared her throat and gave her head a quick shake. Without saying another word, she turned to unlatch the heavy metal gate leading into the courtyard behind the house.

Sena followed, stepped into the courtyard, took one look around, and stopped dead.

The house itself was cute. It had probably started out as a miner's shack, like most of the homes in Owen Station, and been updated and added on to over the years. Good bones. Nothing fancy.

But the *courtyard.* Punched tin, star-shaped lamps that had to have been handmade in Mexico hung from the widely-spaced beams of a wooden pergola. In the center of the space, a sturdy tile-covered wooden table. Four wooden chairs, painted a rich cobalt blue, looked like they'd been snatched right out of La Casa Azul. Beneath their feet, traditional terra cotta tile, handcrafted from clay only found in Saltillo. Inset, tiny Talavera tiles gave the floor a pop of color and were lined up in such a way that they led directly to a tile-covered fireplace and two wrought iron armchairs in the corner. It was like stepping through a portal in the space-time continuum. And she suddenly had no idea where—or when—she was.

"Are you okay?"

Hazel looked concerned, which made Sena realize that she was doing the O now. She closed her mouth and tried to steady herself.

"How...who...what..." Sena took a breath. "*Where* did this come from?"

"What do you mean?" Hazel cocked her head sideways, confused.

"Well, your house...I mean, no offense, but it's so...so..."

A tiny smile tickled the corner of Hazel's mouth. "Ordinary?"

Sena shook her head hard. "That's not what I meant. I mean..."

"Poor?" One eyebrow shot up.

"No!"

Hazel's blue eyes twinkled. "I'm sorry. I'm just giving you a hard time. You want to know what this traditional Mexican courtyard is doing in back of an Irish miner's shack, don't you?"

"Well, yes. Yes, I do." Sena took a deep breath and felt her stomach muscles unwind. A little.

"Okay, well." Hazel turned on her librarian voice. "My great-grandfather came to Owen Station from Chicago answering an ad for mine workers. He built this house after my great-*great* grandfather gave him permission to marry his daughter—my great-grandmother—the *first* Hazel. They were Irish—my great-great-grandpa and grandma immigrated here. But Hazel-the-first was born in Nogales."

Sena's eyebrows jumped as she was yanked back through the portal. She was totally in the present, now.

"Don't look so shocked," Hazel said, waving her hand at Sena's designer dress. "I actually *do* look like I'm from here. Anyway, before my great-grandmother Hazel left Nogales and moved into this house, she insisted that this courtyard be built to remind her of home—and of the woman who had been her best friend since childhood, a girl from a Mexican family." Hazel spread open her arms. "We're standing in it."

They stood beside each other in silence for a minute, feeling the air start to cool as the sun slipped behind the mountains.

"The story I've heard my whole life is that their friendship, in the late 1800s, was as dangerous as it was unlikely. The details of how they met and how they became friends have been lost. But we do know it wasn't long after this courtyard was built that fighting along the border made crossing too dangerous. The two governments tried to stop it by building a wall that sliced right through the middle of the city, dividing families. Splitting the community. The people and land on the northern side of the city were claimed by the US. The southern side by Mexico."

"That was when the first border wall was built," Sena said quietly. "I know the story well."

"Oh my goodness. Of course you do." Hazel's cheeks signaled her embarrassment.

"Go on. What happened then?"

"All we really know is that Hazel-the-first never saw her friend again. Over the years, this courtyard has been updated a few times. Like this tiny casita my dad built before he passed. But it's kept this same character, this connection to my great-grandmother and her friend. It's always been extra special to me, even though she was gone long before I was born. I love that I carry her name, Hazel Eileen. And when my mother died, this little house became mine."

A strong gust of wind blew through the courtyard, whipping up and scattering the mesquite leaves that had gotten stuck in the corners, dried and crispy from the summer heat. Mango had been sitting on the tile hearth, appearing to be eavesdropping, but she leapt up and scooted in close between Hazel's legs. The monsoon season hadn't officially started in Owen Station yet, but a sudden heaviness in the air signaled that it wasn't far away.

Sena's chest felt tight and she realized she was struggling to breathe. She knew all about the kinds of walls that divide people from each other. Some of them political, some religious, some cultural. Some went right through families.

Sena didn't mean to start talking. It just sort of happened.

"It's been...I don't know...six years? Maybe seven, since I've been back to my family's ranch. All those years, my world has been filled with concrete, glass, and steel. The only addresses that mattered were penthouses—or started with *http*. I couldn't have been further away from the mesquite tree that shades my family's patio. This place reminds me of it. Of home."

"What happened?" Hazel asked quietly. "Six or seven years is a long time."

It took a minute for Sena to answer.

"I was there for my first niece's baptism, my youngest brother's girl."

Hazel was still. Listening.

"It was a very short visit. Just a few days. I had to get back to work."

Actually, Sena had just been named to the Forbes 30 Under 30. She was a Silicon Valley wunderkind. Everyone except the one person who mattered had made a big deal out of it. It devastated her. Of course, her mother defended him. She always did.

"Mom, why isn't Dad proud of me?"

"Sena, what are you talking about?"

"You know what I'm talking about. Dad has always been my hero. I loved doing chores beside him, hearing his stories, learning the business. But he's barely talked to me since I was thirteen. I can still ride, rope, and shoot better than the boys. I love them both but you know I'm smarter than the two of them put together. It never seems to be enough for him, though. Nothing is."

"Oh, sweetheart." Her mother shook her head sadly, handing her foil packets of homemade tamales and warm flour tortillas to take with her on the long journey back to San Jose. "Your father can't be more proud of you than you are of yourself."

Sena stared at her mother in disbelief.

What did that even mean? But that was all Mom said. When it came to cooking or riding or honoring the dead, the family was careful to pass on all of the old traditions. When it came to figuring out matters of the heart, you were on your own.

"Earth to Sena."

Sena looked down, surprised to see Hazel's hand gently touching her elbow. Her eyes slowly came back into focus and she tried to feel her feet connected to the ground, this ground, in Owen Station, with Hazel, in this moment, now.

"Oh, I'm sorry, Hazel." Sena's voice sounded far away, even to her. "What were you saying?"

Hazel tilted her head, puzzling out a smile. "Actually, *you* were talking. You were starting to tell me about your family...your home."

An uncertain silence hung beneath them. Finally, Sena spoke. "You know, it's been a long day. I think I'm ready to check in...if the place is ready, that is."

She avoided eye contact, sure that Hazel was wondering what the hell was wrong with her. Sena wasn't sure herself. All the bravado she marched in on had disappeared in a flash, like the blinding sun that had just dipped behind the bluff. From blazing hot to desert chill, just like that. What would she see in Hazel's eyes, if she dared to look? Confusion, maybe. Or worse. Ridicule. Disdain. That's how people reacted to weakness. Wasn't it? They pounced. They killed. They consumed. Only the strong survived. That's what Sena had been taught by the world she'd been living in.

Hazel pressed the keys to the casita into Sena's hand, holding it for just a few seconds longer than necessary, and told her to knock on the back door if she needed anything. Sena slowly lifted her head. She was shocked when the only thing she saw in Hazel's eyes, which had faded to a soft shade of gray, was a reflection of her own sadness.

After unloading her car, Sena stripped out of her dress and threw on a comfy cotton T-shirt, unpacked her suitcases, munched on the raw veggies and hummus she had been traveling with, and climbed onto the antique bed. Cross-legged on top of a vintage box quilt—which looked like it could have been made by Hazel's great-grandmother—she popped open her laptop and pulled up the real estate listings Knox had sent. There were a lot of them to read through, but Sena knew exactly what she was looking for. She put together an email with instructions and the list of places she wanted to see the next day and shot it off to the Realtor-slash-barista.

Sena's phone sat on the bedside table staring at her. Earlier in the day, when she was feeling brash and confident—you know, like *herself*—she planned to call her mother, to let the fam know she was back in Arizona.

Then there was the heat, a courtyard that felt way too much like home, the story of an impossible relationship, a whole family of strangers who were apparently all dead but at the moment felt more present than her own, an eccentric redhead who somehow seemed to be able to *see* through Sena's carefully constructed barriers, a very unfriendly pussycat, that stupid wall, old wounds, ancient insecurities.

Fuck!

It had been a long time since Sena had let herself think about these things. Even longer since she had felt this vulnerable. She'd been living in a world where everything, including invisible things, could be measured and analyzed and warehoused in data bytes. Where calculus was the key to understanding anything that mattered. Where emotion was irrelevant. Math didn't care if you felt good about two plus two equaling four, or bad about it. It just *was*. It's what attracted Sena to the field in the first place and why she couldn't wait to get out of her hometown, away from her family, with all of their unspoken expectations and judgment. She preferred working in a space where your value could be tracked on a spreadsheet or determined like a geometric proof, using indisputable fact and reason. Not left to the impossibly illogical whim of someone like…

Dad.

Sena picked up her phone, shoved it into the nightstand, and slammed the drawer shut. Her family didn't know she was coming. They could wait.

She closed her laptop and set it aside, then slipped under the crisp white sheets.

What was happening? She hadn't been prepared for the impact of being so close to home, and all the memories it was bringing to the surface. And nothing could have prepared her for Hazel. Somehow this small-town, techno-phobic, slightly-haunted librarian had managed, without even trying, to poke a hole in the emotional blockade Sena had spent decades constructing.

That's not how things were supposed to go down.

She was supposed to be going down. On Hazel. Right now. Her pussy began to throb and she let the memory emerge of Hazel's bare arm grazing against her, perky nipples peeking through that white tee, a round tight bottom. Rolling over onto her back, she licked a finger and slipped her hand inside her panties. This never took long. Conjuring an image of a beautiful woman beneath her, begging to be entered, to be filled, Sena could climax in seconds. But as she lay there in the casita, sensing Hazel was just steps away, unfamiliar images wrestled for control. Hazel under the sheets, nestled between her legs, licking and sucking. Hazel on top, pinning her hands to the bed, biting her lip, her neck, her nipples. Sena kept stroking, more and more frantically, aching for satisfaction, as she fought to drag Hazel back onto her own turf, with Sena in control, where she belonged. But the more she fought it, the further away she was from relief.

"Dammit all!" she yelled, whipping off the sheet and springing out of bed. "You need to get your shit together, Sena." Her voice bounced sharply against the walls and ricocheted back at her. A short but effective sermon.

In spite of a long shower and thirty minutes of her favorite relaxation app, Sena dreamt hard that night—memories and fantasies and terrors. She wouldn't be able to remember enough to make sense of it all.

Racing bareback across the desert on Alegre, the stallion's long mane whipping in the wind. Rachel...her first real girlfriend... storming away...screaming...you and your daddy need therapy! A gaggle of spoiled USC brats. Hey, Mexico...When you gonna come clean my room? A rooftop club in LA. Or San Fran. Music thumping while she finger-fucked a blonde under the table. Expensively dressed patrons obliviously sucking on overpriced martinis nearby. An orange tabby. No, wait, it's Puma. He is eating something. He looks up. His eyes are stone. Turquoise. A house on fire. And rain. The smell of creosote. A child alone. A girl. No. A boy. Is that me?

She woke up at some point. Or thought she did. A swirling green light in the far corner of the casita. Then a woman. Graying reddish hair. Fading freckles. An emerald green dress, unprocessed cotton, scratchy and rough. Long billowy sleeves. A silver brooch with a pearl inset. Standing beside her bed.

Who are you? Why are you here?

What? What do you mean why am I here? Why are YOU here? I paid to stay in this casita while my own home is being repaired. Who are you?

You know who I am.

No, I don't. Who are you? What do you want?

Love.

Excuse me?

Freedom.

I don't understand.

You will.

I don't...

You do.

Sena was groggy when her alarm went off and couldn't remember the last time she had such an awful night's sleep. Or the last time Puma had appeared to her in a dream.

Her abuelo told her Puma always had a message for her when he appeared. But her grandfather was long gone. She was grown now and she had left the old world, the world of spirits and stories and superstition, behind. She was a mathematician, for God's sake. Rational.

But that woman last night. So. Real.

And she looked familiar.

"Get a grip, Sena." She spoke sharply into the morning stillness that filled the casita, pushing off the blanket and sheet, feet hitting the cool tile floor.

It was just a bunch of weird dreams. Forget about it. You've got shit to do today. A fortune to make. A librarian to check out. Ha. See what I did there.

She sat on the edge of the bed and tapped her tablet to do a quick email check. Nothing that couldn't wait. Then she pulled on running clothes and headed out to the courtyard to stretch before her very early morning run. But when she threw the door open she was greeted by the strange tabby, sitting on the welcome mat, staring up at her, as if it had been waiting, blocking her way.

Sena and Mango eyeballed each other for a long minute.

"I can do this all day," she finally told the cat matter-of-factly.

Mango blinked first. The cat stood up, arched her back, and started circling between Sena's legs, rubbing and bumping her head, signaling the contest was over. Sena crouched down and gave her a good scratch behind the ears.

"Well, hello there, kitty cat. It looks like we have a friendly pussy on our hands, after all."

Sena stood up and did a few quick stretches. As she took off down the driveway and out onto the mountain roads, it occurred to her. For the first time in her life, she desperately wanted to be running toward something. Instead of just running away.

CHAPTER FIVE

INNER SANCTUM

The air was a little cooler at this hour, before the sun popped up over the bluffs, but it was going to be another record-breaker. Hazel leaned against the counter as coffee percolated on the stove. Gazing through her kitchen window, she drank in a view of the courtyard. Okay, actually she was drinking in Sena.

Hazel lay awake thinking about her half the night.

Sena was sitting in one of the blue wooden chairs under the pergola, in running clothes, having a mug of something and a piece of that rhubarb pie, a laptop on the table in front of her. She was painfully gorgeous. Firm, flexing calf muscles. Smooth thighs, shimmering in the early dawn light.

A flock of butterflies darted in and out of Hazel's stomach and then dashed straight down her middle. This made it a little easier to ignore the quiet voice—make that a loud one—trying to box her in. And keep this dangerous woman out.

Frankly, Hazel was sick of that voice, the same one that convinced her to break up with Abby—her college crush and, she thought, the love of her life—and drop *everything*, when she came home to take care of Mom. Mom didn't ask her to do that. Abby wanted to come with her. But, no. There was that voice. The one always whispering. Be responsible. Be careful. Be good.

Why didn't that voice ever say be *happy*?

Sena was terrifying. Brash. Boldly marching into the future. Determined to drag everyone else in town along with her. But she was exciting, too. And there was something tender underneath it all. Something vulnerable. Hazel didn't know exactly what happened in the courtyard yesterday, but *something* knocked Sena off balance. Could anyone blame her for wanting to bend forward, inch her way in, discover what soft secrets might lie beneath all that bravado?

Apparently yes. Someone could blame her. That annoying voice screaming at Hazel to pull the window shade and turn away.

Hazel scowled, clicked off the timer signaling the coffee had percolated to just the right strength, turned off the heat, and removed the wet grounds. She poured herself a cup of dark brew, just like Grandma used to make, and then she glanced back through the window. What she saw almost made her drop the pot.

Mango was circling through Sena's legs, doing that headbutt thing normal cats do—marking Sena with her scent. Signaling that Sena was part of her safe zone. Bonding.

The tabby was notorious among Hazel's friends. She sort of put up with Delaney—but she didn't like anyone else. Not even Knox. Lace called her Mango the Impenetrable. And when it came to renters staying in the guesthouse, forget about it. Mango would sit on the back wall glaring at them as they came in and out of the courtyard, hissing if they got too close to Hazel's back door. Yet, here she was. A smitten kitten.

Hazel squeezed her eyes shut, trying to silence that annoying voice. If even *Mango* liked Sena, then what could be the harm in…

Girl, you need to get laid!

Hazel could hear Delaney's voice shouting in her head. And that was all she needed to make a quick decision. Hazel took action before she could change her mind. She pushed the window open a crack and called out, "Good morning, Sena! How'd you sleep?"

"Not bad." Sena called back, turning toward Hazel's voice. "How about you?"

Hazel paused, weighing possible responses. "I was too hot to sleep."

A grin slowly stretched across Sena's face. "Yeah, well, I've been known to do that to people across six or seven states."

Hazel's breath caught in her throat. This woman was something else. So sure of herself. It was exhilarating. She threw her head back, flung open the back door, and stepped out onto the patio, a cup of black coffee in hand. "I bet you have."

She strode toward Sena playfully, wearing a light gray pencil skirt that looked like it'd been pulled from Grandma's closet— because it actually had been. The sleeves were rolled up on her white T-shirt. And she had a killer pair of Fluevogs on her feet. She knew she looked fantastic.

"Wow. Just wow. Hazel, you are full of surprises."

Hazel struck an impish pose, one hand on her hip. "You like?"

"I do, indeed."

Sena did look impressed, and Hazel watched her eyes feasting on the ensemble she'd put together. A pair of small silver hoop earrings. An oversized watch on a leather band that hung loosely on her wrist. And one of her father's old neckties, slipped through the skirt's belt loops, fastened on her hip by Great-grandma's brooch.

But, all of a sudden, Sena looked like she had seen a ghost. She went from dazzled to dazed in a millisecond, her face frozen in place.

"What's wrong, Sena?"

"I'm...not...sure..." Sena answered as if in a trance. Then her hand reached slowly toward Hazel's brooch.

Just before Sena's fingers reached the smooth pearl, a shock of heat blasted Hazel in the middle, like the brooch was suddenly on fire, nearly knocking her off her feet. Sena yanked her hand back, as though she felt it too, and shot out of her chair with such force it tumbled backward.

"Sorry," Sena cried, eyes wide, hands in surrender mode, in midair. "I'm sorry!"

They stared at each other for half a minute.

"What...just...happened?"

It was a question without a rational answer. One of many Hazel had asked herself since Mom died.

"I have no idea."

"Static electricity?" Sena finally proposed as she slowly lowered her hands.

"It *is* awfully dry this time of year," Hazel said shakily.

It wasn't, though. Not even a little. They were on the edge of monsoon season and, although the rain hadn't started yet, the air was damp with promise. But it seemed as good an explanation as any.

"Maybe it's just my magnetic personality." Sena shrugged and gave Hazel a crooked smile.

Hazel's shoulders relaxed a little and she smiled back. Sena picked up her chair and sat down. Hazel sat next to her.

"Well, just keep your magnetism away from my watch."

Sena's eyebrows waggled. "What does *that* mean?"

"My watch." Hazel held up her right fist, shaking the timepiece into place. "It's a 1968 Timex Sport Classic. Mechanical. Magnets and mechanical watches don't mix."

Sena screwed her face into a question mark. "A *mechanical* watch? You mean you actually have to wind it up?"

"No, silly. This is a self-winding model. There's nothing electronic about it at all. If you popped it open, you'd see all the gears."

"Where in the world did you get such a thing?" She said it like nothing existed before Apple.

"Grandma gave it to my grandfather on his fiftieth birthday." Hazel paused, remembering family gatherings and happy times. "I really appreciate its simple beauty. Also, it reminds me that a family's love is timeless."

Hazel felt her cheeks grow warm. That was a dumb thing to say. First of all, it just sounded dumb. Also, it was insensitive. Especially given what Sena had shared about *her* family last night. Hazel felt bad.

But Sena was so focused on the vintage timepiece, she didn't seem to notice. "Does it work?"

"It runs like a charm."

Sena was amused. "You know, Hazel, we could be characters in a comedy. High-tech Silicon Valley meets low-tech librarian. Pandemonium ensues."

"Pandemonium is what might happen if I'm late for work and the Thompson sisters can't pick up the new sci-fi novels I said I'd have waiting for them."

"Well, we can't have that, my dear. You should get going. We both should." Sena jumped up, extending an open palm dramatically toward Hazel, a hand Hazel gladly took.

As Hazel rose from her chair, Sena bowed slightly and brought the back of Hazel's hand to her lips for a chivalrous kiss. It was nothing, really. As chaste as it could be. But it sent an electric current up Hazel's arm, through her heart, and right down to the tips of her toes.

A satisfied grin skipped across Sena's face. She released Hazel's hand, flicked her laptop closed, picked it up along with her empty mug and plate, and turned toward the casita. "Oh, by the way," Sena said brightly over her shoulder. "I'm meeting Knox later this morning, to look at some available properties. But he suggested I stop by the library first. He wants me to see pictures of what this town looked like in its heyday. He thinks I need a history lesson before I start changing things. He said you could hook me up. See you in about an hour?" Then Sena flashed a smile, stepped inside the casita, and closed the door.

What the...what?

Hazel stared at the closed door, unable to move. Every cell in her body was on fire from the unexpected touch of Sena's lips. It's not like she didn't go on dates. She did. At least a couple a year. And she had sex. With people. Every so often. Jane, who was plugged in next to Hazel's bed, was her most reliable companion in that department. The point is, she wasn't a nun or anything. But it had been a very, verrrry long time since she wanted anything or anyone as badly as she wanted Sena right now. She was pretty sure she was going to have to change her panties before she went to work.

But what the...what?!

Sena was going out real estate shopping with Knox later that day. She had money. She had a plan. She was here to buy up as much of the town as possible and turn it into the next Silicon Valley.

You heard her. Concrete and glass and steel.

That's what she was going to do to Owen Station. Bulldoze beauty. Trample on history. Drive up prices. Change her town in all the worst ways. Destroy her father's legacy.

Sena Abrigo might be beautiful. Brilliant. Bold. Funny. Surprising. Tender, even. Magnetic enough, apparently, to give her a shock.

Someone I could fall head over heels in love with.

No, no, no. Hazel wasn't falling in love with anybody. Especially not Sena Abrigo. Sena was the *enemy*.

As she stood there, staring stupidly at the door through which Sena did her disappearing act, something bumped up against her leg. Mango.

"I'm sorry, my little friend. But you've got it all wrong."

She took one last look at Sena's door, ducked back into her own kitchen, put some kibble in Mango's dish, and hurried into town.

Halfway to the library, Hazel realized her heart was racing. By the time she was pulling into her parking spot, her mind was, too. How could she have wanted something so badly, knowing how bad it would be for her to have it? What was wrong with her?

She never wanted to see Sena again.

She wanted Sena to start kissing her and never stop.

She was more confused than she had ever been.

The only thing she was really sure about was that she wanted to kill Knox.

He waved at her from across the street, through the window of Banter & Brew, as she bolted up the library stairs to unlock the thick wooden doors. She waved back out of habit, but she didn't mean it in her usual—*Hey, Knox, good to see you!*—kind of way. It was more like—*Hey, Knox, I hope you're happy. Because this is ALL YOUR FAULT.*

It was, too. It was his fault Sena was in Owen Station in the first place—he didn't have to answer her email, help her find a house. It was his fault for not googling her, to know that she didn't belong here. His fault Sena's house wasn't ready. His idea to have Sena rent her casita. Now he was taking her real estate shopping. And he was sending her to the library. *Hazel's* library.

It was one thing to have Sena sleeping across the courtyard. Flirting with her. Sending shock waves of who knows what right through her middle. Making her feel tingly in places and ways nobody had done in...never mind. But now, thanks to her old friend Knox, Sena was headed to the library. A sacred space. A place where knowledge and memory and *history* were preserved. All things Sena, clicking away on her laptop, making plans to buy up Owen Station and turn it into the next tech mecca, didn't seem to care much about.

This was an unpleasant but necessary reminder that this flirtation—or whatever it was happening between them—was a very bad idea. Hazel wasn't a teenager anymore, no matter what her hormones were doing. She needed to stop acting like it.

Hazel hated it when that little voice was right.

She decided right then and there that if Sena was coming to the library for a history lesson, Hazel was going to make it count. She was going to be all business.

B.U.S.I.N.E.S.S. Line of work. Profession. Vocation. Calling. BUSINESS.

Protecting the legacy and the history of Owen Station *was* her calling. Hazel wasn't going to forget that. She threw her shoulders back, grabbed her cleaning kit, stopped off to give her hands a good wash, and headed upstairs to the small Rare Books and Special Collections Room to get ready.

Like a priestess entering the Holy of Holies, Hazel paused to give thanks before she stepped into the cool, dimly lit room. Her ritual of gratitude seemed to subdue whatever spirits were hanging around in the stacks that day. A silent hush greeted her. Moving quickly and deliberately around the room, she reverently lifted each book from its shelf, using a small brush to dust off the cover, checking each spine for telltale signs of decay or infestation. They were all in perfect condition. Of course.

Finally, she slipped on a clean pair of white cotton gloves and opened one of the long drawers in the vintage document cabinet marked *Owen Station: 1880-1920*. After selecting a few photos of the old downtown and a map from 1918, when Owen Station was bustling with enterprise and high hopes, she laid them carefully on the large wooden table in the center of the room.

The distinctive squeak of the library's front door opening and a loud voice in the distance broke the silence. "Helloooo! Hazel... are you here?"

Hazel inhaled sharply and closed her eyes. Just the sound of Sena's voice made the room spin. The back of her hand burned where Sena's lips had brushed them earlier. The high priestess suddenly felt like a sacrificial lamb.

She exhaled long and hard, until her lungs were empty and her head was clear. There was nothing to be afraid of. Right? Nothing was going to happen. Nothing *should* happen. They couldn't be more different. Sena said it herself. High-tech. Low-tech. Sena wanted to build a new future. Hazel wanted to protect the past. And that was just for starters. Sena was on a mission to literally dismantle everything Hazel cared about.

"Helloooo!" Sena was getting closer.

"I'm upstairs," Hazel called back. "Come up and hang a quick right into the stacks."

To her credit, Sena appeared almost reverent when she stepped into the hushed room, wide eyes sweeping across the shelves, maybe searching for the spirits she'd have to be dead not to sense. She was maddeningly beautiful. Tight, white jeans. A coffee brown, silk button-down, unbuttoned low enough to reveal just a peek of a lacy black bra. Wraparound lariat necklace with silver hoops and a turquoise stone. Very expensive cowboy boots.

All the blood drained from Hazel's face because it was surging to her groin. Her squeaked greeting was basically inaudible.

"Hello again to you, too, Hazel." Sena grinned as she shrugged a fancy leather backpack off her shoulder and dropped it onto a chair.

This was embarrassing. Sena looked so relaxed, so confident. Hazel could hardly form enough words to make a sentence.

"What is this place?" Sena asked seriously. "I mean, of course, I've been in a library before. Before I could carry one in my laptop, that is. But I've never seen anything like this."

"This is our Rare Books and Special Collections Room." Hazel stood a little taller. She was presider over secret knowledge and sacred stories. So she should darn well act like it.

"Interesting. All these things are digitized, I hope. Some of this stuff looks like it's older than—oh, wow!—are these books covered in...*leather*?" Sena reached out to grab one from its shelf.

"Don't touch those!"

Startled, Sena snatched back her hand.

"Those are a 1910 set of Harvard Classics. And, yes, they are bound in Moroccan leather."

"Leather bound, eh?" Sena turned slowly with a sly smile and took two steps toward Hazel. "I like the sound of that, don't you?" When Hazel didn't move, Sena took two more steps forward, until she was close enough for Hazel to catch a scent of the prickly pear soap she left for guests in the casita.

Hazel still couldn't move.

Why didn't she just run away?

She wanted to.

She didn't want to.

Maybe swirled in the air like the ubiquitous dust old books attracted.

U.B.I.Q.U.I.T.O.U.S. Omnipresent. Inescapable. UBIQUITOUS.

She was trying so hard to think of something, anything that wasn't Sena. Trying to *think*.

Sena didn't seem the least bit conflicted. Her full chest rose and fell steadily. Locks of silky dark hair draped along her strong square jawline. One eyebrow arched, pulling the corner of her mouth upward along with it. She looked deep into Hazel's eyes and stepped forward again until they were almost nose to nose.

"So, I came for a history lesson." Sena was practically purring. "Teach me something."

Hazel blinked. "Um. Okay." She moistened her lips with her tongue and swallowed hard. "The Harvard Classics are fifty books thought to be the essence of a liberal education."

"Uh-huh. Go on..."

Hazel wasn't sure her legs were going to hold her up, but somehow she managed to produce actual words. "They were compiled and edited by Charles Eliot, who was the president of Harvard at the time. This set is from a very limited edition, given to this library around the same time that my great-grandparents arrived, by our town fathers, who hoped Owen Station would be a civilized place to live and work."

"Civilized? Hmmm..." The corner of Sena's mouth ticked further upward. Hazel stared at it, wondering what it would be like to taste it.

"Uh-huh." Hazel nodded weakly. "Civilized."

"And did they succeed? Did Owen Station become...civilized?"

Hazel couldn't breathe. "Um...I'm not sure." She closed her eyes, told that little voice to shut up, and willed Sena to lean in and kiss her.

"Hazel?"

Hazel snapped open her eyes. Sena was staring over her shoulder.

"What *are* those?" Sena asked. Then she stepped around Hazel to stand beside the large wooden table covered with old photographs.

Hazel turned, too, and moved to stand beside her.

"These are what you came to see." Hazel sounded a little squeaky in her own ears but at least she was able to talk. "These are photographs taken during Owen Station's heyday. Right around the turn of the twentieth century."

"And this?"

"That's a map of Owen Station, from 1918."

"Show me around."

Hazel pulled the map closer—and Sena moved closer, too. They were shoulder to shoulder. Touching. The scent of prickly pear was overwhelming. Every hair on the back of Hazel's neck was vibrating and everything below Hazel's belly button was screaming for attention. But Sena seemed wholly focused on the map.

"This is Main Street, right?" Sena asked, pointing.

"Please don't touch it, Sena." Hazel was back on the job.

"I'm sorry. You're wearing gloves. These are precious documents. My bad."

"It's okay."

It turned out Sena wasn't uncaring. She was just untrained.

Hazel used the map to give her an overview of the city. Back in those days, there were three main sections of Owen Station, all connected by trolley. There were the mines themselves, of course. Then there was downtown, built right in the center of the fanciest neighborhoods, where the captains of industry and finance lived. It was abandoned after the mines closed and the captains moved on to extract and exploit somewhere else. But Main Street—and the entertainment district nearby—was where life happened for the people of Owen Station. It's where they shopped and played. Where they danced and drank. Where they hung out on the street corners, swapping gossip and recipes. It was everything.

Tracing her gloved finger along Main Street, Hazel described every building. Who designed it. When it was built. The litany of occupants over the years. The year her father led the massive effort to renovate it.

"Your father sounds like a visionary...I think I would have liked him."

Hazel turned toward Sena. She was so beautiful. And she actually seemed interested in what Hazel was saying, in the buildings, in the history. It was an irresistible combination.

"I think maybe Dad would have liked you, too."

Sena took Hazel's gloved hands in her own and gently squeezed them. "Will you tell me about him sometime?"

Hazel stopped breathing. There was the question Sena verbalized—will you tell me about your dad? But a very different question was dancing in Sena's eyes. *The* question.

Hazel needed to answer.

Go ahead, answer her. Tell her no. You're not kissing her. Not now. Not ever.

But Hazel didn't want to say no. She was tired of saying no. No to love. No to adventure. No to life. She needed to *feel* something again. The stomach-dropping thrill of a roller coaster. The dizzying high from looking over the edge of a canyon. She wanted to feel like *herself* again. Adventurous. Creative. Free.

Willing that irritating little voice to shut the hell up, Hazel gave an almost imperceptible nod. That was all Sena needed.

She slowly stripped off one white glove and brought Hazel's naked hand to her lips. Peering up through lidded eyes, she kissed the underside of Hazel's wrist.

Everything suddenly got very fuzzy. Was this what people meant when they said they couldn't see straight?

Hazel closed one eye and tilted her head, trying to bring Sena's face into focus. Her deep brown eyes looked up at Hazel. Smiling, Sena dragged her tongue right down the center of Hazel's open palm, to the tip of her middle finger, which she kissed and licked and then slowly sucked inside of her mouth.

Hazel sank backward against the table, her legs dissolving beneath her.

Her watch ticked softly on Hazel's wrist as Sena's tongue stroked and slid between Hazel's fingers, but time was no longer actually passing. Hazel was swirling now, floating in the air, with the *maybes*, with the dust, circling the two bodies below.

"Do you want me to stop?"

Sena sounded like she actually would, if instructed, and that snapped Hazel back into her body. She made sure the next words she spoke were sharp and clear.

"No, Sena. I do not want you to stop."

With that, Sena released Hazel's hand. She slid her own hands down Hazel's sides, grabbing her waist, and lifted Hazel's backside up onto the table.

Whatever was left of Hazel's defenses—and they weren't much to start with—had been destroyed. Hazel shifted on the table, leaned back, and opened her legs. It was an impulsive, instinctual invitation that Sena did not miss. She reached down and gripped Hazel's ankles, owning them, and then dragged her fingers up Hazel's calves. When she reached Hazel's knees, she pushed them open farther.

Hazel gasped and threw her head back, eyes squeezed shut, unable to resist but also unwilling to acknowledge she was allowing this to happen. Her lungs hurt from holding her breath.

It hadn't just been a long time since Hazel had been touched like this. It had been so long since she believed she could be.

It happened slowly. The house got darker and darker as Mom's illness worsened. She heard that Abby had a new girlfriend and moved to California. Then the funeral and all the deadening details that had to be managed after someone you love passed on. Then, the silence.

A silence that Sena shattered when she swaggered into Banter & Brew. Now here Hazel was, surrendering to Sena's hot desire and her own. Feeling terrified and electrified and more alive than she had felt in years. Sena was everything Hazel was not and exactly what Hazel needed.

Hazel leaned back, opening, granting access, giving permission, begging for more. Sena's probing fingers teased their way upward from Hazel's knees, along the inside of her thighs, to just below her panty line. Hazel heard a guttural groan and realized it was her own.

She was ready to give Sena whatever she wanted.

Instead, Sena chose that moment—*that moment!*—to withdraw her hands from beneath Hazel's skirt. She chastely kissed the inside of Hazel's elbow and handed back her arm. If the mission was making Hazel insane with desire, then mission accomplished.

When Hazel opened her eyes, Sena was grinning back at her.

"Well, now. Since I know you have to get back to work—I mean, the Thompson sisters might walk in at any moment, right?—and Knox is waiting for me—how about if you let me take you to dinner tonight? We'll have more time for history lessons and, after dinner, let's plan on going back to my place for dessert."

Hazel's entire body was on fire. She had no words.

She pulled her knees together, sat up straighter, and tried to wrestle control over the torrent of emotion coursing through her heart and mind. Disbelief. Embarrassment. Lust. Terror. She knew she looked ridiculous. She *was* ridiculous. She didn't care.

Sena was waiting for an answer. Again.

All Hazel could manage was a nod.

"Great, then, it's a date." Then Sena picked up her leather pack, threw it over her shoulder, and walked out of the room.

Hazel, on the other hand, had to will her wobbly legs to stand. Everything from the neck down felt foreign, like it all belonged to someone else, someone she used to know, someone who had been dead, who had forgotten how to breathe, how to feel, how to love.

She steadied herself against the long wooden table, heart pounding, groin throbbing, skin on fire every place Sena had touched it.

Oh my God. I have a date.

Chapter Six

A Threat

Sena thought about heading back to the casita for another shower. A cold one. What the hell was wrong with her? She should have checked "fucking the redhead" off her list that morning. Hazel was practically begging for it. Sena was used to that. And on any other day, with any other woman, Sena would have been more than happy to give it to her.

Sure, it was fun to play with her. Leave her wanting more. But that wasn't the real reason Sena pulled back in the library. She wasn't sure exactly what it was, but there was something different about Hazel. She was…sweet. And not in a fake way. It seemed completely unselfconscious. Like when she went all librarian in the courtyard yesterday morning, and then got embarrassed for giving a history lesson that Sena had lived firsthand, and when she lost it over those old books. But more than that, Hazel made *Sena* feel different. She kept making Sena feel *seen*. And, okay, this was weird. She made Sena feel safe. Hazel had a family story for every occasion. And, yes, it stirred up troubling memories and feelings. But it also felt nice. Really nice. There was a warmth there that Sena hadn't realized she'd been lacking. A sense of belonging. Love.

Oh, for God's sake.

Sena didn't have time for this. It was her first full day in Owen Station and there was hella work to do. She threw her Brunello

Cucinelli laptop bag onto the front seat of her car, switched on the ignition, and roared off to meet Knox. He was waiting for her outside the old YWCA building, just a few blocks from Banter & Brew right on the edge of the historic district.

"Mornin', Sena." He scratched the stubble on his chin and looked uncertainly at the dilapidated three-story. "Are you sure this is where you want to start?"

She didn't bother answering. Knox would learn soon enough that Sena always knew what she wanted. And went for it. She looked up at what she planned to make her first commercial real estate purchase in Owen Station. The first of many.

"This must have been magnificent, once upon a time. As you probably know, this building was designed in the early 1900s by the first woman licensed in Arizona to work as an architect. The Owen Mining Company built it for the YWCA to run as a boarding house for young women coming to find work—and maybe a husband—out here on the edge of civilization."

Knox looked at her sideways. "You sound a little like Hazel."

Sena squeezed her eyes shut behind her aviators and gulped as the sound of Hazel's name sent a heat tracking missile up through her middle.

I bet she's still wondering what hit her.

Sena certainly was.

Knox cleared his throat, apparently expecting an answer.

She tried to refocus. "That's very funny, Knox. It shouldn't surprise you that I do my homework. Plus, I took a few architecture classes at USC. Even thought about majoring in it for a hot minute. It's always been an interest of mine. But Hazel is in a category all her own."

"Yes, she is," he smiled. "How's it going with her, anyway?"

"Couldn't be better." Somehow she managed a straight face.

"I'm so glad." His shoulders relaxed and he took a deep breath. "Hazel is a very special person, you know. Not just to me but to a lot of people in town. She's been through a lot. Too many losses for somebody our age."

Of course. That explained the haunted vibe and all the past-tense stories of family members. "I've been picking up on that. I know her father died when she was young."

"He did. Hazel idolized him. But she's lost everyone else, too. Her grandparents. Her mom."

"She doesn't have siblings?"

"No. No one except for the family she's created—including me. But she still shows up, you know? She really cares about people. And about this place."

Knox was a tall guy, maybe six-two, so she had to look up to look him in the eye. He didn't say anymore. His eyes said it all. Sena had better be careful. Hazel had a community of people who cared about her. A family of sorts, even if they weren't actually blood related. And friends. All things Sena forgot she was missing.

Hey, hombrecito!

The word just popped into her mind out of nowhere—*little man*—Sena could still hear Quique, Vic, and Pancho calling to her from across the field. Her dad's lead ranch hands. Even when he stopped paying attention to her, they were there. They were there for her after Abuelo died, too. Teaching her things. Taking her with them to repair fences or bed the stalls. Encouraging her to be independent, to be brave. She *did* know what it was like to be loved. But it all felt like so long ago and so far away.

"You okay, Sena?" Knox was studying her.

"Yes, yes. Of course." Shifting back to the building she'd come to see, she asked, "You're sure the town's open to selling this eyesore?"

"If the price was right, most of the people on our town council would sell their own kids," he said flatly.

"Don't start this again, Knox." As they were searching through listings at Banter & Brew yesterday, he had given her the lowdown on small-town politics, a waffling mayor, a greedy council, and an anti-development group called Save Owen Station—SOS, for short. They were lobbying town leaders to stop exactly the kind of growth she hoped to spark. That's where she lost her patience.

"What precisely do these 'SOS' idiots want to save Owen Station *from*, anyway? Prosperity? Opportunity? The future?" The more she thought about it, the more pissed she got.

Across the bar yesterday, he had thrown his hands up in surrender. "Fair enough, Sena. I do think it's possible for Owen Station to grow in a way that benefits everybody, not just wealthy developers—no offense—and honestly, I'd like to see that happen. It's just that, at the moment, the town doesn't have a plan. If you've got enough money, the zoning department—by which I mean *Dan*—will give you a green light to do whatever you want. History and humanity be damned. And he's got the mayor's unspoken approval to do it. It's creating all kinds of resentment and anxiety for a lot of people. And, on top of what we've all been through over the past few years, that's giving some of the nastier characters in town an opening. We've been lucky so far—the town's managed to avoid the ugliness you see out there. But it's just a matter of time, I think, before it seeps its way in. I'd hate to see you get caught in the middle of it all."

She only had one thing to say. "I've dealt with worse."

And she had, too.

Like that asshat of a CEO she worked for. When she told him she was leaving Silicon Valley to launch a new venture, he didn't even try to hide his contempt.

"That's a nice vision, Sena."

He was such a patronizing prick. Getting his picture on the cover of *Time* magazine the year before didn't help. He literally sneered at her.

"All the noise you're hearing right now about 'diversity' and 'inclusion' is just that. Noise. Nobody—let me say again—NOBODY actually gives a shit about it. Also, good luck finding enough women and, quote P.O.C. unquote, to make your little dream come true. Like it or not, guys like me actually drive innovation and make this sector great. But, hey. Good luck, sweetie."

Sena burned with rage and told him to fuck all the way off before executing a perfect 180 and sweeping out of his office, head held high. But his words still rang in her ears, joining the chorus of subtle and not-so-subtle put-downs she had endured over the years.

She'd be damned if she was going to let a couple of small-town Luddites listening to too much talk radio get in her way now. Standing in the shade of history, she looked up at the old Y and snapped her fingers to get Knox's attention. "Tell me what I have to do to make this deal."

"Well, it's not on the market. So you have to make an offer that will make the mayor's eyes pop."

"I can do that," she said impatiently. "What else?"

"It'll go a long way with the SOS crowd if you promise not to knock it down. Renovate it, instead."

She rolled her eyes. "We've been over this, too, Knox. I need a state-of-the-art apartment complex—at least double the size of this building—for the coders and entrepreneurs I'm bringing to town."

"SOS is going to hate that, Sena."

"Hate *what?* Most of the people living in this building will be *women*, coming here for opportunity and a new start, someplace where they can be as amazing as they dare. It'll be like reliving history, for God's sake. I've hired a woman who will help me design something that nods to the original building, and even incorporates parts of the old building into the new. It's not my fault the town let it go to hell. But at this point it'd cost too damn much money to bring this old thing up to code, much less make it a place with the kinds of bells and whistles tech whiz kids need."

Knox stood staring at the decaying Art Deco building looming silently before them. "The YWCA closed down and sold it to the city probably thirty years ago. It's been abandoned for at least two decades," he finally said quietly. "I get it, Sena. I don't know if everyone else will. But I do."

The rest of the day was a little less controversial. They spent most of it outside the historic district, in Owen Station's old downtown. Hazel wasn't kidding. It looked like a ghost town. Six blocks or so of boarded up storefronts and abandoned office buildings.

"A mule-drawn trolley used to connect this downtown area to Main Street and the entertainment district," Knox explained.

"Eventually, they built an electric streetcar that went from here all the way to the railroad station on the other edge of town. The station's gone now, just like everything else. When the mines closed, the guys who owned these businesses packed up and moved on."

"The bars stayed open," Sena noted.

"You always need booze...especially while you're watching your town die."

They stood in the middle of the empty street as Sena looked down one side and up the other.

"I'll take it," she said decisively.

Knox cocked his head to the side and peered at her curiously. "What do you mean, *take it*? Take what?"

"All of it." She took off her aviators so he could see her looking him in the eye. "I want to buy all of downtown Owen Station. What's left of it, anyway."

Knox's eyes grew wide and he swallowed hard but didn't say anything. What was there to say?

As she led him up and down the abandoned blocks, snapping pictures with her tablet, she shared her vision. One full block would be a high-tech co-working space. Over there, a maker space. There, a research and development center. Here, a business incubator. She'd bring in 3-D printers, build a lab, make available whatever equipment her entrepreneurs might need to design the next world-changing technology. She already had two women-of-color-owned start-ups ready to relocate. They'd have their pick of real estate and help anchor the development.

"No one just *works* all the time, though." She shifted gears. "We'll need to bring in the kinds of businesses and amenities that make life fun...for *women*. Wine bars. A green salon. Farm-to-table restaurants. A big, beautiful dog park. A cinema that shows indie films...a community garden...high end consignment shops...a video arcade and comic book store..."

Knox snapped his head around to look at her.

"That's right, Knox." She grinned. "*Video games and comic books.* Geeks are geeks, no matter what we look like on the outside."

She could hardly contain her excitement. She could see it all so clearly. And she was making it happen.

"I'd love to get that streetcar up and going again, too. An electric one, not the one with mules," she laughed. "And we'll need a great micro roaster and coffee shop on this side of town. Maybe it's time for Banter & Brew to expand?"

Knox gave her a lopsided smile. The poor guy looked shell-shocked.

"How about if we go start working on some paperwork," he asked.

She was so ready. Ready to do something new, something that *mattered*. It sucked that she couldn't do it back home, but that door had closed long ago. It sucked that she couldn't make it happen in Silicon Valley, but that wasn't a surprise. She was going to build a whole new world, starting right here, one where you could succeed if you were creative enough and willing to work hard enough. Where it didn't matter whether or not you had balls. The people she was going to bring to Owen Station were going to change the face of technology. Literally. And that was going to change everything.

"Sounds great, Knox. I'm just going to grab my drone and shoot some pics from above. I want to send them to my architect so we can start laying out the development."

An hour later, she was perched on a stool inside Banter & Brew with her laptop open, looking at aerial photos. Knox, who had sent his barista home early with a bad case of cramps, was making an iced latte to Sena's specification. Skim milk. No syrup.

"Seriously, Knox. This town couldn't be more perfect. Ninety minutes from an international airport. Close to major interstates and cross-border highways. All the infrastructure in place to build. Well, I'll have to do something about getting reliable high speed in here. But that's doable. People are going to love it here. It's gorgeous. Great hiking, mountain biking, camping. All the things young professionals love to do. Plus, there's plenty of affordable housing. Everybody is so sick of the real estate market in Silicon Valley. It's just as bad in Seattle. And who wants to live in Wyoming? Honestly, I don't understand why this hasn't happened before."

"Why what hasn't happened?" Knox set the latte on a napkin to catch the sweat already pouring down the outside of the glass.

"Any of it. Why hasn't somebody figured out something to do with that deserted downtown? And I don't just mean tourism. I mean something that'll bring good jobs back."

"I don't know. Lots of reasons I guess. Some folks are waiting for the mines to reopen."

"But it's been decades."

"Yeah, I know. But there's still lots of copper in these hills. They just didn't have the technology to reach it forty years ago. Once they do and the price of copper is high enough—thanks to the demand your kind of tech creates—scientists in Japan have figured out a way to use copper nanoparticles instead of pricier metals in next gen electronics—they'll be back."

Sena tilted her head and looked up at Knox. She had read that article, too. She liked this guy more every day.

"Okay, but even if mining does make a comeback, why pin the economic future of a town—much less a whole region—on one industry? Especially one that threatens this incredible landscape." She was impatient with this conversation.

"You're not wrong." Knox put down the towel he was using to dry glasses and leaned across the counter. He spoke quietly, just loud enough for Sena to hear. "I said there are a lot of reasons. One of them is sitting right over there." He nodded in the direction of three men sitting at a table along the back wall.

Sena looked over her shoulder to see them staring at her. They laughed when they saw her looking at them, and then turned away to form a whispering huddle.

"SOS?" Sena guessed, swiveling back to Knox.

Knox nodded. "Save Owen Station. And don't look now," he said quietly, picking up his towel to pretend-wipe the counter, "but we've got company."

"You new to town?" The man's voice was gruff and he was not smiling as he leaned an elbow on the counter, uncomfortably close to Sena.

"You know damn well she is, Sirus. Leave her be."

Knox's language shocked Sena, but his menacing tone seemed to bounce right off the guy.

"I'm just coming over to say hello," Sirus growled. Then he turned to Sena with a sickeningly sweet smile. "Hello, sweetheart," he drawled. "Welcome to Owen Station."

"Hello, Sirus." She snapped her laptop shut and spun around on her stool so that she was facing him. Sitting up straight, she was exactly eye to eye. "My name is *Seh-na*...not sweetheart. Make a note. Now, what can I do for you?"

He shot a sneer in Knox's direction. "I see the little lady here is all business. What fun is that?"

"I think you came over here to talk to *me*, Sirus," Sena said steadily, crossing her arms. "So, let's talk. What do you want?"

"I don't want anything you're selling," he snarled. "But I am interested in what you're buying. I hear you've got your eye on the old Y."

Sena glanced at Knox, who shrugged. "It's a small town," he offered helplessly.

She looked back at Sirus. "So what if I do?" It wasn't really a question. It was a warning.

One of his nostrils flared and his eyes narrowed as the fake smile melted into a single curled lip. He stared openly at Sena for a long minute and then took a short step back. Under lidded brows, his eyes raked their way down her body. It was enough to make most women shudder with disgust. And fear.

Sena leaned forward, making him look her in the eye. "Not in a million fucking years, you little dick."

He snorted and looked away. "Nice friends you got there, Knox." Then he took several long strides across the café to rejoin the men at his table, who slapped him on the back chortling.

"Assholes," Knox said under his breath.

"The world is full of them." Sena took a deep breath and felt the adrenaline rush start to subside.

"Yeah, I'm sure. That particular asshole is my landlord."

Sena raised an eyebrow. "Are you serious?"

"Deadly."

"Oh shit, Knox. I'm sorry. I hope I didn't just make life harder for you."

"Don't worry about it. But it's good for you to know what you're up against. Guys like that don't care about anything…except people thinking they have the biggest swinging you-know-whats in town. Sirus owns this whole building. It's named the Goldstone after his great-grandfather…in fact, he owns this whole block. It's been in his family for generations. His dad was an okay guy. Helped Mr. Butler—Hazel's father—renovate Main Street back in the day. But Sirus is different. He doesn't care whether a new development is good for Owen Station or not. If it threatens his place in the pecking order, he's against it. And you, my dear Sena…" His face softened into a crooked smile. "You are definitely a threat."

She couldn't argue with that.

Knox headed off to the kitchen to handle the dishes his barista had let pile up as Sena started uploading photos for the architect. The connection was slow. Annoying. But it also gave her an opportunity to look more closely at the pictures she had taken.

No doubt, the first commercial buildings in this frontier town had been a variety of wooden and adobe structures.

She might have known for sure if she had taken a bit more time with Hazel's pictures. And she probably should have felt guilty about not doing that, but she didn't. Instead, she closed her eyes and let a wave of heat flow through her middle.

Dinner—and dessert—could not come soon enough.

She cleared her throat and shifted forward on the stool, trying to rein in her body and refocus on the photos on her screen.

The oldest remaining buildings looked like they were mostly designed in the Queen Anne style, probably from the late 1800s. She recognized the elaborate roof lines, overhanging eaves, polygonal towers. Most of the newer buildings, like the old Y, had features from the Art Deco period popular in the 1920s. Clean lines, playful ornamentation. The tallest was eight stories. It must have had an elevator.

She would have loved to have seen them in their glory days. And she would have loved to have known the people who dared to dream up this town, out here in the middle of nowhere. Some of the buildings still bore their names. Frank Woolworth. Ansen Phelps. William Dodge. All men, of course. But there were women, too, like Mary Colter and Anne Rockfellow, who designed so many of these earliest buildings. They would have been far more interesting. Living life their way on the old frontier. Challenging convention. Elbowing their way into rooms where only men had been. Putting new materials and construction processes into practice. Changing the landscape of the Wild West.

She leaned in closer to study the photos she had taken. They were all just boarded up windows. Empty streets. Dilapidated interiors, half-visible through decaying roofs.

It was clearly time for new dreams. And people who were brave enough to make them happen. If that made her a threat, so be it.

CHAPTER SEVEN

PROS AND CONS

*O*h *my God, did that really happen?*
Hazel hadn't been able to think about anything else since Sena left her in the Rare Books and Special Collections Room.

For once she had let herself do what she wanted, what felt good, whether or not it made sense. Even if it wasn't the smart or responsible thing. She could just imagine Delaney doing that "you did it" dance and the things she would say in that high-pitched singsongy way she used when she was bouncing out of her skin excited.

Girrrl! It's about darn time! You gotta let yourself have fun, Hazel! You need a warm body to hang on to, somebody real who will love you and be there for you. You deserve that. And don't tell me you've got me and Knox and Lace and all the other people who love you to death in this town. It's not the same. You need to let yourself find that one special person whose heart belongs only to you, and to do that you need to take some risks. And you did it! You really, really did it!

Delaney would have been thrilled.

Hazel, on the other, wasn't sure what to think.

She hadn't felt this way in years. Forget that. She had *never* felt this way. Every cell in her body was vibrating, squealing like they'd just been zapped with the light of a thousand suns. She could see things she'd never seen before. Like the dancing, flying, breathing, living colors on the book spines lining the stacks. Bumblebee yellow. Tiger orange. Rose red. Crocodile green. She had been pulled through the back of the wardrobe and landed upside down in Narnia. She wasn't sure the world would ever look the same again.

But she *liked* her world the way it was. The way it had always been. It was reliable. Steady. Safe. She'd been buying her clothes at the vintage shop for years, partly because it took the smallest bite out of her paycheck, but also because when she pulled on a pencil skirt and snapped on a brooch, she loved seeing her grandmother's reflection in the mirror. It felt almost sacred to stir up a pot of potato soup in the same enameled cast iron pot, using the same recipe she inherited from her mother. It was the real reason she started wearing Grandpa's watch a few years back. She knew she couldn't turn back time, but she sure as heck wanted to be able to hear the tick tock of it.

It made her friends nuts. They got into it the last time she had them over for dinner. Knox was standing in the hallway, looking at the rows and rows of framed family photos on the wall, grimacing. "It's like a museum in here, Hazel."

She snapped. "Honestly, Knox. What's wrong with a museum, if you're preserving the things that you have loved most in your life? What's wrong with honoring the people who have made you who you are?"

"Nothing," Lace said softly. "Nothing at all, honey. Unless your attachment to what *was* prevents you from embracing what *could* be."

Lace the philosopher.

Delaney the busybody.

Knox the overprotective brother.

Why did they always have to have an opinion about everything?

It's not like their lives were perfect. Delaney was madly in love with the new pastor in town, a guy named Bexley. He seemed earnest enough, like he actually believed he was on a mission for good, so it wasn't hard to understand why Delaney had fallen so hard. But he had no idea she was even interested. None. Zero. Zilch. Knox and Lace had been divorced for years but were still business partners and best friends. They both dated other people, but who in the world would want to fall in love with, much less marry one of them. Two's company but three is definitely a crowd. It's not like any of her dearest friends were experts on their *own* lives, much less anyone else's. Much less hers.

Hazel sat down at one of the long mahogany tables in the research room, where she spent long hours studying as a teenager. Knox gave her a first kiss at that table, a sweet peck on the cheek. That library was filled with memories, one of the reasons she loved working there.

She stretched her hands out across the table and leaned over until her forehead was pressed against the cool wood. As much as she hated to admit it, her friends were right. She *was* more comfortable surrounded by the past. History was knowable. You could catalog and curate it. It didn't sneak up on you, toss you onto a table, bust you wide open, threaten to upend your whole life, and leave you dripping with confusion.

Dammit, Sena.

Hazel bolted upright in her seat. And that was another thing. Hazel prided herself on having a strong enough command of the English language that she didn't need vulgarity. Then Sena marched into town and twenty-four hours later Hazel was swearing like an old miner. What was Sena going to turn upside down next?

The answer to that question turned out to be lunch, that's what.

Knox was nowhere to be found when Hazel got to Banter & Brew at one o'clock. Her usual time. *Their* time. When they would catch up on the day's business and enjoy each other's company. It was usually the highlight of her day. They had been doing this together since before Banter & Brew was even officially opened. Hazel would spend her lunch hours there giving Knox advice and helping him refinish furniture, organize the kitchen, hang curtains.

The gum-chomping barista on duty said Knox was out on business. "Showing some properties to that new señorita in town. You know, the one who sizzles when she walks." The girl waggled her eyebrows and wiggled her hips. It wasn't clear if she was trying to be funny or suggestive. She was neither.

"Yes, I know who you mean." Hazel rolled her eyes, trying to look like she didn't care. "Is my quiche ready?"

"Sorry, hon. We're all out."

Hazel gasped and fell back a step. "What did you say?"

"I said we're all out." She opened a palm and used the other hand to sweep it, like she was clearing a table. Sign language for *all gone*, as though Hazel needed help understanding.

"How...how can it be gone? Knox knows it's quiche day. You're telling me he didn't put aside a piece for me before he left? You're telling me that—"

"It's all gone, hon. Yes, that's what I'm saying. How about a grilled cheese, instead? They're looking good today."

Hazel was stunned into silence. Her heart was beating louder by the second, louder even than the old swamp cooler that was gasping for breath. This girl clearly did not understand what was happening. She was new in town. Came from Chicago or somewhere out east, following a boy who was trying to make it as a sculptor. Or a songwriter. Or something. Hazel didn't care and didn't see what Knox saw in her, and right now she was the closest target for Hazel's hyped-up-on-hormones frustration.

"No, I don't want grilled cheese." Each word clinked on the counter like an ice cube. "Today is *Wednesday*."

Hazel didn't even wait for a response. She turned around and marched right back to the library.

Now, she was standing in the middle of the card catalog and her stomach was growling as she watched dust dance through the rays of afternoon sunshine pouring through the beveled glass windows. She didn't know how long she'd been standing there, trying to make herself think about something other than Sena.

Her oldest friend—and Sena—were out there somewhere, collaborating on how to wreck the town.

Sena—and her ruined lunch hour.

Sena—and that weird electric shock in the courtyard.

Sena—and the sadness that floated behind her eyes.

Sena—and her new best friend, Mango.

Sena—and those terrifying, thrilling, maddening moments in the Rare Books Room.

Okay, it wasn't working. She could not stop thinking about Sena.

She checked her Timex. Still hours to go till closing time and her date with...

"Disaster!" she barked into the silence, swinging wildly between hot anticipation and unmitigated dread.

She needed help. So naturally she went to the place she'd been going forever, or at least since she was about eight, whenever she was upset or confused or lost. Her spot in the library was right inside the colorful children's section. She flopped down into the weathered leather chair in a corner, near her favorite books.

"It's not possible to orgasm just because someone kisses your wrist and tickles your thigh, is it?" she asked Curious George, picking up a book worn ragged from generations of eager readers, knowing it was ridiculous. But, heck. That little monkey had been in every kind of trouble imaginable over the past seventy-five years.

"Come on, George. Ask the Man in the Yellow Hat, if you don't know. Because I thought for a minute this morning that could actually happen!"

She fell back into the chair cackling and tried to catch her breath. "Okay, Hazel. Stop being so dramatic."

She tried to shake the thought that she was losing her mind, got up, and walked over to the return cart, checking to see if anything needed reshelving. Again. For the fifth time that day.

It didn't.

Then she wandered to the periodical shelves, to see if they needed to be tidied up. There were fewer and fewer magazines and newspapers in print every year, so the racks always looked half-empty, anyway. And she had already tidied them at least three times that day.

Finally, she stepped behind the thick, hand-carved wooden counter, where she had checked out and checked in hundreds of books over the years, and caressed the smooth, cool surface.

Before she was eight years old, Hazel had scoped out all the best quiet corners of this building, places where she could disappear into a good story. She knew the Dewey Decimal System by heart before she was nine. After Dad died, the summer she turned thirteen, she spent even more time there. Mom never had to wonder. She was always lost in a book, whisked away to a life or a universe where she could be someone, almost anyone, else. With a book, you could take off on wild adventures, skim over the bad parts and jump to the place where the heroine wins the day. You didn't have to wake up every morning knowing that everything terrible was still true. Especially now that her family was all gone, most of the people she loved best in the world were alphabetized by author on those shelves. Hazel was a sucker for the classics, too. Samwise Gamgee and his love of hearth and home. Cassie Logan, who stood courageously against injustice and intolerance. Meg Murray, who never lost faith that we can do and be better.

She looked again at her mechanical Timex, faithfully ticking away on her wrist. That was a record for the day. Twelve and a half minutes without thinking about Sena. What it would be like to taste her full lips. What she would look like when she slipped out of those tight jeans. How she would finish what she started in the Rare Books room.

Hazel had to make a decision.

And she had to be rational about it.

She knew exactly what to do.

She reached under the counter and pulled out the 1914 Underwood she stored there—she had found it in the back of a storage closet when she took the job. Mr. Miller, the recently retired antique dealer, refurbished it for her. She loved the click-clack of the keys and the way letters looked hand-crafted on the page. She used it mostly to capture her thoughts for a short story or novella she hoped to write one day. Those thoughts didn't come to her now nearly as often as they used to.

She sat down, took a deep breath, tucked a fresh sheet of typing paper into the roller, shoved her glasses up into the proper position on her nose, and lightly placed her fingers on the keys until the clicking began.

Dear Sena,

She stared at the black letters on the page.

"Wait, what am I doing?"

Her voice echoed across the vastness, bouncing off those long wooden tables where she had spent so many hours reading and dreaming about where life might take her.

Apparently, she was writing a letter to Sena. Hadn't planned to. But, there she was. She cocked her head, staring off into nothing, trying to gather her thoughts. The clacking beneath her fingers startled her. She was writing.

You are the most beautiful woman I have ever seen. You are also terrifying and I hate what you are planning to do to my town. And I can't stop thinking about you. You make my body want to do things it's never done with anyone. I can't wait to let you tear my clothes off.

She stopped, read back what she had written, and erupted into hysterical laughter. "Oh my God—I mean *goodness*." She silently scolded herself for her language.

"I *am* losing it." Writing a letter to Sena—especially *that* letter—wasn't going to happen. She ripped the paper off the roll and crumpled it into a ball.

"Let's try this again."

At the top of a new sheet of paper, she typed:

Should I keep my date with Sena tonight?

Pros and Cons

She started with the cons.

She's a developer

She so rich, she thinks she can just sweep in and take over my town

She loves computers and flashy new things—I love history and meaningful old things—we have nothing in common

I'm perfectly happy with life the way it is

She stared at those words for a minute. Then she pulled out a little jar of correction fluid, painted over the word perfectly, and typed the word mostly in its place. She was *mostly* happy with life. Wasn't that the best anyone could hope for?

She took one last look at the list. And then added:

She scares me

She read those last three words again. "Why on earth would she scare me?"

Her fingers answered her own question.

She makes me swear, makes Knox forget what's really important, and wants to pull me into an uncertain future when all I want to do is stay bundled up in the past

"Wait a minute. Who's writing this, anyway? Delaney? Let's move to the pros."

Pro number one flew from her fingers onto the page.

I want to f$%k her!

She shook her head and squawked again. "Holy Hannah, Hazel! You have a one-track mind. Also, let's be honest, you'd rather have *her* do that to you."

She shook her head and kept typing.

She has great taste in shoes
Mango likes her
I think Dad would have, too
Delaney says I need to get laid
Delaney is right
She is playful and it's fun sparring with her
She makes me see things in a new way
My heart races when I'm near her
I think there's more to her than meets the eye

Hazel sat back on her stool, reviewed the list, and then added one more to the pros. This time she knew exactly what she was typing.

It's probably time to move on

She took a deep breath as she reread her own startling admission and held it for a long minute before slowly exhaling. On second thought, she wasn't at all convinced it was time for any such thing. Move on to where? To what? Why? What was wrong with right where she was?

She reached for her jar of correction fluid but was distracted by the sound of the heavy wooden front door opening. She held her breath and tried not to panic. What if Sena had come back to finish what she started?

Oh no.

Oh please.

Hazel hopped off her stool, ready to run in one direction or another, she wasn't quite sure which. Fortunately, she didn't need to decide that. Yet. An older white couple pushed their way inside the library dressed in matching moisture wicking shirts and vented explorer hats. She recognized them right away.

Tourists.

Since the Owen Station Library was on the National Register of Historic Places, Hazel was used to people from out of town stopping in, hoping for a tour. She loved every opportunity to share the million historical details she had crammed inside her head. People always got way more than they bargained for on the Owen Station Library tour.

And today they were a welcome distraction.

"Hi there!" She used the corner of her T-shirt to wipe her glasses clean and popped them back into place. "How can I help you?"

The taller of the two women had a ramrod straight back and cropped gray hair under her cap. She was the first to extend a hand, a stiff gesture of greeting. "How do you do? My name's Alex. This is my wife, Amanda."

"Nice to meet you. I'm Hazel, your friendly neighborhood librarian."

The one called Amanda was far more expressive. Her hat was perched on top of a mass of long purple hair. Or it was probably purple when it was first dyed. It was sort of a purplish, brownish gray now. "Please, call me Manda!" She opened her arms wide to declare their arrival. "We're new to town!"

Hazel tried not to laugh. "You don't say."

Alex cleared her throat. "We're here looking at property. Knox sent us over here to meet you. He said you know things."

"My wife retired from the military." Manda nodded toward Alex and shot Hazel a wink. "She's very straightforward. And friendlier than she looks. I teach Women and Gender Studies at the university. Maybe you've heard of me. Amanda Free." She took a little bow. "My first book *Free to Fly, Feel, and Fornicate* is quite famous."

"Of course." Hazel raised a brow and nodded knowingly. Published in the late eighties, the one copy she had in the library hadn't been checked out in decades.

"I absolutely *love* teaching," Amanda continued, punctuating every sentence with a hand flourish. "And I am *very* good at it. Provocative! Fearless! Voted most engaging professor ten years in a row..."

"In the nineties," Alex interjected matter-of-factly.

"Yes, yes. In the nineties *and* in the early aughts. Before everyone became so worried about being politically correct."

"It's been a challenging time," Alex said.

"Yes, yes. Whatever!" Manda waved it off. "The worst thing is that, since the pandemic, they've been making me teach online. And I just *hate* it. Hate it, I say! It's taken all the fun out of it for me."

Alex took Manda's hand stiffly and bent over to give it a little kiss.

Manda's face blew bright red. "Oh my dear, you are making me all tingly!"

Hazel grinned.

When Alex straightened back up again, she looked at Hazel. "Amanda is thinking of retiring early. We need something new to do. We think this would be a good place to do it."

"We're thinking we'd like to relocate here to Owen Station and open a little shop." Manda looked so excited. Like no one else had ever had this idea.

"We're deciding between an ice cream shop," Alex paused, "or perhaps a pet store. Pet supplies, that is. We would never actually sell pets. Not when there are 6.5 million of them in shelters who need homes."

"We have five dogs," Manda explained, "and Alex is very serious about adopting animals. Well, she is serious about most things."

This time Manda grabbed Alex's hand and gave it a little kiss, which made Alex smile. Or, at least, Hazel thought it looked like a smile. Manda continued, patting her sizable belly, "And I clearly love ice cream!"

Hazel couldn't help but be amused by these two. "So..." she said with a twinkle, "Knox is correct. I do *know things.*"

This odd couple was a good reminder at just the right time, that not everything (or everyone) new was bad, just because they were new.

"What is it you need to know?"

Hazel spent hours orienting them to all things Owen Station, at the end of which they decided they were definitely going to open a pet store. Or sell ice cream. Or maybe antiques. Or cheese. In a building on Main Street. One that Hazel's father was responsible for preserving. They loved that idea. And, they would absolutely be back. Manda predicted it dreamily. "This seems like our kind of town."

Hazel did not disagree. They exchanged contact info and asked Hazel to make some introductions to other PLUs in town. Using air quotes, they explained that PLU stands for "people like us." Old lesbians were so cute.

As the two women left, Hazel checked her watch again. Ten minutes until closing. She went back to the Underwood, reread her list of pros and cons, and decided she didn't need to edit it any further. She pulled the page from the machine, crumpled it, and tossed it into the trash beneath the desk.

Then she started quivering at the thought of what she was about to do.

She picked up the phone and dialed Sena's number. It was a relief when it went right to voice mail. "Sena, if you want to know the real Owen Station, the Miner's Hole is the place to start. Meet me there for a drink before dinner. See you in about thirty."

Thirty minutes felt like a long time from now. Long enough to chicken out.

CHAPTER EIGHT

DARKNESS

The Jameson was helping Hazel ignore that annoying voice, which was screaming at her to hop off the barstool, go home, and forget all about this next rendezvous with Sena. But she wrapped her ankles around the stool legs to prevent herself from running away, just in case, and took another swallow.

Sena showed up exactly thirty minutes after Hazel left that message. She was either a control freak, which seemed entirely probable. Or she was as eager to see Hazel as Hazel was to run the other way.

It was dark in the Miner's Hole no matter what time of day it was. But tonight Hazel was not unhappy about the dim light. Sena was clearly having a hard time adjusting, after being out in the late afternoon sun. Hazel could see her just fine. And she was. Fine.

F.I.N.E. Handsome. Striking. Exquisite. FINE—informal, slang.

"Oh my God, Sena. Why do you have to be so beautiful?"

"What'd you say, Hazel?" Ricki was drying glasses, grinning at her.

She'd been behind the bar at the Miner's Hole for longer than Hazel had been alive. Her great-grandfather was one of the first African Americans to be inducted into the National Rodeo Hall of Fame—Ricki loved the reaction she got from tourists when she told them that one-in-four of the old West cowboys were Black. This bar had been in her family for almost a century—Great-granddad's picture hung over the door—and Ricki didn't miss a thing.

Hazel hadn't realized she'd said anything out loud. The last thing she needed was everyone in Owen Station talking about how she had a date. With anyone. Much less, with Sena. And, if Ricki knew, everyone would know.

"Oh, nothing, Ricki. Nothing."

As Sena slowly made her way through the bar, past the TouchTunes, through a group of regulars setting up an impromptu darts tournament, Hazel replayed their encounter in the Rare Books and Special Collections Room that morning. Sena's tongue licking, sucking her fingers. Strong hands teasing their way up her thighs. Dark hair in a tangle. The sweet smell of prickly pear. The edge of the cool wooden table beneath her. The brink of eruption.

Hazel's bra-less nipples hardened against her soft white T-shirt as she thought about it, and the tingling heat, which started just below her navel, crawled all the way down her legs and back again. She was afraid they wouldn't hold her if she stood up.

So she didn't.

She sat still on the stool as Sena leaned in to kiss her on the cheek. To anyone who wasn't paying close attention, it probably looked like a friend's chaste hello. So, Hazel didn't have to worry about that drawing Ricki's attention—or anyone else's, for that matter. But then Sena's hand slipped slowly down to the small of her back, lingered for a moment, and then slid even lower to cup her bum. Her voice was smooth and soft. "I don't think this day could have been any longer. I couldn't wait to see you tonight."

Hazel's stomach did a somersault. Her brain shriveled up, rolled out her ear, across the hundred-year-old wooden floor, and out the front door. Which was the only way to explain the words that came out of her mouth next. Not, what the hell was that in the Rare Books room? Not, how could you leave me like that, oozing frustration? Not even, you totally owe me a piece of quiche.

Instead, she mumbled back, "I had a hard time focusing today, too."

Sena kissed her sweetly on the cheek. "I can't say I'm sorry." Then she moved her lips close enough to Hazel's ear that her breath tickled. "I promise to finish what I started."

A hot flash that originated between Hazel's legs exploded on her cheeks, and her high-pitched squawk was so startling it even made Ricki, who had heard it all in thirty-five years behind the bar, spin to see what was happening.

"I love how easily you laugh, Hazel." Sena's eyes glistened.

"Do I?"

Did she? It certainly didn't feel like there had been much laughter in her life lately. Maybe not for a long time. Sena was seeing something new. Or maybe she was making something new happen.

Sena gently traced Hazel's jawline. "Yes, Hazel. You do. Laugh easily."

Hazel pinched her nose, shoving her glasses up, to rub her eyes. She knew all about fight-or-flight options in the face of a threat. Apparently, there was a third one. Laughter. She opened her eyes to find Sena still smiling at her.

"It's just something you bring out in me, I guess." Hazel left out the part about how Sena also terrified her.

She had to pull herself together. "Let me buy you a drink."

When Hazel called Ricki over, the bartender gave Sena the once-over, nodded approvingly, and then, when Sena looked away, she licked her lips suggestively at Hazel, who scowled back. Sometimes, living in a small town was like walking around in your underwear. In broad daylight.

Sena ordered a Mexican beer and a shot of top shelf tequila. Well, as top shelf as this little town could manage. Ricki set it up with a slice of lime and a greasy saltshaker. Sena pushed them both away with the back of her hand.

"Tequila this good is meant to be savored." She tossed her hair back, thrusting her chin in the air, and held the glass up to examine the golden liquid. "Shooting it is a waste, something gringos do when they want to get drunk fast—no offense. But even if I were to shoot this, I wouldn't need lime or salt—I take my tequila straight— without training wheels, as my brothers like to say."

Hazel laughed. "Brothers? That's right. You mentioned them yesterday. How many?" Hazel was thrilled to be talking about something normal. Something that didn't make her feel like reality was slipping away. Something safe.

Sena took a sip. "Two. Jesús and Junior both tower over me now, but they'll always be my littles. When they were toddlers they followed me everywhere. Like puppies."

Hazel smiled. "I can totally see it. Sena's shadows."

"Exactly. One time I made floppy ears and tails for them out of some old dish towels. They wore them all day, yipping and yapping at my heels. It was annoying as hell." She laughed. "I never did that again."

Sena's laughter trailed off and she grew quiet, sipping on her drink, staring off into the distance over Hazel's shoulder. Hazel just waited. When she looked back at Hazel, her eyes looked a little moist. Or maybe it was just the lighting.

"I hate how far apart we've grown over the years."

Hazel nodded. "You said it's been a long time since you've seen them…six or seven years? Did something happen?"

"It's not like there was a single event or anything. Things just…I don't know."

"Just what?"

"I guess I just got tired of feeling invisible."

Hazel could not have been more startled. She leaned toward Sena, as if by drawing closer she could make more sense of this. "*You*? Invisible? I can't even imagine that."

Sena sniffed out half a laugh. "I'll take that as a compliment."

"Seriously. What do you mean *invisible*?"

"It's hard to explain. My dad is pretty much the center of the Abrigo universe—and was the center of mine for a long time. I followed him everywhere. He taught me how to ride a horse…how to read the night sky…how to tell when someone is lying to you… how to make a good deal. Everything. But then, when I was in middle school, between seventh and eighth grade, he just stopped…"

Sena looked away again.

"Stopped what, Sena?"

She turned back toward Hazel. Her eyes were steel, but her voice was shaky. "Stopped *looking* at me, talking to me, doing things with me. It was like…I don't know. Like I didn't exist to him anymore."

"Oh my gosh, Sena. That must have been awful."

"It was. And it made it even harder to be myself—with *anyone* in my family, really. I felt like I was fading away, until one day, it just didn't seem like it mattered whether or not I was in the picture anymore. I talk to my mother every few months when she calls with the latest update on my nieces or nephews. But she doesn't ask much about my life—and I don't offer. What's the point?"

Hazel reached out and touched Sena's hand. "I can't even imagine how confusing and painful it must all be." Hazel's eyes grew moist. When Sena's eyes met hers, they looked like they might be wet again, too. But she gave her head a quick shake and seemed to bounce back.

"Sorry. I don't talk to many people about things like this." She sort of half-laughed. "How about you, Hazel? You don't have any siblings, do you?"

It was a pretty basic question. First-date-worthy. It made sense that Sena would want to shift the conversation away from herself, and this probably seemed like a safe direction to go. But the simplest stories can be the hardest to tell.

"That's right." Hazel was surprised when her voice caught in her throat. She paused until she was sure she could finish her answer. "I'm an only."

Don't cry, dammit. You're being ridiculous.

Hazel dipped her head hoping to shield her glistening eyes and pretended to shove her glasses back into place. It didn't work. Sena saw right through it.

"Oh, Hazel. I'm sorry. I didn't mean to upset you."

"It's fine."

"It doesn't look fine." Sena smiled warmly.

"It's just that…my family means everything to me. I honestly never missed having brothers and sisters when I was growing up. I kind of liked being the center of attention—the only child, the only grandchild. But now, with both my parents and all my grands gone, sometimes it would be nice not to feel so…alone." As alone as you could be in a town filled with a thousand ghosts, anyway.

"I can tell how much they all mean to you, Hazel. You talk about them a lot. It's like they're all still *here*. I can be completely surrounded by my family and still feel alone. You're lucky to have such a strong bond with yours."

This was what Delaney and Knox didn't get. They almost made Hazel feel bad about wanting to keep her family alive. Sena seemed to understand.

"I wish I was half as close with my family as you are with yours. You actually make me feel kind of guilty about how far away I've allowed myself to become. I'm thankful I still have them—my parents and my brothers, anyway. My grandparents are all gone. I especially miss my grandfather. He died not long after…after things got so weird with my dad." One tear slipped down her cheek and Hazel gently brushed it away.

"Well, this is the weirdest first date I've ever had." Sena smiled as she sniffled. "I've never said these things to anyone."

Hazel took her hand and smiled. "I guess you make me laugh. And I make you cry?"

Sena broke into a grin and sang the next line in the old REO Speedwagon song.

"Oh my God! My parents *loved* that song." Hazel could remember her mom and dad singing it at the top of their lungs in the car, radio blasting.

"Mine, too." Sena laughed.

Hazel took her by the hand. "Come on. Let me introduce you to my heroes. The people who built this town."

She led Sena to a wall behind the pool table, which was covered with old photos. Hazel gestured with her whiskey tumbler, ice clinking, toward a faded black-and-white photo of four dirt-caked men, miners holding pickaxes, wearing hard hats. "That man on the end, with his lunchbox at his feet, is my great-grandfather. He built the house I'm living in. He was also part of the crew who, on their one day off a week, helped build the cathedral up on the hill. But he spent every working day of his adult life underground, in the dark. I've never been able to wrap my head around what that must have been like."

Sena took a swig of beer, squinting at the photo. "You look a little like him, you know."

"You think?"

"Yes, I do...he was handsome."

The way Sena was smiling at her made Hazel all tingly. She tried not to get too distracted by it. "I remember hearing my dad talk about how they used mules in the mines back then, to haul equipment in—and ore out—of the shafts. It was so dark down there, the sun would be too much for them. So the miners just kept them down there. Eventually the animals would go blind. They went into the dark and never came out."

They both took a long drink and stood side by side in silence. In the background, pool balls cracked against one another, Ricki was telling one of the regulars it was time for him to go home, and Easton Corbin was singing a love song.

Hazel kind of hated how good this felt.

Finally, Sena stirred. "It's so strange to look at old photos like this, isn't it? Who do you think took them all?"

"I don't know." Hazel shrugged. "Somebody with a Vest Pocket Kodak, I imagine."

"A what?" Sena shook her head, amusement scrawled across her face. "Hazel, you are just the cutest. Do tell. What is a Vest Pocket Kodak?"

Hazel felt the heat rise in her cheeks. Should she be flattered? Embarrassed? Maybe a little bit of both. "A Vest Pocket Kodak—otherwise known as the soldier's camera because they were made just as World War I was breaking out. They were small enough to fit—you guessed it—in a man's pocket. It took most of the pictures on the battlefield—and here in the mines. It cost about six dollars to buy one—pretty affordable back then, even for a guy making just four dollars a day."

"You know," Sena said lightly, "for someone who says she doesn't like technology—who Knox tells me won't even keep her phone charged—you sure do know a lot about it."

"As long as it's at least a hundred years old, sure."

Hazel didn't mean for that to come out so sharply. But her mood had soured at the mention of Knox. Sena seemed to sense something wasn't right.

"Wait. What's wrong?"

"Nothing."

Sena's brows furrowed and she crossed her arms. "What do you have against technology?"

"I don't have anything against technology."

Sena leaned back. She wasn't smiling anymore. "Do you have something against *me?*"

"Well, now that you're asking." Hazel poked her chin in the air. "Actually, yes."

"Okay, well, let's hear it, Hazel. Say what you need to say."

This wasn't how things were supposed to go. But, whatever. This conversation was going to happen eventually.

"Well, for starters, I know you were out looking at real estate with Knox today."

"Yes, I was. It was a great day, actually. I saw several properties that have a lot of potential. In fact, I've already made an offer on one of them. And I sent some photos to my architect. As soon as she puts a plan together, I'm going to make an offer on a lot more."

"You're certainly moving fast, aren't you?"

"Are you surprised? I'm not afraid to go for it when I see something I want. Or *someone.* And I want to make this a reality, Hazel. What I'm going to do here will change a lot of people's lives for the better."

Hazel snorted. "Look around, Sena." Her hands swept across the bar. "You are literally standing in the middle of history. In the shadow of these extraordinary people who built this town with their bare hands and the help of some mules. If it was up to you, everything they dared to dream and fought to build would be gone. Flattened by a bulldozer. Replaced by some godforsaken who-knows-what kind of concrete and steel high-rise or whatever. This town isn't yours to conquer, Sena. You are taking something that doesn't belong to you."

Sena looked like she had turned to stone, but somehow words came out of the slit that used to be her mouth. "Is that so? Well, let me tell you something, Hazel. This land belonged to someone else when *these men*," she waved at the photos on the wall, "arrived. And those people, who lived here before—who hunted and loved and died and made a life here on this land—they were *my* people. This is as much my land as anyone's."

Hazel paused. That was a fair point. More than fair. But, still.

"You know what?" Hazel threw her hands up to deflect whatever Sena might aim at her next. "Whatever. We can't fix the wrong that was done in the past. But if you do everything you say you're going to do, it's going to ruin this town for everyone who lives here right now. Property values will go up. Taxes will go up. Rents will go up. People like Ricki here—people like *me*—won't be able to afford to live here anymore. We can hardly make it now!"

"First of all," Sena hissed, "if I do what I *say I'm going to do*, this town will have good paying jobs for the first time in... how long? Fifty years? Sixty? And *these* jobs won't strip the land of its beauty. They won't kill people with toxic chemicals. They won't crush people in underground accidents. They won't up and disappear the moment every valuable thing has been extracted from this land. Secondly, believe me..." Her voice dropped two octaves and her words were sharper than the three-inch spines on a saguaro. "I am very aware of what can happen when colonizers descend on a people and make life unsustainable. You don't think I have a plan to ensure fair and sustainable housing for the people who already live here?"

"How am I supposed to know that, Sena?" Hazel's pitch was as high as Sena's was low. She probably sounded like she was on the edge of hysteria because, well, she was. "For as long as I've been back in Owen Station, out-of-town developers have been flowing in and out of here. They've snatched up historic houses, torn them down, and built monstrosities in their place. And the houses they haven't torn down, they've turned into short-term rentals, putting this town on the edge of a housing crisis no one is prepared to deal with. They're buying up land all around us, and have already started throwing up big box stores that will shutter every single small business on Main Street. MAIN STREET. The street my dad died trying to save. They don't care about this town. They don't care about the people who live here. They have one goal. Make as much money as possible. And screw everyone else."

"Well, I'm not like everyone else, Hazel. Frankly, I'm not like *anyone* you've ever known. I see what this town has been. I am in awe of the women and men who had the imagination and the guts to make it happen. Here. In the middle of these mountains. Surrounded by desert. Before electricity. Before running water. Before the railroad. With their bare fucking hands. I am in awe of your *dad* and what he was able to make happen after the industrialists stripped this earth of its resources, and pulled out as soon as there was nothing left for them to exploit. I want nothing more than to honor the vision and the achievements of those who came before me. But I'm going to do it in a way that also honors the people who lived on this land for centuries before your people even arrived. I have a vision that includes everyone, Hazel. Not just rich white men. *Everyone.* And the fact that you can't see that…that you *won't* see that…makes you as blind as those mules. And twice as ignorant."

Hazel fell back a step, her mouth half-open, ready to hit back. But she had nothing to say.

She dashed to the bar and shouted good night to Ricki, who was trying to explain to a belligerent tourist why she wouldn't keep serving his very drunk wife. She dropped a twenty on the bar to cover her drinks and Sena's and started toward the door.

Sena followed and, when they got outside, she grabbed Hazel's elbow from behind.

"Hazel, what just happened?"

Hazel snapped around to face her. "I have no idea, okay? I'm sorry. You're right…about the history of this land. About…everything." Hazel looked away. It was too hard to look Sena in the eye. "I didn't mean for things to unfold this way. I honestly…I don't *know* what's wrong with me or why…why I'm so *stuck*…in what used to be."

Hazel let Sena take her hand—and that's when her tears started to come. "It wasn't always like this, Sena. And I'm not sure why or

how it happened. It was…after my mom died…after *everyone* died.
I just sort of…I think I just lost my…"

Hazel stopped. There were no words to say something she had
never said before.

"Your what…?" Sena asked softly.

"I don't know." Hazel was having a hard time getting the words
out. "My way…? My dreams…? My…self. I lost *myself*, Sena. It's
like I went down into the darkness and never came out." Hazel
covered her face with her hands and her shoulders began to shake
as the tears flowed.

"Just like those mules." Sena put her arms around her and held
her close. "Oh, Hazel, I'm so sorry. I didn't mean those things I said.
I don't want to hurt you."

When Hazel could breathe again, she untangled herself from
the embrace, still holding Sena's hands. Sena's brown eyes looked
deeper, richer than before, filled with flecks of copper, the color of
the Mule Mountains, warm and strong. Hazel couldn't help herself.
It didn't matter that they were standing in the middle of the sidewalk
or that she could see herself teetering on the edge of a precipice,
her whole carefully constructed world in danger of collapsing. She
leaned in and gave Sena a kiss. Okay, it was only a kiss on the cheek.
But she hadn't made a move like that on anyone for so, so long.

Before she could step away, though, Sena's hand was on the
back of her neck, pulling her closer. She could feel Sena's soft lips
on hers, the tip of Sena's tongue beginning to probe, their bodies
meeting, pressing together, heat rising, the two of them exploring,
searching, trying to understand through touch what could not be
grasped any other way.

"Oh, hey there, Hazel." A cheerful man's voice interrupted
them.

It was Pastor Bexley, out for his evening stroll through town.
Correction. *Assistant* Pastor Bexley. Delaney's secret crush. So
secret the good reverend had no idea.

Hazel pulled away from Sena quickly, looked at Bexley, then
back at Sena, horrified at the way her two worlds were colliding. The
old world of Owen Station, where she knew everyone and everyone

knew her, where even her daily lunch menu was set in stone, and nothing new ever happened, where it might be dark but at least it was stable and safe.

And the new world that Sena represented, where everything was upside down and every step she took was a risk, where she had zero control over her thoughts or her emotions, where daylight was even more blinding than the darkness she had wrapped herself in, where not even *lunch* was safe.

Heat flashed across her face. How could she have been so stupid?

S.T.U.P.I.D. Ignorant. Foolish. Naive. STUPID.

Sena reached out to grab her hand. "Hazel, what is it? What's wrong?"

But Hazel was too quick for her. She wrapped her arms around herself, tucking her hands out of sight and out of reach.

"I'm so sorry I interrupted!" Bexley looked mortified. "I didn't mean to. Please, carry on with…oh my goodness…just carry on!"

Hazel ignored him.

"I can't do this, Sena. I just can't."

"Do what?"

"Whatever this is. You and me."

"But, I don't understand. Why not? I thought we were really connecting. Hazel, I've shared things with you—things I've never shared with anyone. I don't know why. I didn't plan on this. I wasn't looking for this. In fact, this was the last thing I was looking for. But I like being with you. I like how I *feel* when I'm with you. I feel safe. I feel *seen*. Do you know how many times this has been true for me? In my entire *life*? I can count the times on one hand. I could describe all those times to you in about five minutes."

She turned toward Bexley, who was still standing there, rooted to the ground, apparently unable to move. "Hey, Rev—you got five minutes? I'll tell you all about it. Seriously, that's all it would take."

The poor guy turned green and looked like he might throw up.

Sena whipped back toward Hazel. "Are you hearing me?"

"Yes, I'm hearing you. And that's the problem, Sena. I'm not ready for any of this. It's too much…too fast. I've only known you

for a few days. I know you have good intentions. At least I think
you have good intentions. But you are about to turn my town upside
down. And you're *already* turning my life upside down. You're
making me feel things I...I...I don't think I've *ever* felt before.
You're making me *do* things I've never done before. I mean, really?
Really? The Rare Books and Special Collections Room. Do you
know how hard I work to keep that room free from contamination?
What was I thinking?"

Hazel put her hands over her face. Seriously, what had she been
thinking?

"You are changing everything, Sena. Everything. My cat has
lost her mind. I can't get anything done at work. I didn't even have
quiche for lunch today."

"What? Hazel, what are you talking about?"

"QUICHE, Sena. I always have QUICHE on Wednesdays.
Today is Wednesday. Get it?"

"No! I don't get it at all. You want quiche? Let's go. Right now.
I'll find you some quiche. I'll fucking *make* you some quiche—
sorry, Rev. Wait, no, I'm *not* sorry. What the hell are we talking
about?"

And then Sena started to cry.

Bexley took a step toward her but stopped.

And a thousand, million arrows shot right through Hazel's
heart. "Oh my God. Sena, I can't. I can't. I can't."

"You...can't...*what*, Hazel?"

"I can't go through it all again. Don't you see? I've lost
everyone. It hurts too much. I'm looking at you right now, and I
can see how hurt and confused you are, and it is breaking my heart.
I can't deal with this, with you, your family, your big plans. Any
of it. I like my life just the way it is. I like my little house and my
quiet job. I like knowing what I'm going to eat for lunch every day.
I like not worrying about whether the person I love is going to get
sick or get hurt or up and *die* on me. I like how simple everything
is. Predictable. And you are the least simple, most unpredictable
person I've ever known."

Hazel stood up as straight as she could.

"I'm sorry, Sena." And, actually, she didn't feel sorry at all. "I just can't do this."

As she turned to go, racing back toward home and history, leaving Sena standing beside the bewildered minister in the middle of Main Street, Hazel knew this was the way things had to end.

CHAPTER NINE

MUJER FUERTE

Sena's eyes popped open the next morning with Hazel's last words ringing in her ears.

I just can't do this.

She had been so angry, after the initial shock of watching Hazel walk away. It made no sense. She and Hazel were right at the start of something. Sena didn't know what, exactly, but she knew it was something different than anything she'd had before. Something good. And Hazel just turned and ran away.

That minister, who was still a sickly shade of green, apologized a half dozen times for interrupting such a "special moment," as he kept calling it. Sena was finally able to shake him loose, with assurances that she would be okay.

But she wasn't.

Sena had long ago mastered the ability to bury her disappointment and hurt.

Thanks, Dad.

It sucked, but it worked. Sena channeled all of those bad feelings into school, into sports, into work, making her the best at whatever she did. She buried those feelings so deep, she forgot they were even there. But not this time.

For the next few weeks, Sena spent mornings huddled with Knox, making offer after offer on old properties. Her architect flew in from Chicago and they set up shop at a back table inside Banter & Brew, ignoring the stares and whispers from Sirus and his goons. The firm she had chosen went back to 1939, deeply rooted in history while on the cutting edge of sustainable design. The hours flew by as they worked together. But Sena was careful to clear out before one o'clock every day. The last thing she wanted was to be face-to-face with Hazel. It was hard enough getting a glimpse of her through the window each morning as she waved to Knox and scampered up the library stairs. It was torture knowing that Hazel was sleeping just steps away every night.

Sena spent afternoons on the phone, pitching her vision to the most innovative women across the country, or marching around her new house, barking orders at the workers. Knox had warned her the problems with these old houses were always worse than they first appeared. He wasn't kidding. A hundred years ago the booming town was a free-for-all. Houses sprang up all over the place. People hooked up their sewer laterals to the city main however they wanted, quick and dirty. No one thought twice about it when new houses were built on top of them. Now the lines were old, leaking, backing up. The line from a neighbor, two houses down, ran right underneath Sena's house. Fixing it meant getting permission from the neighbor in between, dealing with an overwhelmed and under-resourced town, and major construction Sena hadn't planned on. It was a big stinking mess.

A perfect metaphor.

The whole situation with Hazel was ridiculous. Completely and utterly ridiculous. There had been so many women. Most queer but more than a few just curious. Begging for Sena's attention. They embarrassed themselves in bars and boardrooms, at the gym, in the middle of gala dance floors, everywhere and anywhere. Sena could have any woman she wanted.

Except Hazel.

Sena had never let her guard down like that before. Not even with Rachel all those years ago. What had she been thinking? She hadn't been in town for more than forty-eight hours before she was falling for a redheaded technophobe wearing her grandmother's clothes. Pouring her heart out. Playing show-and-tell with her open wounds. Crying, for God's sake. Sena Abrigo. *Crying*. Did she really think Hazel would be any different than all the rest? That she could *trust* her? That she would be *safe* with her? That maybe, for once in her life, she might be able to find someone who would actually *see* her? All of her. Good. Bad. Ugly. And love her for who she really was?

For a very brief moment, Sena dared to think Hazel could maybe be that person. She wanted to pick up all of their broken pieces and put them together, to create something beautiful and whole. Sena wanted to be there to wipe away every tear. She wanted Hazel's laughter to fill every day. She wanted to taste those lips and let the heat that ignited between them fill her every night.

How idiotic. Now Sena was planning her every day, every outing, around avoiding her. It was a small town. You couldn't walk down Main Street without bumping into a dozen people you knew. And they both lived on the same postage-stamp-sized lot. Hazel must have been doing the same thing. The only creature Sena ever encountered at Casita Butler was Mango, who had perched herself on the adobe wall overlooking the courtyard. Watching. Waiting. As if wondering when all the drama would end.

Sena poured herself a glass of Malvasia Bianca, one of her favorite local whites, and pulled a smoked salmon pasta dish out of the fridge. She hadn't had time to find her own chef yet. Thank God for Williams-Sonoma's delivery service. Not only was the restaurant scene a big zero in Owen Station, going out would have chanced running into Hazel. And honestly it wasn't much of a sacrifice to skip out on what passed for nightlife in Owen Station.

The worst part of the day was always when she crawled under the sheets at the end of it. Alone. That night, like every night since Hazel lost her damn mind and ran away, went on forever. Sena slept fitfully, tossing and turning. In her dreams, Puma came to her again.

She is riding. Sena on Alegre. Rachel on the back of a Paso Fino. They stop. Tie up the horses. But, wait. The sun is so hot. Blinding. Rachel...no, it's Hazel...throws a leg over to dismount. They are lying together under a shade tree. Hazel begs her to make love. Sena reaches out to embrace her. I just can't do this. And Hazel is gone, vanished into the air. Puma is there, instead, his yellow eyes open. Staring.

And then, the greenish light. The woman. By the side of her bed.

Why are you here?

Go away.

Why are you still here?

I've already told you.

You are free.

I don't know what you're talking about.

You do.

I don't.

You will.

Sena got out of bed the next morning feeling groggy and without a plan…except to get the hell out of town for a while.

The sports car felt powerful beneath her, and she gripped the steering wheel hard, flying through the tunnel that tore through the Mule Mountains, speeding past cypress trees and cottonwoods, across the rugged Southern Arizona landscape.

Abuelo used to say the desert was a place where even the plants would kill you if you were not careful, where only the strongest—or most adaptable—survived. She had forgotten how much she loved this land. Growing up here had made Sena tough. At least that's what she told herself as she watched it all stream by in flashes of copper red, sage green, and a hundred shades of purple. She hoped it was true.

Large white clouds floated low in the sky. After hours of cruising through back roads, she entered the pastoral Sonoita Valley—wine country. Few outside of the most adventurous connoisseurs knew that this high desert country south of Tucson was the next frontier in high end, old-world style wines. The California snobs Sena went to school with thought it was hysterical when she would talk like this.

They could go fuck themselves.

She hadn't seen a car for miles when she flew past a new, hand-painted wooden sign for Mujer Fuerte Winery, alerting her to the well-tended vineyard along the road. Curious, she hung a quick U-turn and entered the long, dirt drive to look for the Strong Woman promised on the sign. Or maybe to find one inside herself.

The tasting room wasn't a room at all. It was a piece of reclaimed barn wood resting on two wine barrels, on a patch of desert grass, under a sun sail, on top of a hill with breathtaking views of the Patagonia Mountains. It was stunning. And a strong breeze made the heat bearable in the shade. An old Airstream was parked about thirty feet away and the clothesline nearby made it clear somebody was living in it. Size two jeans and T-shirts hanging from the line made it clear that somebody was a woman. There wasn't a customer in sight.

"Hey there, how's it going?" The laundry clearly didn't belong to the woman pouring wine behind the folding table. She looked like she was maybe in her late thirties. Her bronzed skin said she spent a lot of time in the sun. And something about the way she was standing there in her Wranglers and a pair of brown leather Ropers, sun-kissed hands on her hips, facing outward, greeting the stranger coming toward her like it was a new dawn, like there was nothing to fear, made Sena think she had a few scars under that smile. She looked like she could damn well face anything life threw at her.

Sena popped her sunglasses off and dropped them on the table. "Honestly, I've had better days."

"Well, let's see if we can change that."

The woman was wearing a T-shirt with the Mujer Fuerte logo and her sun-streaked, chestnut brown hair was pulled through a matching baseball cap in a ponytail that reached down past her shoulders. A short-haired, black and white dog—Australian Shepherd, maybe—was lying at her feet.

She extended a hand. "Name's Tessa. And this here is Bleu."

Sena shook her hand. "Sena."

"Happy to meet you, Sena. Now, what's your pleasure? I've got three great reds, two surprisingly good whites—a third I'm not crazy about, to be honest with you, although the 20-somethings seem to like it—and a pretty fabulous rosé. Taste 'em all for twelve bucks."

Sena pulled out her wallet and tossed a twenty on the table. "Start pouring."

Tessa knew her stuff. She described the aroma and color of each wine, the sandy, gravelly soil that gave them depth and made them so peppery.

"How'd you end up here, anyway?" Sena asked between pours of the first and second reds.

"Ah, good question. My ex and I owned a winery together in Marin County. I was both the brains and the brawn in that operation, but she insisted on keeping it in the divorce. So I sold my share to her, escaped to Arizona and bought this vineyard—which is twice as big and half as expensive as the one I left behind. Bought it from a couple of engineers out of Phoenix who found out winemaking is harder than it looks. My daughter came with me. She's turning twenty-one this year and is bunking with me in the Airstream while we work to put this place on the map."

That explained the teeny tiny tees.

"What's it been like for you—here in Arizona?"

Tessa put the bottle down and looked out at the vineyard over Sena's shoulder. "Well. So far, it's been a beautiful place to start over. And business has been good—the past few years were tough in a lot of ways, but we came through it okay. More than okay, actually. We created an open-air tasting room—a safe space for people to come and hang out—and built a pretty loyal customer base that way. But, water's huge. It's not that we need a lot of it. Grapes need a lot less water than most fruit, which makes it a good crop in a high desert region like this. It's the mega farms that need a ton of water, and they're digging wells so deep they're sucking up all the groundwater. They're mostly owned by big corporations whose stockholders don't give a damn about long term sustainability or the people who live here. But it's still the Wild Wild West out here. Nobody wants to regulate it."

"Sounds about right." Sena grew up in the middle of it all.

"Yeah. And, I guess on a personal note, you can't imagine how hard it is to be taken seriously as a winemaker when you own a pair of ovaries…even if they are bigger than the biggest set of balls."

Sena arched an eyebrow. "I spent the past fifteen years in tech. I think I know a thing or two about what it's like to not be taken seriously."

"Touché."

After Tessa poured the last tasting into Sena's glass, she capped the bottle. "You're a good listener." She peered out at Sena from beneath the ball cap, as if trying to read her mind. "What's *your* story?"

Sena considered a half dozen ways to respond. Finally, she answered with a shrug. "That's a good question."

What was she supposed to say? That a month and a half in the middle of a nowhere town had taken the mighty Sena on an emotional roller coaster? That she was feeling a little unhinged and exhausted after weeks of shitty sleep? That she felt haunted...by the ex who walked out, an emotionally distant father, and the horse she left behind? That she was seeing *ghosts* and that Puma had been showing up again in her dreams? That she was so damn lonely... and pretty sure she had scared away the first woman in more than a decade that she actually wanted to...*what*? Trust? Laugh with? Cry with? Love? Not a chance. That was way more than she was able or willing to share.

Skipping right over Tessa's question, she raised her glass with a tight smile. "Tessa, it's been nice talking. These wines really are spectacular." Then she turned and headed out to sit alone in an Adirondack chair at the edge of the sun sail.

Five minutes later, she had company. Tessa took the seat next to her. Bleu wasn't far behind. Tessa had a bottle and two glasses in hand. "Pretty spectacular view, isn't it?"

Neat rows of grape vines spread out in front of them, giving way to a purple-hued savannah. A creek ran through the property, on the other side of which was a forest of velvet ash and mesquite, and lush grassland as far as the eye could see.

"You look like you could use some company."

Sena looked at her out of the corner of her eye, hoping her noticeable lack of a welcome would send a message. But the winemaker didn't take the hint.

"This is a 2015 Sagrantino from my first vineyard." Tessa held the bottle up for Sena to admire. "One of the wines I'm most proud of. It's an Italian varietal, not one you find in the States very often. I'm gonna plant a section of it right over there."

She tilted her head and looked knowingly at Sena. "Usually this grape needs to be blended with something else…because it tends to be too broody on its own."

What the hell? Was she taking a shot?

Tessa responded with a grin and a wink, as if she heard Sena's thoughts, and kept going.

"I aged it two years in barrel, two in bottle. That's enough to ground it, I think." Taking her time, she carefully poured the deep red liquid into each of the glasses and handed one to Sena. "It takes time and a little work, but it's worth it. See what you think."

Sena took the glass and watched mesmerized as Tessa swirled, sniffed, sipped, and swished.

"I don't know." Sena frowned. "I think there are some things time probably can't fix."

Dammit. She did sound broody.

A few wrinkles appeared in the corners of Tessa's eyes and a gentle smile slowly lifted her cheeks until her eyes all but disappeared. She settled back into her Adirondack.

"I don't know exactly what's going on, Sena, but I've stood across a bar from about a thousand people and heard about a thousand stories and I know that whatever burdens you're carrying, they feel heavy. I've also been through a thing or two myself. If it helps, I want you to know that I'm a living, breathing example of how a little time and a little work can make all the difference."

Sena was disturbed to feel tears forming behind her eyes again. What the hell was wrong with her? She had cried more in the past few weeks than she had in the past ten years. She didn't trust herself to speak, but Tessa's kindness made her feel vulnerable enough to acknowledge to herself that she was tired. Damn tired. And not just from a lack of sleep. She was exhausted because *she* was *exhausting*—and she was sick of the fake ass life she had built for herself. Sick and tired of hiding. Hiding behind her looks, her brains, her money. Hiding from her family. Hiding from herself. And she was so tired of being alone. She shook her head and closed her eyes.

Tessa was quiet until she opened them again. "Let me guess. Judging by that fancy car you pulled up in and the way you're dressed, it's not money trouble."

Oh my God. Really?

She was just wearing those old...

Oh fuck it.

Sena rolled her eyes and muttered. "No, it's not money."

Tessa threw up one know-it-all eyebrow and kept going without a pause. "You're a little too young for a midlife crisis. And a little too old to still be fighting with your parents..."

"Are you ever too old to fight with your parents?"

The laugh started in Tessa's belly. "No, I guess not. But I'm also guessing that's not it. Or at least not all of it."

Tessa sat up and turned to look Sena up and down through squinted eyes. "Okay, lemme see...my guess is...you're in transition because you got sick of the bullshit in your first career, but you're hitting roadblocks you didn't expect as you try to shift, *or* you just found out your ex is getting married, *or* you're in love with someone who isn't sure he...or she?...loves you back."

Tessa sat back with a satisfied smile. "How'd I do?"

Sena couldn't help but be impressed. "You nailed the work thing, which freaks me out a little. But my ex isn't getting married. Or, if she is, I haven't heard and frankly I don't care."

Tessa nodded knowingly. "*She.* Got it."

"And I'm *not* in love...I don't think." She scrunched up her forehead and slipped lower into her chair, as if trying to disappear. "But honestly, I wouldn't mind if I was. Even though I can't believe I'm saying that. And, damn, if I didn't blow it somehow."

Tessa sighed sympathetically. "I'm sorry, Sena. That sucks."

They sat looking at the mountains in the distance. It felt good just to be in the presence of someone who didn't seem to want anything, who was willing to just...*be.* Sena realized that, on top of everything else, she missed having friends.

"You know…" Tessa's voice was soft. "When my wife left, I thought I'd never be able to breathe again. She was my everything." Bleu got up and put her head on Tessa's lap. She gave the pup a scratch, then swirled her glass again and took a deep sip.

"How long were you together?"

"Fourteen years. We met when my daughter was just three years old."

A gust of wind carrying the scent of creosote blew a lock of hair into Sena's eyes. Soon rain would fill the dry desert washes, bringing new life.

"I feel like a fool," Sena said as she brushed her hair back over her shoulder. "You've just lived through the breakup of a fourteen-year relationship, and I'm a mess because…oh, I don't know… because I met someone who made me feel."

Tessa tilted her head sideways, so her ear was aimed at Sena, as though expecting to hear more. Finally, she just asked. "Made you feel…*what*?"

"Made me *feel*," Sena said, dropping that last word like a bag of sand.

"Got it. What's her name?"

"Hazel."

The word tasted as bitter as a handful of jojoba nuts plucked under an unforgiving Sonoran sun.

"Well, Hazel must be a pretty amazing woman to have gotten under your skin like this."

Sena couldn't help herself as the tears that were cresting behind her eyes finally broke free. "I don't know what's wrong with me." Even her nose was dripping. "This is so unlike me."

"Love'll do that to you."

Sena groaned. "Reason number 834 for why not to let it happen to you."

After a few moments, Tessa shifted around to look directly into Sena's eyes. "Here's the funny thing. I don't regret one minute of it. I could probably list all 833 of those other reasons not to fall for somebody. But here's the truth. All the joy and all the pain love has caused…it's made me who I am. It's taken a while, but I'm finally finding my way. I'm figuring out how to have a relationship with my daughter, paying attention to what I need, and I have the best view in the state. I feel grounded." She swirled the Sagrantino in her glass thoughtfully. "A little bit like this wine. I feel...whole. I'm even thinking about starting to date again. My kid says I'm living my best life." She smiled. "And she's not wrong."

Sena prided herself on being strong. But in the presence of this honest-to-God mujer fuerte, who was confident enough to be open and real, who was willing to even *think* about giving her heart away after all the pain she had endured, who knew how to love both others and herself with grace and joy, Sena felt deeply unsettled. Whether she intended to or not, Tessa had held up a mirror, and Sena did not like the wounded woman she saw in the reflection.

Whatever might happen next with Hazel, Sena decided right then and there that she needed a change. She needed to stop being so damn scared and trust herself. Yes, she might get hurt. But she was tough, resilient. And she damn well wasn't going to spend the rest of her life alone. '

She picked up her glass and tipped it in Tessa's direction. "Here's to living our best lives," she toasted, thankful for the strong woman beside her, and the one she hoped to become.

Before she left, Tessa invited her to join her and a few friends at the Triple D for drinks and maybe a little dancing.

"The Triple D, huh? Is that still there?" Sena laughed. "I haven't been since summer break my last year at USC."

"It probably hasn't been cleaned since then," Tessa joked as she wrapped Sena in a hug to send her on her way.

"You know, I think a night out with some new friends is exactly what I need."

"Alright then." Tessa pulled a card out of her jeans and handed it to Sena. "We're going this Saturday. Let me know if you decide to come."

Bleu followed Sena out to her car, as if to make sure she got off safely. Sena climbed in, hit the ignition, and hung a right out of the parking lot, back toward Owen Station and whatever a new future might hold.

CHAPTER TEN

FRISKY BUSINESS

Hazel spent weeks sneaking in and out of her own house like a burglar. She waited until she was sure Sena was tucked in for the night to slip Mango's food outside the back door. And, except for work, lunch at Banter & Brew, and quick trips to the grocery store, where she made sure Sena's car was nowhere to be seen, she hunkered down at home. She had made such a scene in front of Bexley—it was humiliating. But worse, she couldn't shake the image of Sena standing there looking confused and hurt, with tears streaming down her cheeks. Hazel wasn't about to chance running into her in the driveway or anywhere else in town.

How was she supposed to explain what happened? She wasn't even sure she understood it herself. But she regretted nothing. She had been faced with a life-or-death moment. Literally. As in, if she stayed one more moment on that street with Sena, her old life was going to have to die. And she'd seen enough death in her thirty-three years, thank you very much.

That didn't mean she didn't cry herself to sleep that night…or every night since. It was impossible not to second-guess herself. Her heart told her she was an idiot for running away from the chance at a new life, a grand adventure, and maybe even a shot at love. And her body was in all-out rebellion, aching for Sena's hands on her bare skin and another taste of those cinnamon-flavored lips. Even George and the Man in the Yellow Hat seemed to look at her like she was out of her mind. She did her best to steer clear of that corner of the library. In fact, she was doing her best to not see anyone. It wasn't hard to be stuck at home. This had been the worst monsoon season on record. Almost the end of August and still no sign of rain. The heat was unbearable, and people weren't just squirrely, they were getting mean. It was all making Hazel very cranky.

She hunched over the counter, scowling as Knox set her usual tuna fish sandwich down. "When in the world is Sena's house going to be ready, Knox? It's been weeks, already."

"Happy Friday to you, too," Knox said, unsmiling. Of course, he had found out what she did to Sena from Lace, who heard it from Delaney, who heard it from Bexley. Turns out there had been other people on the street that night, too, including one of those stupid ghost tours. Hazel hadn't noticed any of them. She hadn't cared then. Now she did. Everyone in town was talking about what happened. Except they didn't actually know what happened. Because Hazel wasn't even sure she understood it. But that didn't stop them from talking.

"You know I can't discuss my clients with you." Knox clipped his words. He had been working closely with Sena on her development plans. She was in there with him almost every day. Once in a while, on her way to work, she thought she caught a glimpse of Sena through the window. Knox tried telling Hazel about it and seemed to think that what Sena was doing was going to be good for Owen Station, that she was working closely with community members and planning things that would honor the legacy of the town. But Hazel didn't want to hear about it. She didn't want to hear anything Sena-related.

"I just want my house back."

And my life.

As whiny as Hazel sounded, she wasn't surprised Knox spun off down the counter to take an order from a couple of regulars. Plumber Joe and Electrician Joe—that's what people called them to avoid confusion—waved hello.

She ignored them, tucked her chin down, hunched over her plate, and poked at her sandwich.

Why hadn't she ordered something else? Nobody else cared what day it was. There was no universal rule that said you couldn't have a grilled cheese on Friday. Or a turkey sub. Or whatever. There wasn't even a rule that you had to eat at Banter & Brew. It didn't matter what she ordered or where she ate, anyway. She'd lost her appetite when she lost Sena.

When Delaney called the house the next day, she immediately regretted picking up. Delaney insisted Hazel come with them for girls' night out.

"I'm not in the mood, Delaney."

"You're pouting, Hazel. It's not attractive."

"I'm not pouting. I'm busy."

"Doing what? Another crossword puzzle? Another idiotic SOS meeting?"

"It's none of your business."

Delaney laughed. "Girl, you *are* my business. And right now business sucks. You need to get out of that house before you shrivel up and become the town's next old cat lady. Besides, Lace and I miss you. You've been MIA since everything happened with Sena. Enough is enough. I am picking you up at eight and you *better* be ready. If not, I'll drag you out in your nightgown."

"I don't wear a nightgown."

"You know what I mean. Go take a shower. Put something fun on. And *be ready.*"

Delaney clicked off before Hazel could argue.

She arrived right at eight in the bright red Wrangler she'd been driving for a decade. Hazel was ready. Once Delaney got something in her head, there was no use fighting it.

She had taken a long shower, lukewarm to help cool off after the day, and gotten dressed. Jeans, a simple silky top, and boots. She chose one of her mother's favorites, a silver necklace with a roadrunner pendant, which had a small turquoise stone for an eye, to top it off.

Delaney honked to let Hazel know she was there but didn't get out of the car. She was that confident Hazel was coming. "You look great," she said coolly as Hazel hopped in.

"Are you sure you're not a lesbian?" Hazel had made this joke a hundred times. "This car is a dead giveaway, you know."

"Are you sure *you* are?" Delaney raised one eyebrow high enough to lift the equally bright turquoise cowboy hat she was wearing.

"Not you, too." Hazel muttered it, hopefully sounding as exasperated as she felt.

"What do you mean, *not you too*?"

Hazel clicked her seat belt, grumbling. "Knox is still mad at me."

"Nobody is *mad* at you, Hazel," Delaney said sharply. "We just don't understand you. It's almost like you don't *want* to be happy."

Hazel opened her mouth to fire off a defensive retort, but Delaney cut her off. "Sena is really great, you know. Knox has been helping her make friends. He introduced her to the mayor and council. They're all excited about her plans for the old downtown. That place has been an eyesore for decades and an embarrassing, constant reminder of how great this town used to be. And the old Y ladies are ecstatic! She asked a bunch of them to be on an advisory committee to design the new building. Which...was...*brilliant*. Everybody's feeling hopeful about the future of this town for the first time in decades. And she's done it all so quickly. But *you*! You're moping around like—"

"Not *everybody* is excited about what Sena is doing," Hazel snapped.

"Oh, you mean Sirus and that bunch of grumps?"

"They're not grumps, Delaney. They care about this town, about our history."

"History mystery. Blabbity blab. They're grumps who don't want anything to change."

"That's not true. We just want change to happen the right way."

"So it's your way or the highway? I get it."

Hazel was sick of hearing about it. She reached over, spiked the volume on the radio and slumped down in her seat to pout.

"See what I mean!" Delaney shouted over the music. She reached over with a big grin and ruffled Hazel's hair. "You need to let yourself have a little fun, my old-fashioned friend."

Hazel shouted back. "Why do you think I'm in this Jeep with you, flying to Frisky Business on a Saturday night?" Delaney was annoyingly good at chasing the gloom away and Hazel smiled in spite of herself.

Frisky Business, which sat out on the edge of town, was Owen Station's only adult toy shop. Lace opened it in the Owen Mansion after she and Knox split up. It was a crime the way the Owen family had let that place get so run down. Jack Owen, one of the original mine owners, had been the first in Arizona to order a house out of the Sears Modern Homes and Building Plans catalog back in 1917. Unlike Hazel's great-grandfather, who used scraps to build his new wife a home using a Sears plan—the home Hazel was still living in—Mr. Owen had twenty-five tons of material delivered by railroad from Cairo, Illinois. He paid extra to have the parts for indoor plumbing and electrical wiring installed, even though it would be a year and a half before the town's infrastructure stretched far enough out for him to hook up to it.

The house had been vacant for years when Lace made a cash offer, using her more than generous divorce settlement. Knox invested in the business to help her get started, too. He wanted to be sure Lace would be okay because, well, because he loved her and always would. He wished it wouldn't have taken an affair with that buxom blonde motorcyclist who whizzed in and out of town that last summer they were married for her to admit that she could never be happy married to a man. Even if that man was Knox. But he was glad they both finally figured it out.

Lace lived in the back three rooms of the Owen Mansion now and ran the shop in front. She opened the door before they could even knock, gave Delaney a quick kiss, and threw her arms around Hazel. "Hazel, honey! It's so good to see you. Come in, come in!"

"What's up with that, Lace?" Delaney cried. "How come she gets the hero's welcome and I get a peck on the cheek?"

"Oh, Delaney, you know I love you. But Hazel's been all the town can talk about for the past few weeks. Come on in, Hazel. I want to hear all about it."

"Well, sure." Delaney hit Hazel with an accusatory stare. "I'd love to hear what our favorite librarian has to say for herself, too."

Hazel exaggerated a sarcastic kissing face as she bumped past her into the living room.

Merchandise was everywhere, but there was a sitting area in the center of the room with a well-worn, red-velvet-covered, Queen Anne couch, built by hand in the late 1800s. It had come with the house and it was Hazel's favorite spot. Delaney plopped down in one of the old, comfy chairs Lace had picked up at the Miller's antique shop. A heavy wooden coffee table sat between them, covered with the latest issues of feminist magazines. Yes, actual print magazines. There were so many reasons to love Lace.

When they were all settled, Lace filled three wine glasses, each etched with the Mujer Fuerte logo. Delaney's eyes sparkled as she took a glass. "Nice choice. The owner comes to town about once a month to get her hair cut. Name's Tessa. Have you met her yet? She plays on your team." She gave Lace a large, lusty wink and Lace froze with her glass halfway to her lips.

"Hmmm, I'll take that as a yes." Delaney laughed as she toasted herself and took a big gulp.

"Yes, we've met." A pale shade of red crept up Lace's smiling face. "We're actually developing a very nice friendship. We're both business owners. Had to pivot when everything went nuts a few years ago—figure out how to launch our own online shops—navigate government loans—things like that. Now we're having trouble finding workers. You know. We have lots in common."

Delaney chortled. "Sure...you're *friends*..."

"Yes, we are. And that's all I'm saying about that."

Lace was still red but she flipped around on her chair and rubbed her hands. "Enough about me, Hazel. What is happening with *you*?"

"Nothing's happening." The monotone she adopted wasn't meant to be as smart-alecky as it came out. Something *did* happen, but nothing *was* happening. Nothing good, anyway. And Hazel did not want to talk about it.

Lace's singsong voice matched the silly grin on her face. "That's not what I hear."

"Why? What'd you hear?" Hazel frowned.

Lace clapped her hands enthusiastically and practically squealed. "I heard you and that new developer in town were hot and heavy, love at first sight!"

"That sounds like something Delaney would have said." Hazel shot daggers in her direction.

"Well, it's true, Hazel. You *were* hot and heavy. And it's about time, too." Delaney was indignant. "But then you had to go and freak out on her. My Bexley said you babbled a bunch of things that didn't make any sense. Something about quiche. And Johnny Ryan, who was giving a ghost tour that night and saw the whole thing, said he heard you say you had sex in the library. But then you just ran off, leaving poor Sena crying in the street. That's what my Bexley said. And now Knox says you're avoiding her. Heck, you're avoiding everybody!"

Hazel locked her jaw, steeling herself against the memory of pain scrawled across Sena's face. And she went on the offense. Because everyone knows that's the best defense.

"*Your* Bexley," she scoffed. "That's precious. You shouldn't be giving me such a hard time when the love of your life doesn't even know how you feel! Also, *no*, Delaney. I most definitely did not have sex in the library." Hazel jumped an octave with each phrase and her cheeks were on fire.

"Whoa, ladies." Lace held her hands up to stop the squabble. "No reason to get testy."

That's when Hazel turned her sights on Lace. "And what about you, Lace? You haven't been in love since Knox."

"Well, at least she gets a nice piece of tail once in a while," Delaney cut in.

"Oh come on now, it's more than once in a while." Lace laughed, mockingly covering her heart with her hands, as if Delaney's words hurt more than Hazel's. "And besides…" She winked at Hazel "I'm at least open to the possibility of having my heart stolen away. We were all so happy when it seemed like you had maybe finally found somebody, Hazel. We're all worried about you, hon."

"Well, there's no reason to. I'm fine. Life is good."

"Uh-huh." Lace looked skeptical. Delaney's mouth dropped open, like she couldn't believe Hazel would even say such a thing.

"What? Why are you looking at me like that? Life *is* good. And I don't need some out-of-town developer…"

"*Gorgeous* developer," Delaney interjected.

"*Brilliant* developer." Lace piled on.

"Ambitious, Strategic. Kind. *Rich*…"

"Okay, okay, I get it! Sena's amazing. Everyone thinks so. Blah, blah. And I've heard her plans. I know she has good intentions—at least I think I do. But, the fact is, when I look at her, all I see is trouble. You know darn well that SOS is going to fight against every single thing she wants to do. It's just too much, too fast. This is *not* going to end well for anyone, least of all this town."

"I'm sorry, Hazel, but that is just BS," Delaney said. "Stop hiding behind that SOS garbage."

"It's not garbage, Delaney. Why won't anyone listen to me? *My father died saving Owen Station. I am not about to let that be for nothing.*"

"Hazel, do you hear how crazy that sounds? I'm sorry for all the loss you've had—you know I am. I've been here for you through all kinds of rough times. And I'll *always* be here for you. But your dad died twenty years ago. You have to let it go, hon. You have to let yourself live your own life."

"That's right, Delaney. It's *my* life. And I don't need Sena or anyone else messing it up."

"How could falling in love mess up your life, Hazel?" Lace asked softly. Leave it to her to ask exactly the right question, in exactly the right way.

Yes, what would be wrong with falling in love?
Would that really be so awful?
Millions of people do it every day. Why not you?

Hazel slumped down in her chair hoping Lace and Delaney would take a hint. She did *not* want to talk about this any further. Thankfully, Lace got it. She began regaling Delaney with the details of her current fling. They never lasted long with Lace. Three months—that was her rule. She said things got too complicated after that. Hazel was only half listening, her eyes wandering as she sipped wine.

They were sitting in what would have been Mrs. Owen's parlor, but the walls were covered with racks carrying all kinds of adult toys. Vibrators. Strap-ons. Nipple clamps. Some things Hazel couldn't quite identify. In the built-in buffet, which the mine owner's wife probably used to store her china, every imaginable kind of dildo was on display. A basket of butt plugs sat beside a bucket of bright, multicolored condoms with a sign that read, "Free—take one and give one to a friend. Peace, love, and safe sex."

When she spied the colorful "Hanky Panky" panties, she lost it.

"What's so funny?" Both Delaney and Lace asked at the same time.

Hazel was covering her mouth, having nearly spit out her wine.

"I'm sorry," she said between gut-wrenching guffaws. "I was just thinking about what old Mrs. Owen might say about those Hanky Pankies on her buffet, right where her silver tea set used to sit!"

Hazel's hysteria was contagious and before long they were all laugh-crying until a loud crash, like somebody dropped a bowling ball on the old wooden floor above them, stopped them cold.

Delaney dove to the floor screaming, covering her head with her hands. "What the hell was that?"

After a startled pause, Lace doubled over, howling with laughter. "Girls! That's just old Mrs. Owen. I think she's letting us know *exactly* what she thinks about those Hanky Pankies."

Delaney got up off her knees slowly. Her eyes, as round as one of Mrs. Owen's silver serving plates, were glued to the ceiling. "Are you *kidding* me? You always said this place was haunted, but I never thought…I never thought you really meant it!"

There was a reason a whole ghost industry had grown up in Owen Station. The oldest hotel in Arizona was right in the middle of town and, after a hundred years of guests checking in, more than a few were rumored to have never checked out. True Owenites didn't believe the official stories the tour guides told, of course. But they did believe in spirits. People had lived in that desert for thousands of years, long before the invasion of western beliefs and practices, and their descendants were still a powerful force. Pilgrims from around the world traveled to the Southwest—to find power in the vortexes of Sedona, healing in Yavapi County's hot springs, a spiritual connection in the Superstition Mountain wilderness. Owenites were surrounded by reminders that some things just can't be explained. They accepted that as fact.

So it wasn't hard to mess with Delaney. Lace brushed her fingers through her short hair, smiled mysteriously, and spoke in a hushed tone, like they were sitting around a campfire in the dark. "Well, maybe now you'll believe me when I tell you I have a roommate who doesn't pay rent. That's why I won't move into the upstairs bedroom."

"You stop that right now, Lace Arnold Reynolds!" Eyes bugging out of her head, which was swiveling back and forth looking for other signs of ghostly trouble, Delaney looked every inch that friend who gets picked off first in a horror flick.

It was all so funny that Hazel almost forgot, for a moment, that her heart was bruised, her body was aggravated, and her friends were disappointed. "Have you ever actually *seen* her?" Hazel whispered, eyes on the ceiling, just to heighten the comedy.

Lace cackled, pretending to study the contents of her glass. "This blend is good, don't you think?" She took a slow sip, continuing to stare spookily at Hazel and Delaney over her glass.

"Come on, quit teasing, Lace. Tell us *everything*," Hazel begged, egging her on.

"Okay, okay. No." Lace put her glass down and sat up straight, like she was getting serious. "I've never actually seen her. But I

always know when she's come for a visit. And I do mean *come...*"
She paused dramatically.

"Do you see that bright red dildo on the shelf all by itself, right above the panties?"

Hazel and Delaney both nodded.

"About twice a week, I find that dildo on the floor in the morning when I come in to open the shop. Always *that* one. Vibrating up a storm, bouncing all over the floor. Like somebody got caught in the act and dropped it before scurrying away."

Hazel squawked with delight and joined Lace in uncontrollable laughter. But Delaney looked terrified. She grabbed her purse and jumped out of her chair. "I think I'm ready to go."

She was out the front door and down the stairs before Hazel could take a last swallow of wine. She and Lace quickly collected their things and followed.

"See you later, Mrs. Owen," Lace shouted up at the ceiling as she flipped off the light and locked the door behind her.

Delaney was at the wheel when Lace and Hazel hopped in. Thanks to Mrs. Owen, no one seemed mad at her anymore.

Hazel knew it was all coming from a good place. Her friends were worried about her. Heck, she was a little worried about herself. Maybe it was time to let herself have a little fun.

Just like every girls' night—almost always the third Saturday of the month—they were headed to the only lesbian bar south of Phoenix, since The Closet closed in Tucson. The Triple D was known for bad food, bland beer, and surly bartenders, but it was packed every weekend—except for that year and a half when no one went anywhere, especially not where there would be a crowd. Tonight, loud country music spilled out into a parking lot filled with pickup trucks and Jeeps, Harleys, and a long line of Priuses. Two denim-clad women leaned against a wall near the door, making out. A large woman sporting a crew cut and a Black Eyed Peas T-shirt was taking a ten-dollar cover charge. "Have fun and stay outta trouble, ladies," she said as they pushed through the swinging saloon doors.

Inside, a couple dozen women jostled around pool tables and a live, all-female band was killing it in front of a crowded dance floor. Hazel, Lace, and Delaney headed to the worn wooden bar, which looked like it had been around since Doc Holiday roamed the desert, and squeezed onto a couple of empty stools. A steer skull hung on the wall in front of them, right next to somebody's old wooden cane, a hunting knife, a framed magazine cover of John Wayne, a six-year-old calendar, and a metal sign that said "3 Things I Don't Like—Hot Beer. Cold Women. Assholes."

She'd seen that old sign a hundred times at least, but tonight a little shiver shot up Hazel's spine. She felt guilty of at least two out of three.

The place was dark and needed a good dusting. But there wouldn't be a single man hitting on, ogling at, or drunkenly asking them what "women really want." And that made the Triple D the only bar within a hundred and fifty miles where that was true.

When they finally managed to flag down the bartender, they ordered a round of shots. Jack Daniels. It wasn't Irish, but it would do.

Delaney waved off three invitations to dance within the first ten minutes. Her bleached blond hair, big smile, and bodacious curves were like catnip in a no-kill shelter full of frisky felines. She didn't mind the attention, even if it wasn't her flavor. She just came to dance, drink cheap booze, and hang with her friends.

Hazel leaned close and shouted into her ear. "I love you, Delaney."

She meant it, too. Delaney had been rock solid ever since she moved back to Owen Station to take care of her mother.

"You ought to!" Delaney grinned.

Hazel hopped off the stool and took Delaney by the hand. "Let's dance! Come on, Lace. You, too!"

They threw back what was left of their whiskies and joined a line dance that was just getting started. They stayed for another couple of songs, two-stepping until the band slowed it down, easing into an old Chely Wright tune.

By this time, Lace had found a dance partner, a cute brunette in a fitted tee, cutoff shorts, and blue cowboy boots with gold stars cut into the leather.

"That's Tessa! You know, from the winery. I cut her hair." Delaney yelled over the loud music. "It looks like our Lace really has found a *friend*."

They exchanged grins, gave Lace a thumbs up, and headed back to the bar.

Delaney was ordering another round, lost in a sea of women trying to catch the bartender's eye, when Hazel heard a voice so close to her ear she could feel the warm breath on her neck.

"Is this seat taken?"

Hazel's heart froze, but a tremor went through her body. She didn't need to turn around to know that Sena was standing right behind her.

CHAPTER ELEVEN

TRIPLE D

S ena never imagined running into Hazel. Which was stupid, come to think of it. It was a small town. It was bound to happen at some point. And why wouldn't Hazel be out having fun with friends? What did Sena expect? That Hazel would be home alone, eating frozen dinners, stewing on how her life had gone so wrong, aching to touch the woman sleeping just steps away, worrying that she had missed out on the chance of a lifetime, fixated on how to make it right, wondering if that might be possible somehow? Hoping beyond hope that it was. Well, yes. That was what Sena expected. Because that's what Sena's life had become.

But here was Hazel. Looking relaxed and happy. Like nothing had ever happened. Sena grabbed her fitted black dress at the seams, adjusted it with a flip of her wrists, and threw her hair over one shoulder. Then she stood tall and marched herself over to where Hazel was sitting. She was glad she was wearing her favorite boots because she was suddenly in a shit-kicking mood. Hazel had some explaining to do.

"Is this seat taken?"

Hazel jumped.

"I'm sorry. I didn't mean to startle you."

"You didn't…I mean, you did. I mean, it doesn't matter." Hazel swiveled around on her stool to look at her. "Oh, hell."

In the dim light, Hazel's blue eyes were dark as the desert sky in moonlight. Sena melted. Right then and there. A snowball on the side of a sand dune. She didn't want to be angry. She couldn't be. She didn't know how Hazel had done it, but this quirky, unexpected woman had pierced a hole in the wall that had grown around her heart. Even though it still hurt that Hazel had run away, and she was confused as hell, that hole had become a crack, and each day bits of that wall were falling away. She would always be thankful for that.

Sena lightly brushed Hazel's cheek with the back of her hand. "My favorite librarian swears like a truck driver, I see."

Hazel flinched again. Her face was hot against Sena's hand and her eyes hardened as she pulled away. "I'm sorry, Sena. I guess I have no idea what else to say."

"How about, it's good to see you, Sena?"

Hazel's gaze thudded to the floor. "I'm not sure that it is."

Sena reached out a finger to lift her chin, but Hazel shivered hard at the touch. This was not going well. So, impulsively, Sena did the one thing she hoped might turn things around. She told the truth.

"I've missed you, Hazel."

And there it was.

She traced Hazel's jawline with a finger, down along her neck and across the deep edge of her silky tank top, and Hazel's body shuddered. An electric current shot up Sena's arm, down the middle of her body, exploding between her legs.

Panic erupted in Hazel's eyes and she grabbed Sena's wrist. "Please, stop." Her voice dropped to something just below a whisper. But it was loud enough for Sena to hear. "I can't."

Sena immediately dropped her hand and stepped away, as if she'd been slapped. Just then, the crowd around them thinned and a blonde in a turquoise cowboy hat turned toward them.

"Well, hi there!" The woman shoved three glasses toward them. Wearing an infectious grin, she swung her head to look at Sena, then at Hazel, and back again.

"Lemme guess. You must be Sena. I don't know how we've gone this long without meeting, but I've heard a lot about you. In fact, the whole town's talkin' 'bout you. Welcome to Owen Station! Thanks for the good work you're doing."

"And you must be Delaney."

Delaney nodded and handed her a glass. "Whiskey okay? I figured you might need one when I saw Hazel here just about jump out of her skin."

Sena nodded gratefully and, feeling a little shaky, reached out with both hands to take the glass. Delaney rolled her eyes and shoved a glass at Hazel.

"I got *you* a double."

Then Delaney turned her grin back on and swiveled toward Sena. "I see you've found the infamous Triple D."

"Actually, I spent some time here one summer when I was in college."

"What?" Delaney's eyes popped wide open and her jaw hit the floor. If she was a cartoon, which she actually did resemble, a light bulb would have been exploding over her head.

"Wouldn't it have been an AMAZING coincidence if you two had actually been here *at the same time* back then? Think about how different life might have been."

Hazel interrupted sharply. "I think it's quite a coincidence that you're here *tonight,* Sena."

"I'm not sure what you're implying, Hazel. But it *is* a nice coincidence and I'm very happy to see you." She tilted her head toward the dance floor. "I came with some friends."

"Oh, that's right. I *heard* you were making friends in town." Hazel sounded like a cactus, if cacti could talk.

What in the hell was making her so prickly? Whatever it was, Sena wasn't going to be chased off easily. Not this time.

"Actually, I am making friends. It's sort of a new goal of mine. The friend I'm here with tonight owns a winery in Sonoita."

"You mean *Tessa?*" Delaney's eyes lit up.

"Damn. This *is* a small town." A town Sena was starting to love.

Hazel scowled and slumped over in her seat. "Well, you certainly are hitting it off." She looked at Delaney and then at Sena. "Maybe *you* two should date."

Then she drained her glass in one swallow, slammed it on the bar, and stormed off toward the bathroom. Sena stood there with her mouth open, watching Hazel walk away. Again.

"Well, why are you just standing there?" Delaney held her hands out like a priest sending the people off at the end of Mass. "Go get her."

Sena didn't hesitate. She reached the back of the bar, near the bathroom, just in time to see Hazel push through a rear exit out toward the parking lot. Muttering a string of excuse mes, she followed her through the crowd and out the door.

"Hazel, *stop!*"

To Sena's surprise, Hazel obeyed. But she didn't turn around.

Coming up behind her, Sena resisted grabbing her arm to turn her around. Hazel was going to have to come to her on her own this time or not at all.

"Why do you keep running away from me?"

"I told you." Hazel sounded sniffly, like she was crying. "I don't want to do this. I *can't* do this."

"Is this about the work I'm doing here in Owen Station? Do you still think I'm the enemy? Because, I swear to God. I'm not. I'm doing everything I can to help this town. I mean yes, I want to do something great. I *need* to do something that matters. But I also want to do it the right way. Just yesterday, I met with my advisory board…a lot of them were on the board of the old Y…they're amazing…and we decided we should…"

Hazel turned around and put her hand over Sena's mouth. Her eyes were wet, but they were bright blue again, and they were sparkling in the light of the streetlamp.

"Sena. This is not about your work. This isn't even about the town. I thought it was, but it isn't. I don't even know how to explain it. All I know is that I have not stopped thinking about you. Not for a second. I can't eat. I can't sleep. I bump around in my house all by myself, afraid to go anywhere I might run into you. We were only together for a few days and I felt like I got pulled through a wrinkle in time. Like I was spinning wildly through space. I felt like I was losing my mind. Like my whole world had been turned upside down and inside out. A world I've worked very hard to create. It might be a little boring but it's safe. It's *mine*. I'm just not ready to let that world go, Sena. It's terrifying. *You* are terrifying."

Sena closed her eyes, took a deep breath, and held it. What did you say to that? The truth again? She opened her eyes and exhaled the most honest words she could think of.

"This scares me, too, Hazel. You...have...no...idea."

Nothing could have surprised Sena more than Hazel's laughter. It tinkled like rain, like ice in a glass of agua fresca on a hot day.

"I think it's obvious why *I'm* scared, Sena. Just ask Delaney. Or Knox." Eye roll. Crooked smile. "I'm basically allergic to anything new."

Hazel looked like porcelain, easily breakable, but here she was. Brave enough to see her own silly reflection. Sena reached out and brushed her cheek again. This time Hazel did not flinch. "You are stronger than you look, Hazel Butler."

"Maybe," she said, reaching up to hold Sena's hand against her cheek. "But you couldn't look more powerful if you tried, Sena. I can't believe *anything* could scare you."

Sena didn't know where to start. How could she explain? That the stylish clothes, the attitude, the accoutrement, the high-powered Audi, which all seemed designed to attract attention, were actually part of a well-crafted defense to keep her hidden. Like the Sonoran desert, Sena looked tough on the outside, inhospitable, dangerous even, a place where only the strongest survived. But underneath there was a fragile ecosystem.

"Sena?" Hazel was studying her face, as if looking for clues. She was almost whispering. "What could you possibly be afraid of?"

"Hazel..." Breathe in. Eyes closed. Exhale. Eyes open. Finally, a free fall. "I am afraid of *you*, Hazel."

"How is that even possible, Sena." Hazel crossed her eyes and grinned. "What is scary about *me*?"

Was this as ridiculous as Hazel made it sound? Sena steadied herself by taking both of Hazel's hands and bringing them to her lips to kiss them. Buying herself a moment. Looking for nerve. She found it deep in those clear blue eyes.

"Hazel, I *want* you. I mean, I want to finish what we started in the courtyard. In the library. On Main Street. I want to make love to you."

Hazel stood very still, barely breathing, suddenly looking as frightened as Sena felt. Sena pushed on, carefully pronouncing every syllable, making sure there would be no misunderstanding.

"But…I…don't…think I can *make* love to you…without *falling* in love with you."

"And that…that's what scares you?"

"I've never felt this way about anyone before, Hazel. It terrifies me."

"Why?" Hazel's voice was barely audible above the buzz of the streetlight. "Why is the thought of falling in love so terrifying for *you*?"

Sena looked past Hazel into the distance. "Because love isn't real."

A pickup truck roared through the parking lot blasting Tejano music, and four women hung out the window singing along. In the distance, a coyote called to her mate. Sena refocused and looked into Hazel's eyes.

"How can you say that, Sena? Love is the most real thing in the world. The kind of love my mom and dad had for each other. The kind of love they had for me. The kind of love Knox, Delaney, Lace and I all have for each other. I would be lost without it—literally dead without it." Hazel paused and glanced away for a moment. She was clear-eyed when she turned back. "Love might be the *only* thing that is really real, Sena. It's more real than the books we write, the businesses we launch, the money we make. It's more real than the houses we build, the clothes we wear, the gadgets we invent. Love is the only thing that endures."

Sena was silent. Could this be true? She had seen the love in Hazel's life. In her friends. In her family…even though they were all long gone. She could see it now, in Hazel's eyes.

Sena dipped her head, dropped her eyes, and let the truth, her truth, slip out. "I want that, Hazel. I need that."

Hazel didn't speak. Instead, she took Sena by the hands and pulled her into a dark nook along the side of the building. This time Hazel's kisses were anything but chaste. She explored Sena's lips with her own, sliding and sucking, and dragged her tongue along the entrance to her mouth, teasing and probing. When Hazel pushed her up against the wall, plunging her tongue into her mouth, Sena gasped and opened her legs wide, allowing Hazel to press closer. Sena swelled with desire, returning Hazel's kisses, deep and full.

Until it stopped.

It. Stopped.

Hazel pushed Sena away, a familiar panicky look in her eyes. Sena grabbed her hands, afraid that she'd run again. "Hazel, what *is* it?"

Hazel dropped her head. "Oh my God, Sena. I am so sorry." Tears begin to fall. "I want you. So much. But I'm just so afraid.

"Of *what*, Hazel? Why can't you just let go?"

"I don't *know*, Sena." She dropped her head. "I don't know what it will take."

Terror filled Hazel's eyes when she looked back up. "You're afraid of falling in love because you think love isn't real. I'm afraid because I know that it is. I know what happens when you love someone. You lose them. And I don't think I can go through that again."

"I get it, Hazel. I do. But we can't let our fears control us. I am stronger than that. *You* are stronger than that."

"I'm not you, Sena! Why do you think I hold on to the past? Why have I thrown myself into protecting my dad's legacy and preserving the history of this town? It's safe, that's why! I can immerse myself in memories, connect to something bigger than me, and feel loved without the pain. But then you come along. Dragging me into the future. And I'm scared, Sena. The thought of letting myself go with you is terrifying."

"But, Hazel…" Sena took Hazel's face in her hands and looked deeply into those clear blue eyes. "Aren't you tired of being alone?"

Hazel looked stunned. Then she collapsed into Sena's arms and began sobbing. Sena caressed her hair, her back, letting the tears fall. When the crying stopped, Sena dropped her lips to Hazel's ear and volunteered to end this painful dance for good.

"Hazel, do you want me to take you home?"

Hazel murmured into Sena's neck. "Yes, please," she moaned. "Take me back to the casita, Sena. Make me yours."

That drive back to the casita took a lifetime for both of them to make and Sena knew what she needed—and wanted—to do. Stepping over Mango, who was curled up outside the front door, as if waiting for them to both finally come home, Sena entered the little house backward, holding Hazel's hands. Moonlight flooded through the window as she steered Hazel across the vintage cowhide covering the cement floor, through the small living room, past the galley kitchen and into the bedroom.

They both stood beside the antique bed as Sena unbuttoned Hazel's jeans. Then she gently lowered Hazel onto the bed and pulled them off, letting them fall to the floor. As Hazel sat there, Sena knelt before her and held her gaze as she ran her hands down the full length of Hazel's body. Then she opened her legs and slowly dragged a finger from back to front along the wet center of her panties. Hazel tipped her head back and moaned.

The ceiling fan sent a cool breeze skimming across their skin, making the curtains at the window flutter softly. In the distance, a neighbor's dog barked.

Sena unhooked the leather band of Hazel's ticking watch and carefully laid it on the nightstand. Then she removed Hazel's necklace and her black-framed glasses and gently set them there as well. She tugged Hazel's silky tank top over her head, exposing firm breasts and hard nipples, folded it, and laid it beside the jewelry.

Hazel was passive as Sena ran fingers through her messy, bright red hair. That freckled skin was nearly the same color as her white panties, and goose bumps emerged under Sena's fingers as she lightly ran them along Hazel's collarbone, between her breasts, down her belly, and along the inside of her panty line. Except for those panties, Hazel was completely naked now, her eyes filled with both terror and trust.

"You're trembling," Sena whispered.

Hazel responded with a shy smile.

"Are you sure you're okay?" She would not take one inch more than Hazel was willing to give.

Hazel looked deep into Sena's eyes and nodded.

"You are beautiful, Hazel. So incredibly beautiful." She sat beside her, put her hands on either side of Hazel's face, and held her gently, staring into those deep blue eyes. And then she kissed her. The kiss was deep and passionate, filled with promises too deep for words, commitments Sena wasn't certain she could keep…to be open and real, to stay and not run, to be grateful and careful with the priceless gift Hazel was giving her. She wanted these promises to be true. Both for Hazel's sake and her own.

Hazel was silent.

Sena stood up again and straddled Hazels legs. She ran her hands down Hazel's neck to her shoulders, and then down her arms. When she grabbed Hazel's wrists and squeezed them, gently at first and then harder, Hazel let out another soft moan and Sena began to cream. She was confident and strong, used to being in control, undeniably hungry but more patient than she had ever been. Holding Hazel firmly by the wrists, she raised her arms above her head and then lowered them, putting Hazel's hands behind her back, locking them in place, training Hazel to follow her commands. With Hazel immobilized, Sena buried her face in that smooth, sweet neck, and began covering it with biting kisses. Hazel whimpered, unable to move, feeling the sharp sting of Sena's nibbles. Sena paused.

"Do you want me to stop, Hazel?"

Hazel's eyes were wide with fear and excitement. She shook her head.

"Are you sure?"

Hazel nodded.

"If, at any point, you want me to stop, I want you to tell me, okay? I will stop immediately." Sena spoke clearly, but softly. "My only purpose right now is to make you feel as beautiful as you really are…both inside and out. Completely and totally alive. Are you hearing me?"

Hazel nodded.

"I want to make you scream with desire."

Hazel's words were buried so deep they sounded guttural when they finally emerged.

"I want that, too."

Hazel's willing passivity, her agency in making clear her desire to be taken, lit a fire between Sena's legs. She released Hazel's wrists and swung her around, lifting her up onto the bed and pushing her gently onto her back. Exposing a bush as bright red as the hair on Hazel's head, she stripped off the soaked panties and tossed them to the floor. Then, as Hazel lay there motionless, Sena stood up and prepared to strip off her own clothes.

"Hazel," she said steadily. "I want you to open yourself up. Let me see you."

Obediently, Hazel reached down and parted herself. She was swollen and red. Sena took a deep breath as her own body responded, every inch on fire. She could barely resist the urge to ravish, to consume. If it was any other woman, at any other time... but this was different.

Hazel was different.

Sena was different.

Hazel was trusting her. Opening, not just her body but her heart, a heart that had been broken and bruised. Sena would not take that for granted.

She walked over to the end of the bed, for a better view. "That is perfect, Hazel. Now, lick your finger."

Hazel obeyed and waited for the next command.

"Touch yourself."

Sena was insane with desire and ready to explode. Clearly, Hazel was too. Given permission, she slid her wet finger down to her throbbing clit and began to circle it, thankful for relief.

"No." Sena commanded. "I didn't say rub. I said touch."

She leaned over and reverently placed Hazel's finger right where she wanted it. Close enough to create pressure. Maddeningly close. "Hold your finger right there, Hazel. Don't move it. Don't move at all. Just...hold it."

She pinned Hazel to the bed with her eyes as she shimmied out of her tight dress and let it fall to the floor. Hazel lay, legs wide open, as her eyes gobbled up Sena's body. As Hazel moaned and writhed under the pressure of her own hot finger, the smell of oozing sex made Sena wild with desire.

But she was on a mission. She had been called to set Hazel free. To release her from all that was holding her back, keeping her in bondage, preventing her from moving toward the life she wanted. The life she deserved. Hazel couldn't do it on her own. Sena could help. Wanted to help. Hazel had asked her to do this.

She crawled up between Hazel's legs to kiss and lick the finger that was creating such painful pleasure, carefully avoiding the swollen clit. The muscles in Hazel's belly tensed and a loud moan slipped over her tongue.

"Sena, you are torturing me." A low whine, a plea for release. Her brow furrowed in agony.

"Exactly." Sena smiled, kissing Hazel's tense, motionless finger one more time.

While Hazel watched through widening eyes, Sena reached over and opened the nightstand drawer, pulling out two silk scarves.

"I don't go anywhere without these." Then, like a benevolent goddess, Sena gave her subject leave.

"Okay, Hazel, would you like to be able to rub yourself?"

Hazel nodded. "Yes, please." Her voice was raspy, barely audible, as if she was afraid to move too fast or do the wrong thing and have this privilege taken away.

"Slowly, then," Sena commanded her. "Very slowly."

Hazel circled herself, moaning, while Sena attached the scarves to the antique iron headboard.

As she slipped a scarf around Hazel's free hand, Hazel threw her head back and began to rub faster, harder with the other.

"Oh, no you don't. Not yet."

Sena took the hand Hazel had been using to pleasure herself and tied it to the opposite headboard post.

Then she reached back into the drawer and pulled out a feather.

Hazel opened her eyes wide and then closed them, arching her back, opening herself wide, wordlessly begging Sena to take her. There was nothing Sena had ever wanted more. She wanted to take Hazel from darkness into light, to release her from all that held her back, to help her live again.

She started at Hazel's ankle, lightly brushing the tip of the feather up the inside of her leg.

"Oh my God…"

Hazel's agonized voice was fuel for the fire that burned inside of Sena. Hazel's eyes were still squeezed shut and she moaned as Sena gave the other leg equal treatment.

"I cannot believe how beautiful you are, Hazel. Or how much I want you."

She drew a circle around Hazel's wild red bush with the feather, eliciting a deeper moan. Then she moved up and lay beside Hazel as she dragged the feather straight up Hazel's stomach, toward her breast bone. She brought it under Hazel's chin, causing her to tip her head back. And that gave Sena perfect access to the thing she most longed for—Hazel's lips.

Sena's mouth hovered inches above Hazel's, whose arms were outstretched above her head, wrists bound. Sena was in complete control. She had permission to take what she wanted, to make Hazel her own. Hazel wanted that, too. Needed that.

"Hazel..." Sena whispered.

Hazel's eyes opened slowly. As blue as the Sonoran sky. Sena had longed to float in those eyes from the first time they met. She was safe there. She was seen. Sena laid the palm of her hand softly on Hazel's cheek and gently pulled, bringing Hazel's mouth so close she could feel Hazel's breath on her lips.

When their lips touched, the earth beneath them gave way. Nothing else in the universe existed. Just Hazel's lips beneath her own. Sena was gentle, covering Hazel's lips and cheeks and chin with soft kisses. The feather forgotten, Sena lay beside her and traced the soft edges of Hazel's body with her finger tips. She wanted to touch everything, learn everything there was to know about Hazel's body. What made her groan. What made her shiver. What made her beg. She wanted Hazel to know that she was seen, too. Safe. And wanted.

She ran her fingers along Hazel's long neck and delicate shoulders. She twirled one nipple and then the other, and then slid down the long runway from breastbone to navel. Her fingers lingered in the tender space just beneath Hazel's hips, teasing, diving lower toward Hazel's bush and then back up again. Each time Sena dipped lower, Hazel thrust upward, as if willing Sena's fingers to meet her throbbing wetness. Hazel wrapped her hands around the scarves, pulling, moaning.

"Sena..." Her voice was deep, demanding. *"Kiss* me."

Sena looked into Hazel's eyes and saw the years of longing and the loneliness—and made it her mission to melt it all away. She covered Hazel's mouth with her own.

But Hazel was no longer a passive recipient. Her demanding tongue pushed Sena's mouth open wider. She pulled against the restraints, working to drive her tongue even deeper into Sena's mouth, filling her. Still kissing, being kissed, biting and being bitten, Sena reached up and untied Hazel's hands, which flew to Sena's naked body.

Hazel was free.

She pulled Sena on top of her, her hands racing from Sena's neck to her ass and back again. Then she put her hands on Sena's shoulders and pushed her down between her legs.

Sena did not have to be told again.

"Is this what you want, Hazel?" Sena had one hand under Hazel's ass, while the other softly brushed the inside of Hazel's thighs.

Hazel nodded, her eyes wild.

Sena leaned in and tasted Hazel's opening with the tip of her tongue. "Do you want more?"

Hazel nodded more furiously.

So did Sena. She wanted more than the meaningless relationships, the one-night stands, the empty scx she had in the past. She wanted to be the missing piece in someone's life, the glue that held everything together. She didn't just want to take. Sena wanted to give, to fill Hazel with laughter, and a light that no darkness could ever dim.

She parted Hazel with a finger, found her swollen clit with her tongue, and did not stop until the explosion...and Hazel screamed her name.

CHAPTER TWELVE

ANTARES

S ena waited for Hazel to be the first to say something. Hazel was laying spread-eagle on her back, her eyes closed but a smile tugging both sides of her mouth. "Oh. My. God."

"You look satisfied." Sena grinned. She was a master conductor after a thunderous, symphonic climax. She felt like taking a bow.

"Satisfied? I feel like Sam and Frodo after they destroyed the One Ring."

"I think it was actually Gollum who fell into Mount Doom, *accidentally* destroying the Ring."

"Whaaat?" Hazel turned over and propped herself on one elbow. "You are a Lord of the Rings fan? Those were my favorite books from about age nine to eleven. I must have read them a dozen times over the past twenty-five years. If I would have known this about you, this whole jumping into bed thing wouldn't have taken so long!"

Sena laughed and Hazel leaned over to kiss her before laying back down.

"I'm not kidding, though. I do feel like we just won a great battle."

Sena studied Hazel's face. What a strange thing to say. But Hazel was the strangest woman Sena had ever known. In the best of all possible ways. "A battle, huh? Who was the enemy?"

Hazel turned her head and looked sharply into Sena's eyes. "I was."

Sena flipped over on her side and rested her hand on Hazel's cheek. "You are so beautiful, Hazel." It was silly to keep saying that, but those were all the words she had for what she saw in Hazel. Nothing that Sena could say would capture the light and joy and life that Hazel was radiating.

Hazel brought her hand up and covered Sena's hand on her cheek. Her eyes were pools of crystal blue water, clear. Clean. "And you, dear Sena, have set me free."

Then Hazel closed her eyes and Sena watched her chest rise and fall. She was breathing. Really breathing. Inhaling and exhaling.

When Hazel opened her eyes again, she looked up at the ceiling. "As much as I wanted to let go of the past and...and do *this*...I just couldn't. It was like being bound by invisible handcuffs. Tied to memories. To responsibilities that weren't mine anymore and maybe never were. To commitments I fulfilled a long time ago. No one was keeping me there except myself. My friends told me this for years. I guess I had to see it for myself. But I didn't see it... *couldn't* see it until..." She turned her head toward Sena, her mouth twisted, a jumble of joy and pain. "Until I thought I lost you."

Hazel spoke softly, like her words were coming from deep within a well that had been dry as dust but now was filled. "Thank you."

Sena kissed her softly on the lips. "You are most welcome, m'lady."

They lay smiling into each other's eyes and, honestly, Sena could have stayed there, just like that, forever. But finally, she broke the silence. "You know what, Hazel? You are an enigma."

"Why, whatever do you mean?" Hazel's mocking tone perfectly mimicked a proper lady.

"Well, I never would have expected someone so wrapped up in the past to be so eager to do...new things...especially the first time with a new lover. I'm clearly going to have to learn some new tricks."

"Never underestimate a librarian." Hazel arched her eyebrow and laughed. "We read things."

"Speaking of not-to-be-underestimated, enigmatic librarians... how'd you know what kind of shoes I was wearing the day we met? And speaking of fancy shoe wear, how exactly did you come by a pair of *Fluevogs*?"

Hazel looked embarrassed and a little flustered. "I, um...I..."

"You love great shoes as much as I do?"

Hazel snickered. "You got me. As a matter of fact, shoes are my secret indulgence. Mostly I pick up great pairs at the antique and thrift shops in town, along with all the rest of my clothes. It's amazing what you can find when you know what you're looking for. But after my mom got sick, while she could still get around okay, we took a quick trip to Denver. I found a great fare and we decided on a whim to go see the Rockies. Mom had always wanted that. And while we were wandering around the city, I found—"

Sena shouted. "Fluevogs! Yep, I've been in that store, too. RESISTS ALKALI, WATER, ACID—"

"FATIGUE AND SATAN!" Hazel joined in and they recited together the famous words John Fluevog engraved on the soles of his shoes.

"And...now we are finishing each other's sentences." Sena kissed Hazel again. "I. Love. It."

"You know what I'd love?" Hazel had a mischievous twinkle in her eye.

"Whatever it is...I'm here for it." Sena could go all night long. She was counting on it.

"Oh, I want some more of that, for sure...later. First, I need some food. I am famished!"

"Come to think of it, so am I," Sena said with a grin. "I could *also* eat some food."

Hazel laughed while she hopped out of bed and padded to the closet. "Apparently, I'm not the only one who can surprise." She pulled Sena's old chambray button-down off a hanger.

"Why is that so surprising? I grew up on a ranch. You never know when you might need a good work shirt."

Actually, Sena couldn't remember the last time she wore that shirt. But she was never without it. It was one of the few things she owned that reminded her of her old life, the family that felt so far away. Home.

"Well, I love it. And I'm borrowing it." Hazel slipped it on and headed to the door, barefooted and bare assed. "I'll grab something to munch on and meet you in the courtyard."

Sena watched until she was out of sight. Then she tidied up and pulled a cream-colored silk kimono out of the closet. She shivered as it slipped over her bare skin. Her reaction wasn't entirely physical. If this were any other night, with any other woman, this wouldn't be the end of their date. It'd be the end of the "relationship"—if you could call it that. Hazel would be just another notch on her belt, a trophy on her shelf. Sena was thirteen when she learned the most important lesson of her life. Unconditional love was an illusion. Life was a proving ground and it was dangerous to play the game any other way. The only thing that mattered was being the strongest, the smartest, the best.

But, tonight, she was going to go out into that courtyard in the middle of the night and have a snack, and probably a real conversation, with a small-town librarian. It made almost no sense. But that's what she was going to do.

"I'm going to live my best life." She said this out loud, remembering Tessa with gratitude. "And that's going to start right here. Right now."

The sun had been down for hours and the temps, although still high for an Owen Station night, had dipped to a bearable ninety degrees. The lack of humidity in the air made it almost cool when Sena stepped into the courtyard. She sat in one of the cushioned wrought iron armchairs, took a deep breath, and let herself relax into this new moment. A few minutes later, Hazel emerged from the back door of her house carrying a goody-filled tray.

"What's all this?"

"Oh, just a little something I threw together." Hazel looked very proud of herself. "Handmade corn chips and fresh guacamole from the farmer's market."

"And in the decanter? Which, lemme guess…is from like 1952?"

"I'm impressed! You nailed the decade. And in this decanter, I'll have you know, is a little Bacanora I had sitting around the house."

Bacanora—an agave spirit made only in the state of Sonora, just south of the Arizona border, where hot days and cool nights gave it an unmistakable flavor—was an Abrigo family favorite. What were the odds?

"Hazel, my dear, I do think I could fall in love with you."

Sena couldn't believe those words just popped out of her mouth. But she had never spoken truer ones.

Hazel batted her eyelashes playfully, fanning herself as if she was overheated with embarrassment. "You mean that hasn't happened already?"

Sena laughed and stuck her tongue out as Hazel handed her a glass. But she grew serious as she took a first sip of the golden liquid.

"Oh my God. It's been a long time. It tastes just like the desert… dry…complex…with a little bit of a bite." She took another sip and let magic happen, as long forgotten memories danced through her mind. Good ones. Family celebrations. Sunday dinners. Everyday moments filled with love. "It tastes like home."

"Like home?"

Sena laughed at the puzzled look Hazel was giving her. Then she closed her eyes, opened her heart, and reached for Hazel's hand. "Yes, Hazel. Like home."

They both settled back in the armchairs, side by side, and Sena held Hazel's hand loosely, their fingers entwining, releasing, and then finding new ways to come together. Overhead, the stars went on forever. And off in the distance, heat lightning. "Maybe we'll finally see some rain tomorrow," Hazel said.

But Sena wasn't looking at the sky. Something was happening in the far corner of the courtyard. A sliver of greenish light flickered just above the adobe wall. It began to pulse and the hair on the back of Sena's neck sprang to life. She bolted up straight in her chair.

"Hazel…" she whispered, "do you see…"

But before Hazel turned, the light shot upward toward the sky and was gone so quickly Sena thought maybe she had imagined it. She laughed nervously and squeezed Hazel's hand.

"What was it, Sena?" Hazel's eyes narrowed. "What did you see?"

"It was nothing, nothing."

Hazel frowned. "You don't sound convincing."

"It was just a trick of the light. I think." Sena shrugged. "Nothing more."

Hazel's eyes blinked wide. "Let me guess…was it a *green* light?"

"A green light? Yes! Do you know what that was?"

Hazel inhaled deeply. "I'm not sure. The first time I saw it was the night we buried my mom. It filled up the courtyard and, when it was gone, Mango was here. I didn't know what it was, but it didn't scare me. In fact, it made me feel…" She paused as if trying to find the right words. "Peaceful."

Sena stared at Hazel, trying to take this in. "Have you seen it again since then?"

Hazel nodded. "Yes, a handful of times. Enough to make me do some research."

Sena smiled. "Of course you did research."

"Some people believe that a light like that is one way spirits visit. A green one—as long as it's exuding positive energy, that is—is all about growth and generosity and unconditional love. No one besides you, except for me I mean, has ever seen this one, though. As far as I know."

"You mean, none of your other renters have reported sightings of a pulsating green light…or a woman in their bedroom in the middle of the night? That'd probably look bad in the guest reviews."

"What?" Hazel's eyes were wide again. And, even though Sena had tried to sound lighthearted, Hazel looked terrified. "You saw a woman in your bedroom?"

"Besides *you*, you mean?" Sena laughed. "Yes. The first night I was here. And a couple times after that."

"Didn't you think that was weird? I don't know, maybe worth mentioning to your landlord?"

Sena laughed again. "Not really. I mean, it was more like a dream. I don't think she was *physically* in my room. But, even if she was, I mean...it's not like that would be a new thing. My grandfather helped me understand that they're everywhere, you know? And there was nothing scary about her. If anything, she just seemed sad."

"What does she look like?" Hazel was interrogating now, looking at Sena intently.

"Actually, Hazel..." Sena gently tapped Hazel's freckled nose. "She looks a lot like you. And, if I'm not mistaken, she is wearing your pearl brooch."

Hazel gasped and her hands shot up to her mouth, as if to catch her own breath. "My great-grandmother. Hazel."

A sudden clap of thunder in the distance startled them both and Hazel literally jumped into Sena's lap. After a first terrifying minute, they looked at each other looking ludicrous and then simultaneously erupted in waves of laughter.

Sena wrapped her arms tightly around Hazel, one hand inside the soft button-down, against Hazel's bare skin. "I could get used to this."

Hazel responded with a kiss and eased in, nestling her head against Sena's shoulder. She might have fallen asleep like that, but Hazel's excitement roused her.

"Look! A shooting star!" Hazel pointed at the sky.

This time Sena did look up. She missed the shooting star but let herself be awed by the sky. San Jose, like most cities, was full of light pollution. Owen Station was far from a big city. The sky was vast and dark, like the sky she grew up beneath. It had been such a long time since she had seen so many stars. "Let's see. My dad taught me a little about the night sky. We should be able to see Scorpio at this time of year...right? That's my sign, you know."

"No way. You're not a Scorpio. Are you?" Hazel's sarcasm dripped like desert wildflower honey. "Scorpios like to think they are calm, cool, collected and always in control. They're seductive.

And don't mess with them unless you want to be stung. No, that doesn't sound like you at all."

Sena laughed but she was also a little confused, looking up at the sky. "I'm serious, Hazel. I can see the Dipper…and Cassiopeia. But where is Scorpio? It should be right above us."

"You've been in the city too long, Sena. It's right there. Let me show you."

Hazel stood up and pulled Sena out of her chair by the hand. "Come here." She made Sena stand behind her, to see exactly what she was seeing.

"There…there are the three stars. Do you see them? They're right there, in a straight row. That's her head. And then, follow my finger, there is the curve of her tail. Do you see it?"

Sena's eyes were on the sky, but feeling Hazel pressed against her, her body was on fire again. She squeezed Hazel's arm, just below the shoulder, and felt taut biceps rippling under the surface. She slipped her hands down the length of Hazel's body and pulled her closer.

"You are insatiable, Sena Abrigo."

Sena murmured in her ear. "You have no idea."

Sena had loved finding ways to pleasure Hazel, bringing her to the edge of ecstasy and then backing away, shifting the rhythm, slowing down, and then building her up again, again and again, until finally she had exploded. It had been all about Hazel. And Sena was hungry.

Sena slid her hands down to Hazel's hips, caressing them. She squeezed Hazel's soft, bare ass, and let her fingers wander, first tickling and teasing from behind, then crawling around to the front of Hazel's body to playfully twirl the hair between her legs. It was complete turn-on to have Hazel wearing her chambray. From behind, she slowly unbuttoned the shirt and let her hands find a trail all the way down Hazel's stomach and up again, where she grabbed hold of Hazel's petite, firm breasts. Then she slipped a finger into Hazel's mouth, wetting it, and used it to circle and then gently pinch her erect nipples. Hazel moaned and tipped her head up, leaning back against Sena's shoulder.

Nothing was sexier than the way Hazel trusted Sena to touch her, to attend to her needs. To take care of her. Sena wanted nothing more than to be the person Hazel believed her to be.

She traced a line from Hazel's breasts, down her belly, to open her. Hazel was totally still and Sena imagined the tingling, the swelling, the creamy anticipation of the moment when Sena would enter her again. Sena's body was on fire.

Hazel could hardly speak but she grabbed Sena's arm. "Stop for a minute! Look up!"

Sena paused and turned her gaze upward. Toward the impossible. In the direction of infinity. At this point, willing to do almost anything Hazel asked.

"Right there in the very center of the constellation, Sena." Hazel's words were breathless. "Do you see it?"

"That big star?"

"Yes! That is Antares—a red supergiant, one of the largest stars in the sky. It's hundreds of times bigger than our own sun, if you can imagine. Sena…that is the glowing, beating heart at the center of Scorpio."

Hazel turned around and they stood there, eye to eye, story to story. She placed one hand between Sena's breasts, in the center of her chest, and pressed hard. Sena felt the warmth grow in her chest, beneath Hazel's hand.

"I want this, Sena." Hazel was whispering as if these words were meant for one person and only one to hear. "I'm not going to lie. I am scared to death by all of this. But I want this powerful, glowing heart of yours. I want to hold it and kiss it and care for it. I want to help heal it, Sena. I want it to be whole."

When you're not used to being seen and suddenly someone shines a light on you and invites you to stand in its glow, what do you say? How do you respond? Sena had no words. She just blinked at Hazel through her tears.

Hazel took her by the hand and coaxed her back into the casita's tiny living room. They sat up and talked for hours. Hazel asked about her family, her culture, her experience in Silicon Valley. She asked question after question as Sena shared her plans for the old downtown. She seemed amazed at the support Sena was getting from people in town, including some of the grouchiest, and she seemed genuinely excited about Sena's vision of making a new kind of space for women, and building an inclusive community where they could thrive.

After Sena had said all there was to say, they made love on a bed of blankets, with that supple cowhide beneath them on the floor.

Sena didn't remember at what point they got up, having fallen asleep together on the rug, and got back into bed. But she did remember being awakened again, in the very early hours of the morning. It was as if they had both been lost and wandering through the desert for so long, they were dehydrated and desperate for what only the other could give. A brown-crested flycatcher screeched its pre-dawn song as Sena tossed Hazel over onto her back again and slid down under the sheets.

CHAPTER THIRTEEN

DAYBREAK

The sunlight tickled Hazel awake, and she smiled before she even opened her eyes. This was the best time of day. Somewhere over the bluffs, the sun had risen, but down here in the canyon it was an in-between time. Hazel lay next to Sena, who was still in a deep sleep, and tried to remember every single thing that had happened in the past ten hours. How many times had Sena risen to meet her demand?

Hazel was awake.

Not just physically, but in other ways, too. To a sense of possibility. To hope about what tomorrow might bring. Sena had done that. Hazel never could have crossed over without her.

She lay there, studying every curve, memorizing every arc and every line. She drank in Sena's deep brown hair and her skin, the color of desert sand at twilight. A shock wave of desire shot through her body, but somehow she resisted the urge to wake Sena again. It was Sunday. They had a whole day ahead of them. She kissed Sena very lightly on her bare shoulder and quietly headed over to her own kitchen.

"Good morning, Mango." Hazel cheerfully greeted the orange tabby, who was uncharacteristically waiting for her. "Why, yes, I did have a wonderful night, thank you." When Hazel opened the door to her kitchen, it looked like Mango might follow her inside. "Hey!

What are you doing...oh no! I'm so sorry, Mango! I forgot to feed you last night, didn't I?"

Before she did anything else, Hazel filled Mango's dish with kibble. "Please don't take it out on Sena. It was not her fault." At the mention of Sena's name, Mango rubbed against Hazel's leg purring.

"Okay, Mom, I'm getting the message." Hazel laughed, bending over to give Mango a scratch.

Inside, Hazel headed straight for her bedroom, where she rummaged around in her dresser for a vintage Wonder Woman T-shirt, worn soft from a decade of weekend wear, and her favorite flannel boxers. She went from room to room, opening the blinds to let the light in—how long had it been since she had done that?—and put one of Grandma's Sinatra records on the old turntable in the living room.

Hazel sang along as she washed some fresh fruit for the breakfast she planned for later, and put the percolator on the stove. When the coffee was ready, she filled a mug and headed out to the front porch to pick up the newspaper. Heavy clouds had moved in overnight and they looked ready to release their load, finally bringing relief to the dry desert and a welcome respite from the heat.

Hazel flopped down into an old Adirondack on the porch with the paper on her lap and Mango at her feet. She hated that the *Owen Station Caller* only got published twice a week now, on Wednesdays and Sundays. Honestly, she didn't know what she'd do when the only way she could get news was to turn on a computer. She snapped open the paper just like it was any other Sunday, but what she saw made her dizzy.

The front page was all Sena.

A large picture in the center of the page captured her hopeful enthusiasm, standing in the middle of a dilapidated downtown, surrounded by the mayor and town council, pointing to something in the distance. The cutline said, "New developer Sena Abrigo points mayor and council to the future." A smaller photo of Sena with members of the Committee to Rebuild, all grinning into the camera in front of the old Y, anchored the page. The headline below the masthead blasted: *Will Sena Abrigo Save Owen Station?*

Clever.

The story was surprisingly positive. Surprising because Donald R. Smith, Smitty to everyone who knew him, the town's editor-in-chief for the past thirty years, was never positive about anything anymore. But he was apparently as smitten by Sena as everyone else seemed to be.

Well, almost everyone.

The lead story jumped to page eight, which was also where the letters to the editor started. Members of SOS were out in force. No one called out Sena by name, but they were demanding that the mayor and council pass a moratorium on granting business licenses and building permits to "outsiders"—anyone who hadn't lived in Owen Station for at least five years. If passed, it would essentially put a halt to all new building in Owen Station and slow business development to almost nothing. It would stop people like Amanda and Alex…and kill Sena's project.

"Who came up with this stupid idea, anyway?"

Mango's ears flattened. She didn't hear Hazel angry very often.

Hazel had known some of the letter writers her whole life. That made the words she read all that much more confusing. The little group she helped start, to protect their historic buildings, had morphed into something she didn't recognize. It had happened behind her back. And it seemed to be growing fast.

Then she saw the letter from Sirus. Of course, he was behind it all.

LETTER TO THE EDITOR: STOP ALIENS FROM TAKING OVER OUR TOWN

There, I said it, I'm sick and tired of the language police and I don't care who I might be offending. I'm offended that the gates to our country are always open, allowing anyone to enter, lawfully or not. I am begging our mayor and town council to Save Owen Station from this invasion. Stop giving building permits to outsiders who are destroying our beautiful town. Stop giving them licenses to come in and put our own people out of business. If you don't take action, we will be forced to do it ourselves.

Hazel folded the *Caller* and set it down slowly. A sharp pain shot through her temples.

When she helped launch SOS, it was just after Mom died. It gave her a reason to get up in the morning, helped focus her grief. She felt close to Dad—to all of them. And she really did love all of those old buildings. But that was more than a decade ago. A lot had happened in the world since then. Even in Owen Station, people were angrier, more polarized, exhausted, and afraid. Some people couldn't tell the truth from lies, anymore. At the library, Hazel was constantly trying to counter the latest wacky rumor or irrational "fact" someone read on the internet. And saying the ugliest things had become socially acceptable. There were certain things you just didn't talk about anymore, except with your closest friends. Not if you wanted to keep the peace, anyway.

Well, it looked like Sirus wasn't interested in peace. He wanted a war. And he was building an army.

"What are we going to do about this, Mango?" Hazel asked.

Mango didn't respond. But Hazel knew she had to do something. The monthly SOS leadership meeting was first thing tomorrow morning. Hazel would be ready.

Just then a hungry Gila woodpecker started going to town. Hazel looked up at the telephone pole to see if she could spot it. But then she realized what she was hearing was loud knocking on the back door.

She leapt up from her chair, immediately forgetting every troubled thought, and scrambled back into the house yelling, "Come on in!"

Since almost every stick of furniture in the house had been there for more than sixty years, Hazel's foot race to Sena was the most excitement this house has seen in a very long time. Douglas fir floors creaked noisily beneath her bare feet. The whole house seemed to shiver awake, jostling the vintage picture frames, filled with black-and-white family photos, leaving them confused and cockeyed on their nails in the hallway.

Sena was peeking through the door just as Hazel arrived, a little breathless, and they both stepped into the cool kitchen at the same time. Sena looked absolutely yummy. Black hair loose, tousled from the night. Her kimono hanging loose around her, revealing the outline of her full breasts. Underneath, she was wearing nothing but a pair of cream-colored lacy panties, highlighting her toned thighs and long legs. Hazel almost dropped her mug as a shiver shot through her body.

"You look happy to see me." Sena grinned goofily.

Hazel tried to pick her jaw up off the floor. "I've never been happier."

Then, without asking permission, Sena pushed aside the turquoise vintage plastic canisters and basket of fruit and hopped up onto the tile kitchen counter. The way she commanded her own body and Hazel's space might have been the single sexiest thing Hazel had ever seen anyone do. And, after last night, that was saying a lot.

"You gave me a scare, Hazel. When you weren't next to me this morning, I started looking for a Dear Jane note on the nightstand."

"You should know better, Sena. Why would somebody want just a one-night stand with you, when they could have two?"

"Or a lifetime." A mischievous grin spread across Sena's face.

A lifetime. What would that look like with Sena Abrigo? Constant motion. Boundless energy. Insatiable ambition to change the world. Amazing sex.

Hazel's libido went into overdrive. She didn't even stop to think about it. She pushed open Sena's kimono, exposing her rounded breasts, and began liberating Sena from her panties. Sena leaned back and lifted her bottom just enough for Hazel to slip the panties down and drop them onto the wood floor. But when Hazel began to push her knees open, leaning in for a morning taste, Sena suddenly resisted. Her legs tightened and she put a hand on top of Hazel's head.

"Wow. This is escalating quickly. You're on fire this morning."

Fire did not even begin to describe it.

Hazel didn't move and she didn't look up. Her voice was rough, raspy.

"Wider."

Last night, she had been pliant, allowing Sena to take command at almost every turn, waiting for Sena's direction, following her lead. Sena took her places she had never gone and carried her over the threshold to a new imagination. This morning, Hazel was reborn, confident and eager to offer Sena a taste of what she had been given last night.

Sena relaxed her muscles just enough to allow Hazel to push her legs open farther, one hand on each knee.

"Oh my God, Sena." Hazel took a half step backward to admire the view. "You look like a goddess…"

Hazel lingered on the full, dark bush in front of her. As put-together as Sena looked on the outside, underneath, here in the most secret part of her body, she was untamed, covered with thick curly hair. It was breathtaking. Hazel's gaze crawled upward, hovering over Sena's powerful hips and taut belly, licking up every mouthwatering inch of the view. Sena's kimono had slipped, exposing one shoulder, making her appear unguarded, defenseless. Following the curve of Sena's shoulder upward along her neck, Hazel ran the tip of her tongue along her bottom lip, eager to nibble and bite the tender flesh beneath Sena's ear.

When her eyes finally met Sena's, she was shocked to see Sena looking so…afraid.

Hazel stopped cold. "Are you okay, Sena?"

Sena dropped her eyes and didn't respond right away. Finally, she said quietly, "I don't know."

Hazel froze. She had no idea what to do with this. Sena was so… powerful. Commanding. She was front page news. On a mission. Going for what she wanted. Always in charge. Well, except for that exact moment. Sitting on Hazel's counter. With Hazel calling the shots. Looking exposed. And vulnerable.

Who would Sena be without being on top and in control? What would it mean for her to open herself up, to be on the receiving end, even if the one admiring, commanding, giving was Hazel? Hazel willed every ounce of tenderness that existed in the universe to fill her eyes and voice, praying that it would be just the tonic to release the tightness in Sena's jaw.

She took Sena's hand and kissed it gently. "Sena…please look at me."

Hazel wasn't sure if Sena would. Or could. She waited. Finally, Sena's moist brown eyes met Hazel's and held onto them, as if they were the only thing keeping her from toppling over. Sena's voice trembled.

"This is new. For me."

Hazel squeezed her hand and kissed it again tenderly. "We can stop, Sena. Just say the word. We don't have to do anything you don't want to."

Sena studied Hazel's eyes for a long minute. Then she leaned back against the wall, reached down, and used her fingers to open herself. A single tear squeezed out as she closed her eyes and waited for the touch of Hazel's tongue.

"No, Hazel, I most definitely do not want you to stop."

Hazel took a deep breath and exhaled a silent prayer of gratitude. The gift Sena was giving felt as fragile as a desert bloom. She gently kissed one of Sena's knees and then the other before releasing them. Then she ran her hands up and down the inside of Sena's thighs, savoring the journey. Electricity sent tingles through Hazel's hands, shot up along her arms and then down through the rest of her body, producing an immediate wetness between her legs.

Sena moaned, her eyes still squeezed tight, and she shifted her bottom slightly to be able to open her legs even wider. Hazel leaned in and hungrily ran the tip of her tongue up one side and down the other of Sena's silky inner lips. Sena shivered and, taking that as a good sign, Hazel began licking the tender skin on either side of Sena's swelling clit, teasing, not yet touching it. When she dipped her tongue lower, to taste the bittersweet wetness that hung on the edge of Sena's fiery entrance, Sena arched her back, quivering for more, demanding to be entered.

Inspired by last night's erotic lovemaking, Hazel resisted the urge to plunge her tongue into Sena and bring her to climax, hard and fast. She longed to reciprocate even a tiny taste of the wild pleasure she had been given. Out of the corner of her eye, Hazel saw the bowl of freshly washed strawberries. She hesitated and then reached over to select a small one, ripe and red. The tiny seeds on the skin made it feel slightly coarse to the touch. First, as a test, she very lightly scraped the cool rough tip of the berry along Sena's soft outer lips. Sena's deep murmur of approval gave Hazel courage to go further, and she gently dragged the berry along Sena's silky inner lips. The muscles in Sena's belly tightened and she began to twitch. So Hazel reached over and pulled out the largest, firmest, coarsest berry in the bowl. It was cool to the touch. Dragging it down along Sena's slit, she teased the wet opening.

"Oh my God." Sena shuddered, arching her back again so high this time that it lifted her bottom off the counter. She cracked her eyes open to see how Hazel was creating this unbearable pleasure, looked from the strawberries to Hazel and back again, and then rolled her eyes back.

Hazel carefully dipped the tip of the enormous hard berry toward Sena's wetness, without entering her, as Sena writhed and surged, thrusting toward her, as hungry to be filled as Hazel was to fill her. She teased the opening until her fingers were dripping with Sena's juices. Sena was on fire and Hazel saw her begin to focus her whole energy toward reaching her peak.

"Oh, I'm sorry, Sena." Hazel pulled the juicy berry away.

Sena's tortured eyes widened as Hazel held the fruit in front of her, tauntingly. "I know you want this but…" She paused and grinned wickedly as she brought the large fruit to her own lips. "I am *starving*."

As Sena watched, frozen in place, unable to breathe, Hazel licked her sweetness off the berry and then began to eat it, one tiny nibble at a time.

"You taste delicious, my dear." Hazel spoke from a place low in her throat, pulling words from deep in her groin. "I think I just may have to eat you."

Sena let out a ferocious cry. "Please, Hazel," she pleaded as she gripped the edge of the counter. "Do it." Her voice dropped an octave lower. "Do it now."

Hazel shoved the kimono off of both shoulders, giving her an unobstructed view of Sena's luscious body. She caressed the full length of it with her eyes, while firmly kneading the soft skin, molding it beneath her fingers.

"But are you sure you're ready for me?" Hazel asked, meeting Sena's intense desire with her own. She reached for Sena's breasts, squeezed them hard, and pinched and tugged at the nipples until Sena cried out. Then she yanked her hands down to Sena's waist, to her hips and then under her bottom, lifting and jerking Sena's pussy toward her.

"I have never been more ready," Sena said in a muffled, tortured voice as Hazel buried her face in her folds.

Hazel licked and probed and sucked and bit, looking for the spots that would make Sena moan in ecstasy, the ones that would make her gasp in pain-filled pleasure, the ones that would make her quiver and clench, the ones that would make her melt.

Every cell in Hazel's body existed for one reason in that moment. To pleasure, to please, to rock Sena's world, to bring her over and in.

Sena's guttural groan told her when she had found the spot. "Yes, Hazel, there. Right. There." She grabbed the back of Hazel's head and dragged her closer.

Lips and tongue locked in place, Hazel felt and saw and thought and smelled and tasted nothing else. When Sena's heavy breathing quickened and she began building toward climax, Hazel entered her for the first time, with one and then with two more fingers. Sena screamed as Hazel used her fingers to rock her from the inside. With her tongue, she furiously answered Sena's demand.

Sena's legs pressed tightly around Hazel's head, her hands caressing Hazel's face, twisting her ears, tugging on her hair, keeping her pinned inside. When she erupted, shrieking with sweet relief, delivered from agony, wetness spilled into Hazel's palm and covered her face.

And that's when Sena started to cry. Deep sobs. Tears streaming down her face.

"What is it, Sena?" Hazel panicked. "What's wrong?"

This wasn't how everything was supposed to end.

Hazel did the only thing she knew to do. She kissed and caressed Sena's arms and hands and legs until the weeping began to subside. When she could finally speak, Sena leaned over and took Hazel's face in her hands. Her eyes glistened like melted chocolate. And when she smiled, it cracked Hazel's heart wide open.

"Nothing is wrong, Hazel. Just the opposite. For the first time in my life, everything feels right."

CHAPTER FOURTEEN

SWEET CONFESSIONS

Hazel knew there could be no going back. She would never again be who she was before that moment. She was sure the same was true for Sena. Wordlessly, she helped Sena down off the counter and led her, sharing grateful tears, across the hall, into her bedroom. The room was tiny. A heavy wooden wardrobe stood against one wall next to a matching dresser, on which sat a simple arts and crafts-style frame holding black-and-white studio photos of Hazel's parents, grands and greats on their wedding days.

This was Hazel's safe place. Now, she would make it theirs.

Still holding Sena's hand, Hazel flipped down the crochet coverlet her mother had made before she got sick, and the crisp white top sheet. She stepped out of her shorts and T-shirt and slipped off Sena's kimono. They both shivered, although it was not cold. Hazel climbed in under the sheets first, rolled over onto her back, and pulled Sena down next to her. Sena drew close without hesitation, put her head on Hazel's shoulder, and let herself be embraced.

Sena's tears finally stopped and she was still in Hazel's arms for what felt like a long time. Tenderly, Hazel kissed Sena's forehead. She wondered what it would take for this to last forever.

"Just so you know," Sena whispered into Hazel's shoulder. "Nothing like that has ever happened before."

Hazel gently brushed Sena's hair off her face and tucked it behind her ear. "Nothing like what?"

"All of that. The crying. The...um...so much wetness...that was...crazy."

"Yeah, I thought I might drown." Hazel said it lightly, meant to ease the moment, but Sena wasn't laughing.

"I'm so embarrassed." She buried her face deeper into Hazel.

Hazel managed to wriggle her arm out from underneath her so that she could prop herself up and look Sena in the eye. "You. Have. Nothing. To be embarrassed about."

Sena turned her face away and closed her eyes. The room suddenly darkened, as though thunder clouds had reported for guard duty outside their window.

"Sena, look at me," Hazel pleaded.

But Sena just lay there. Barely breathing. So, after a minute, Hazel was a little more forceful. "Seriously. Look at me."

Finally, Sena obeyed.

Hazel just shook her head in wonder. "I am so grateful."

Sena wrinkled her nose like that was the dumbest thing she'd ever heard. "For *what*?"

What had it taken for Sena to entrust herself to Hazel in that way? Hazel couldn't imagine. Sena Abrigo was a giant. She could have anything and anyone she wanted and was used to taking it. What was it like for her to give herself away, instead?

"I am grateful that you let yourself do that with me, Sena. You let yourself come to me in a way no one else ever has. I feel like I was just given a gift of...I don't know what to call it...trust? I will cherish that, this moment—and you—forever."

Hazel kissed her gently, at the corner of her mouth first and then on her nose. Sena closed her eyes and Hazel brushed her raven hair from her face, pushing it up over her ear and back across her shoulder. She ran her fingertips over Sena's high cheekbones, across the fullness of her lower lip, down the slope of her long, strong nose.

As Hazel lay there, committing this precious moment to memory, another long-buried memory bubbled to the surface. One that she wished hadn't.

Finally, Sena stirred out of the silence and looked up. "What are you thinking about, Hazel?"

Now it was her turn to be embarrassed. Hazel smiled sadly. "I was thinking about the *last* time I had a naked woman draped across my bed."

Sena stayed very still. Listening. Could she hear the longing and the loss and the pain? Hazel hoped so. That was all that gave her the courage to keep talking. "It was a long time ago. Her name was Abby. We were talking about what we'd do after graduation. We had plans to move to California. I was going to write and we'd grow our own food and swim in the ocean every day and get a dog, just be ourselves, open and out and outrageously normal. Free. Then the phone rang. And six months later I was living in my old bedroom, learning to give injections, reshelving books at the library."

"That...that was the last time?" Sena asked incredulously, reaching up to caress Hazel's cheek. "The last time you were *with* someone?"

"That was the last time I invited someone into my bed."

"I'm sorry I didn't come along sooner," Sena whispered.

"Me too."

Those were hard words for Hazel to choke out but, once they were released, nothing could stop the rest. "I've spent so long feeling trapped here. I mean, don't get me wrong. I'm glad I came home. I was thankful to be with my mom during those last years. And, after she was gone, I couldn't imagine being anywhere else. Knox was here for me, and Delaney and Lace. They're my family now. And I love my job—well, most things about it—and this town. I've made a good life for myself here..."

The tears started flowing. "...and it's *suffocating*. I never have to worry about the future because there *isn't* one. At least not one that looks any different than today. I wear the same clothes, eat the same food, see the same people every single day. And then *you* stroll into Banter & Brew looking all sexy and new."

Sena brushed away the tears and smiled crookedly. "I looked sexy, eh?"

Hazel slapped her playfully on the arm. "You know full well you did. Do."

"So, what's the problem?" Sena asked seriously. "Why don't you look happier about it? About…me?"

"I *am* happy, Sena. Happier than I can ever remember being. That's exactly the problem. It's like, after all this time, I've been pulled up out of the darkness, like I…like I can finally see again."

"I still don't understand, Hazel. What is wrong with being happy?"

The next words were terrifying, so Hazel said them quickly before she lost her nerve.

"I'm afraid it won't last—I'm so tired of losing the people I love—I don't want to go through that ever again."

Sena pulled Hazel toward her, until she was tucked safely inside her arms. They each lay there for a long time, lost in their own thoughts, until finally Sena, staring at the ceiling, took a deep breath.

"You know, Hazel. I feel the same way. I mean, I guess my path took me in the opposite direction. I've had more naked women in my bed than I can count…"

Hazel sniffed and gave her a playful pinch.

"Ouch!" Sena laughed. "Let me finish. It doesn't matter how many lovers I've had. None of them ever did what you just did to me. None of them have ever seen me the way you do. Not one. I've never let them."

Hazel tucked tighter against Sena, as she stroked her shoulder and kept talking.

"I can't promise there won't be hurt, Hazel. To be alive is to be hurt. But, since the moment we met, I think I knew I'd found something I didn't even imagine was possible. Oh my God! I will never forget seeing you perched on that stool at Banter & Brew. So cute and sassy looking. In your librarian glasses and adorable Lucille Ball outfit…"

"Lucille Ball? Really?"

"Well, of course. With that crazy red hair and that pencil skirt. You were unlike anything or anyone I'd ever seen. And then when you opened your mouth…everything that came out of it was just so…"

Hazel wiggled out of Sena's arms and propped herself up on an elbow, to see Sena better.

"So what?"

"So...*real*. You have no idea how much fake is out there, Hazel. How many phony smiles and plastic boobs. I'm so sick of it all. And I was sick to death of the person I'd become. Or the one I showed to the world, anyway. Swaggering Sena. Stomp all over you till I get what I want Sena. Tag 'em and bag 'em. And never, ever stay the night."

"I like stay-the-night Sena," Hazel said, leaning in with a kiss.

"And I love your kisses."

Sena took a breath.

"I'm done with that life, Hazel. Being with you—being in this town—seeing the way you love so easily—and how much you are loved—it's made me see how lonely I've been. And how most of that is my fault. I don't know how you did it...but I'm thankful."

Hazel stroked Sena's cheek. "You seem so different than you did just a few weeks ago. I mean, you're *you*. Bold...strong..."

"Amazing?" Sena grinned.

"Yes, amazing. But you're also softer. More vulnerable. It's very sexy."

"I'm glad you think so. Honestly, these last few weeks have been exhausting. Trying to be *nice* to everyone. Making friends. Doing the right thing. Oh. My. God."

She stopped, as if even she knew how that sounded.

Hazel spoke flatly into the pause. "Being nice...yes, that sounds terrible." Then she snorted and they both laughed.

"Seriously, though." Sena continued when she caught her breath. "It has been hard. I used to have a pretty thick wall between me and the world. It's not quite as thick anymore, thanks to you." She playfully popped Hazel's nose.

"That's a good thing, I guess. I mean, yes, it's a good thing. But I feel weird, too. I think it's going to take me a minute to figure out who stay-the-night Sena really is."

She took a deep breath. "I guess we're both just a big mess, aren't we?"

Hazel kissed Sena on her forehead and then lay back down, wrapped in Sena's arms, smiling. Two broken pieces that, together, held the possibility of becoming whole.

Nearly four hours later, a loud crack of thunder startled them both awake. Hazel heard the needle still scratching at the center of the Sinatra album in the other room. A perfect Sunday morning. Lovemaking. Meaning making. Revelations and rapture.

"Time for coffee?" Hazel murmured, more a statement than a question.

Sena gently shifted Hazel out of her arms and turned over onto her back, sweeping her long black hair away from her face and onto the pillow, exhaling satisfaction. "You are reading my mind."

Hazel sat up, twisted around, and flipped her legs off the side of the bed. "Okay, it's made, I just have to warm it up. You can hop in the shower if you want. Hang a right down the hallway."

"Mind if I look around a bit, first?" Sena reached out as Hazel leaned over to pick up her T-shirt and shorts, and playfully pinched her behind. "I'm dying to poke around your underwear drawer and see what secrets they hold."

"Not very exciting, I'm afraid," Hazel said. "I'm an open book."

"Funny joke, Ms. Librarian."

Hazel thought for the hundredth time that day how beautiful Sena looked, even as she poked fun. "Knock yourself out, though," Hazel said, pulling on her clothes. Then she slipped out into the living room to flip off the turntable, making a mental note to replace the needle.

When the coffee was ready, Hazel padded back down the hallway to find Sena leaning against the doorway that led to the dining room. She handed Sena a mug and leaned back into her arms.

"This house is like a museum."

Hazel bristled. "I know, I know. Delaney is always complaining about it. Knox, too."

"I'm not being critical," Sena clarified quickly. "I do find it fascinating, though. Is…everything…in here a family heirloom?"

Hazel laughed. "I don't think any of this stuff is worth enough to qualify as an heirloom. But, yes, it's all been handed down to me from my greats, my grands, and my mom and dad."

"Oh, I don't know," Sena said. "I bet this Chippendale set is worth a lot. That is some piece of furniture."

Of course, Sena would know enough about overpriced, high-end furniture to recognize the elaborate style, the curving cabriole legs and ball-and-claw feet.

Hazel sniffed. "Yeah, that. Definitely not my favorite. But I can't bring myself to get rid of it. My great-grandfather used a design out of the Sears catalog and scrap materials from the Mine's dump to build this house. He couldn't afford to install a working bathroom or electricity, but he had this monstrosity shipped by rail from the Cabinet Shop in Grand Rapids for my great-grandmother, Hazel-the-first. It took him twenty-three years to save up for it. My dad told me that, when the Depression hit later that year, all his grandmother could think was 'I wish we had that money back.' Dad said they only sat in here two or three times a year, on holidays or when the priest came for dinner. Hazel-the-first hated it. Too ostentatious. Too expensive. A complete waste of money. Great-grandpa died about ten years later and she felt like it would be disrespectful to sell it."

Sena was quick to see the irony. "So, let me see if I have this right. Your grandfather saved up all his money, used it to buy a table your grandmother didn't want or like, they used it a couple dozen times, and now you're stuck with it?"

"My *great*-grandparents. Hazel and John. My mom thinks... thought...that he spent all that money on it to try to make up for something he did. Or didn't do. Something to try to win Hazel-the-first's affection. But, yes. We've all been stuck with it. My great-grandmother, her daughter, my mother. And now me."

Sena disengaged from Hazel's embrace, turned around and gave her a peck on the cheek. "I guess there are some parts of your family history you'd like to shake loose, after all, huh?"

Hazel couldn't disagree.

"How about that purple chair in there?" Sena was looking over Hazel's shoulder into the living room across the hall. "Is that a 'shake loose' or a 'hang onto' part of your history?"

Hazel shrugged with half a smile. "Honestly, I can't explain that chair. My mom ordered it online about a month before she died. She knew she was dying. It didn't make any sense to me then and it doesn't now."

The chair was an explosion of color in a room that was heavy with Craftsman-era furniture, various shades of brown. Off-white drapes hung in the front windows.

"Maybe it was your mom's way of telling you that you don't need to feel stuck with things the way they are. Maybe she was setting you free to let your life move in new directions."

Hazel just stared at Sena for a moment. There was more to this gorgeous, driven woman than anyone knew.

"Too much?" Sena asked into the awkward silence.

"No," Hazel said. "But I think that might be the deepest thing anybody has ever said about a piece of furniture."

It might also be true, Hazel thought, and decided she'd have to talk that over with Delaney. Then she cheerfully changed the subject. "How about brunch? I don't know about you, but I've worked up quite an appetite."

Sena licked her lips suggestively. "Me, too."

CHAPTER FIFTEEN

THE STORM

Sena slept in. It had been a long, full, wonderful—but emotionally exhausting—weekend. Hazel had tested her physical limits, too.

Monday morning came way too fast, and by the time Sena stirred, Hazel was already up and out of the house. There was hot coffee in the pot and a note reminding her that Hazel had an early meeting. She signed it with a little red heart.

Hazel made it so easy to love her. Sena practically skipped back to the casita, singing good morning to Mango, who was hanging out near her door, as usual. And she took her time getting ready, even though she had a busy day planned.

Later, she'd make another visit to her new home to see the progress, or lack of it, herself. Knox had never been more right about anything. Buying a hundred-year-old house meant problems under every floorboard and behind every wall. She had no idea how much longer it was going to take to solve them all.

Before she headed over to her new house, though, she was finally going to check out the GSD Co-working Space above Banter & Brew. Knox had been encouraging her to go up to meet the guys and get a sense of what they were up to. He was proud to tell her he opened it quickly, just as soon as he saw interest in the local real estate market pick up. "I knew all those people moving down here to get out of the city would need a place with reliable internet—and maybe an excuse to get out of the house for a couple of hours every day." He hadn't made any real money on the investment yet, especially since most of the city people moved out after the health authorities gave the all clear. But he was hopeful. Sena was looking forward to seeing it.

She checked herself out in the mirror before she headed out. Jeans, boots, and a silk tank top.

"Why, Sena Abrigo. You look like a local."

She was starting to feel like one, too.

Mango was waiting for her when she opened the casita door. The cat issued a loud meow and followed Sena through the gate, leaping into her front yard perch in the desert willow as Sena got in the car. "I hope you have a good day, Mango," Sena called brightly. "Please tell Mrs. Butler I am taking good care of her daughter."

Knox was behind the counter when she popped into the coffee shop. It was a bit too early for the lunch crowd and, thankfully, the creepy SOS guys were nowhere to be seen.

"Well, hello there, Sena. The usual?"

"Give me a cold brew this morning, instead—with a double shot." She hopped up onto a stool.

"Need a little extra caffeine boost after your wild weekend?"

Sena couldn't help the blush that warmed her cheeks.

"Is nothing private here in Owen Station." She returned his grin.

Of course Delaney or Lace would have talked to him already, about Saturday night at the Triple D and the way suddenly Sena and Hazel were a thing again. Or maybe Hazel filled him in, stopping by to say good morning now that she wasn't afraid of running into Sena.

But Sena wasn't annoyed. Knox's laughter made her feel good, like after a monsoon sweeps through the valley on a blistering summer day, leaving cool, clear air behind it. She'd never want to date him or anything, a few college experiments convinced her of that, but she liked him. A lot. The guy might have been small town, but he was a small town visionary. And he had been invaluable to Sena, teaching her about the real estate market in Owen Station, letting her bounce ideas around, introducing her to other business owners so she could listen to what their needs and hopes for Owen Station might be, taking her personally to meet the mayor, hosting coffees so she could meet members of the town council, helping her put together the right group of old Y ladies to serve on the "Committee to Rebuild"—he even thought up the name.

"Hey, Knox…can I ask you a question?"

"Shoot."

"Why are you helping me do this?"

He slowly put down the glass he was drying, leaned against the back counter, and studied the floor for a minute. Then he shrugged. "I guess I just like you, Sena. You're good people. And I trust that you're going to do good things for my town."

He had no idea how much pressure that was. Or what a gift.

After a glass of cold brew and some of Knox's famous banter, she headed outside and around to the back of the building, to the stairs that led up to a glass door with "GSD Co-working Space" stenciled on it.

Everything about the place should have made it perfect for someone to growth hack their way to the top. Eleven-foot ceilings, exposed brick and adobe walls, and sunlight flooding in through the three double hung bay windows. Magnificent. She wanted to love it, especially because it made Knox so proud. There were more people than she expected, maybe a dozen guys. But the homogeneity was stifling, and way too familiar. Although the faces were a little more diverse than they'd been in her California office, they were still mostly white and they were all men. And they were all wearing the uniform—cargo shorts, sneakers, and T-shirts with obscure band names, Che Guevara's face, or some Star Wars saying on them.

Then she heard the whistle. Like she was a dog or something. She didn't see who it came from. It didn't matter. No one called out the culprit, condemned it, or stood up to apologize on behalf of assholes everywhere. Instead, she heard a quiet snickering ricochet around the room.

A guy with an idiotic grin, looking like he could be her little brother, and *maybe* just old enough to have a legal drink shot across the room to greet her.

"Hey, how's it going?"

Sena started to respond but he just kept talking. Right. Over. Her.

"Welcome to GSD! Our little oasis in the desert." He identified himself as the manager and said Knox told him to expect her.

"I saw your picture in the paper yesterday. You're like famous or something."

Then he acted like he wanted to tell her his whole life story, although it was probably just nerves, and he started babbling about how he moved to Owen Station from LA because, "it's Cheap As Fuck here and there's a lot of guys working on some totally savage apps."

When she didn't look that interested, he nervously switched gears. "Come on, let me show you around, introduce you to everybody."

She didn't want to be mean—she hoped those days were behind her—and she almost felt sorry for this young man, but she also wasn't going to just let this one lie.

"How about if you start with the guy who thinks it's okay to objectify women, even the ones who are smarter than he is? The guy with the whistle. I'd really like to meet *him*."

Her voice was loud enough that even the cowards who quickly ducked behind their computer screens could hear her. The young manager didn't know what to do under the ferocious glare of the most powerful woman he'd ever met.

"No?" she asked, sarcastically. "Okay, then."

She adjusted the waistband on her jeans, gave her blouse a gentle yank, tossed her hair over one shoulder, and stood up as straight as she could, which meant she was towering over the poor guy.

"I think I've seen all I need to see here for right now."

She spun around and headed back for the door. Stenciled in bold, black letters on the wall in front of her was this meant-to-be motivational saying: *PUNCH TODAY IN THE FACE.*

"Ha ha!" she shouted over her shoulder, pointing at the words. "Not one of you actually has the balls to do this."

Her laughter was meant to humiliate and she imagined it echoing through the space long after she left. But she was more unsettled by the experience than she wanted to admit. It certainly wasn't the first catcall she'd ever heard, but today she was facing life without those thick walls that had protected her for so long. And she was still new at treading that fragile space between the old Sena and the new.

"Take a deep breath," she told herself as she shoved out of the building and back out onto the street. It had been a whirlwind few weeks or so—and a roller coaster of a weekend. Things were going to be interesting, for a while as she learned to navigate life heart-forward.

Distracted by these thoughts, it took her a minute after she left the building and rounded the corner, to realize that the crowd gathering on Main Street between Banter & Brew and the library wasn't just a bigger than normal lunch rush.

It looked like they were there to protest something.

There weren't many of them, maybe a dozen, but they were clearly riled up. At first, it looked like the focus of the small, angry group was the coffee shop, but then she realized it was the tequila tasting room next door. Two guys from Hermosillo, six hours south of the border, owned it. They were nice enough. Sena spent an evening sampling what they had to offer last week and reminiscing about their favorite places to visit in Mexico. Jorge and Miguel confided that they were a couple, even though they said they liked to keep their private business private. They said they opened up right before the pandemic was shutting everything down—bad luck timing— but they had been doing a brisk business from tourists since things opened up again. They warned her about the rocks in town, under which some ugly people were hiding.

And, just that like, there they were. Out from under. In the open.

Sena's first thought was to go see if the boys needed help. But that was ridiculous. What kind of help could she possibly offer?

Knox. Maybe Knox could help.

The crowd had already more than doubled in size and Sena had to push through the crowd to get from the corner to Banter & Brew.

It probably should have scared her, but it didn't. The handmade signs people were carrying mostly said, *Save Owen Station!* Other messages were scattered throughout the crowd.

History Matters!
Protect Our Businesses!
Close The Border!

Then the chanting started. "Go Back HOME! Leave Us ALONE! We are better off ON OUR OWN!"

Sena was just about to the door of Banter & Brew when Sirus appeared out of nowhere, and stepped right in front of her, blocking her way. "Go back to Mexico where you came from," he growled.

Sena stopped dead in her tracks, mouth open to respond, but unsure which of the five hundred swear words that ran through her head she should spew. Instead, she said the first coherent sentence that came to her.

"You're kidding me, right? My family has been in this state for nine generations, you son of a bitch. I'm not the invader here. You are. Now step out of my way."

The man moved closer to her, shattering whatever personal space she had left, and for a split second Sena thought, "Oh my God. He's gonna shoot me."

She had forgotten, after being away for so long, what it was like to live in a place where every crackpot you meet might be wearing a Glock on his belt or carrying an AR-15 slung over his shoulder. Legally.

She didn't know whether to turn and run or stand her ground. She stood. Just as he was about to…what? Grab her? Push her? Punch her?

Suddenly, she felt two strong hands on her waist, pulling her backward and away from the ugly face in front of her, and heard a familiar voice.

"Back the fuck off, Sirus."

Knox was pulling her toward his shop, apologizing all the way. "I heard them start yelling and came out to see what was going on. I can't believe how carried away this has gotten. I am so sorry, Sena. Oh my God, I am so sorry."

That's when she realized she was shaking. Violently. In fact, she could barely stand. Knox caught her as she started to stumble and she fell against his chest, letting him hold her, just needing to feel safe for a minute.

That minute passed quickly when, over Knox's shoulder, Sena saw Hazel. She was standing in the crowd next to a large woman, who was wearing a jean shirt with "Doc" embroidered on it and holding a sign that said *Small Is Beautiful.*

When Hazel saw Sena, her eyes sprung open and her hands flew to her mouth, and then she started running toward her. But Sena broke free from Knox's embrace to confront her with an upraised palm.

"Stop right there, Hazel. Don't come any closer."

"Sena, I—"

"Is this the *meeting* you had to get to today?"

"Sena, I can—"

"Are you telling me that you are a *part* of this?"

"Sena, I can explain."

"Really, Hazel? I'd really like to hear that. I'd like to know why you're here. And how you would explain being part of *this.*" She flung her hand toward the crowd.

"Sena, I…I'm *not* part of this. I mean, I did help *start* it, but—"

"You're telling me you're behind this little protest?" Sena was having a hard time thinking.

"No! I mean I helped start this group—"

Sena snapped her head toward Knox. How could this be true? She wanted Knox to say something, to make this make sense. He just closed his eyes and shook his head. Then she looked back at Hazel.

"Sena, listen to me. I didn't do *this.*" She swept her hand toward the crowd. "But, yes. I *did* help start Save Owen Station. I wanted to protect our old buildings and make sure we didn't have a bunch of people like you buying up all the houses, sending our property taxes sky high—"

Sena didn't let her finish. She didn't need to hear one more word.

"People like *me*? People. Like. Me. Okay, I get it now, Hazel."

"I didn't mean that the way it sounded."

"You didn't? Funny. You sound just like Sirus."

"What?" Hazel turned a pale shade of green. "Why? What did he say to you?"

"He told her to go back to Mexico where she came from," Knox growled.

"Well, that's just stupid. Sirus is stupid. You're not even from Mexico."

"That's not the point, Hazel! Why do you think the protest is here, in front of this little shop, instead of the town hall? And this chant! What the hell do you think that means? They're talking about people who look like me, Hazel. Is that how you see me, too? Alien? Dangerous? Unwanted?"

"No, of course not," Hazel cried. "I hate what is happening right now! I would never—"

"You know what, Hazel? Forget it. Just forget it. The fact that you don't understand what is wrong with all of this...that you helped *start* this...*that* is the point, now."

"But I *do* understand, Sena. I told you why I started this. It wasn't like this then. None of this was ever supposed to happen..."

"Well, it *did* happen, didn't it."

She turned to Knox. "I've got to get out of here." He nodded understanding.

Hazel panicked. Grabbing Sena's arm, she begged, "Sena, where are you going? Please, wait."

"I'm leaving, Hazel. I can't talk to you right now. I can't be with you. I just can't."

"Sena, please."

Sena turned and faced Hazel. "I thought you were different. Hell, I thought this *town* was different. But I let my guard down way too far, too fast. I thought you understood me, supported me. I thought that, with you, I could finally drop the walls I've been hiding behind. It turns out, you and your friends here are literally *building* the wall."

"No, Sena, no!"

Hazel was crying as she clung to Sena, who was trying to wrench free. Knox put his hand on Hazel's shoulder.

"Let her go, Hazel." Sorrow and rage fused his face, leaving no room for sympathy. Hazel collapsed, burying her face in her hands.

That was the last thing Sena saw before shooting through the crowd toward her car.

Above them, there wasn't an inch of blue sky to be seen. A threatening wind had swept in heavy gray clouds and the humidity level had spiked, making the air almost too thick to breathe. Dust swirled, stinging Sena's eyes as she ran, and she smelled rain. Wet creosote leaves that desert dwellers knew meant a storm was coming. Like her mother and her grandmothers before her, Sena's mother would use creosote leaves and twigs to make a foul-tasting tea that she swore cured everything, flu, colds, upset stomachs. Everything except a broken heart.

"How could I have been so stupid? So *blind*. Sena shouted at herself as she sat behind the wheel, waiting for her hands to stop shaking before she hit the ignition and sped out of town.

A massive lightning bolt streaked across the sky, followed by a terrifying crack of thunder, and the sky opened.

She pictured Jorge and Miguel inside their shop and was relieved. "At least the storm will chase those rats away so they'll leave those poor men alone."

It was not the first time she was thankful for a storm. There was nothing like an Arizona monsoon. Every year, people who didn't know better were swept away to their death. But in Sena's family, as for her people throughout the centuries, its arrival was greeted with gratitude and relief. When it threatened not to come, they used song and sacrifice to call it. Because, without it, *everything* would die.

Sena's tears fell as torrential rain battered her windshield. The wipers, sounding like a feverish drum, worked furiously to clear it. According to the thermometer on her dashboard, the outside temperature had dropped ten degrees since she left Owen Station and it was still falling.

Her cell phone started buzzing next to her. She looked down, saw Hazel's number, and didn't answer. It stopped ringing for a second and then started again. After the fifth call, Hazel finally left a voice message, which Sena didn't bother listening to.

Then, she got a text.

"Well, that's surprising," Sena said aloud. "I wonder how long it took her to figure out how to do that."

Sena, please call me.

"No, Hazel. Not a chance."

After several minutes, another, longer text. Sena had trouble reading it on the seat beside her so she picked up the phone.

I am sorry I was so stupid. I was embarrassed. I was trying to stop it. But this thing has gotten totally out of control. When I saw you there, I didn't know what to say or do.

She slammed the phone back down. "How about saying you know it's fucked up. How about that?" She was still shouting.

I know this is fucked up.

Okay, that was progress.

I knew Sirus was trouble.

I could see this coming. I tried to stop it but I couldn't.

This is all my fault.

"Yes, it is, Hazel. Yes, it is."

I love you.

"Oh for fuck's sake!" Sena screamed as she reached over, shut the phone off and slammed it on the floor. "Are you kidding me right now?"

What would have been a glorious moment just hours ago, Hazel confessing her love, now felt like being shot in the heart. She threw her head back and tried to release the pain in a shattering howl. Angry tears blinded her, even as the storm raged outside.

A deluge of water hit the side of her car as a pickup truck passed her, going dangerously fast on the two-lane road, and she grabbed the wheel, temporarily distracted from her own agony. Looking out the window, she realized that, although she had been driving aimlessly, without direction or purpose, her car was very deliberately taking her somewhere.

Sena was going home.

CHAPTER SIXTEEN

VISITATION

W hat the absolute hell were you thinking?" Knox was so mad at Hazel after Sena drove away. "You knew Sirus was up to no good. I *told* you when I saw you this morning that he was planning something like this. And now look what you've done."

He stormed away. And then the rain came.

Hazel played the whole thing over and over again in her mind. Knox was right.

It was her fault.

Early that morning, she had gone to Banter & Brew. It was supposed to be the regular SOS leadership meeting. She planned to confront Sirus about that letter in yesterday's paper. Not only did he sound like a racist asshole, he had no right to use SOS as a platform for his hateful ideas. And there was no way she was going to let him use those ideas to tear apart her town or the people she loved. She was going to demand that other SOS leaders co-sign a letter with her, apologizing to the community on behalf of the group. And then she was going to recommend that they disband.

But no one from the group was there that morning.

They had canceled the meeting or moved it, without telling her.

"Where are they?" Hazel asked Knox. She was looking around, as if they might be hiding under a table.

"They're not here."

"Where are they?"

"I don't know. All I know is the youngest Murphy boy was in here talking about a big protest—I don't know when and I don't know where and, frankly, I don't care. That SOS group needs to shrivel up and die."

He didn't give her time to agree.

"I mean it, Hazel. There's some good people in it, sure. But they're naive. *You're* naive. You saw that letter from Sirus yesterday, didn't you?"

Hazel nodded.

"Well, you shouldn't have been surprised. It was just a matter of time before Sirus infected that group with his racist bullshit."

Dammit! Why hadn't she seen this earlier? Stopped him earlier?

Hazel sat down at the counter, put her head in her hands, and tried to figure out how this all happened.

In the beginning, she had lent her name, invested her passion, shared her expertise to get the group off the ground. She wanted to make sure Owen Station's history wasn't swept away in a rush to throw up ugly new buildings designed to make rich out-of-towners, who didn't care about Owen Station, even richer. But at some point people in the group started talking less about the buildings and more about Owen Station's *unique culture* and *way of life*. It all sounded innocent. Until it didn't.

Hazel wasn't stupid. But Knox was right about her being naive. She could see everything that was happening in the world around them. The anger, the fear, the violence, the anti-immigrant rhetoric.

She just wanted to believe Owen Station was immune from it all.

She buried herself in the past so that she wouldn't have to deal with the hard stuff.

Just like she had done in her own life.

And now that was threatening to destroy everything—including whatever she had—or hoped to have—with Sena.

That morning, sitting at the counter inside Banter & Brew, Hazel made a decision. She would find out when and where the protest was going to happen. And she would show up. Sirus was probably a lost cause. But Doc and the others? She would talk sense into them. She would fix this somehow. She would make them stop. That's what she was trying to do when she saw Sena.

The next thing she knew, Sena was running, rushing down the street and away from her, shooting painful words, leaving Hazel awash in grief, afraid that everything she had dared hope for was gone. And no wonder. Sena had trusted Hazel—and Hazel had let her down.

After the storm broke, drowning out the voices of the protesters and scattering them like sewer roaches, Hazel raced to her car, where she called and called. Sent message after message. But nothing. She raced back to the empty casita, hoping to find Sena. Again, nothing. She finally collapsed onto the cowhide where they had once been wrapped together in ecstasy, and cried until there were no more tears left.

At some point, she got up and stepped out into the courtyard, where she let the sky weep for her, as the rain beat down upon her face. She didn't know how long she stood there, but she was drenched to the bone when she finally went back inside.

Her own house hadn't sounded like this since the night her mother died. Deathly still. And from somewhere deep inside, somehow more tears came. Everywhere she turned, she was reminded of Sena. Wanting more than anything to just crawl back into bed and escape into sleep, she couldn't bring herself to enter her room. The sheets still smelled like them. She crumpled to the floor, head in her hands. What had she done?

Sena had trusted her. Shared her story. Opened her heart. Let Hazel see the hurt little girl who still lived inside of her, the lonely child without a home, afraid to love and be loved. Sena had given her the most precious gift she had ever received. Hazel had torn it apart. And for what?

Like a lost child herself, Hazel grabbed a blanket and crawled into the lap of her mother's purple chair. That's where she was hours later, sound asleep, when she heard loud knocking at the door and a terrified Delaney calling her name.

"Hazel! Are you in there, Hazel? Are you all right? Open this door!"

When Hazel opened her eyes, the first thing she saw was Mango, sitting on the repurposed coffee table right in front of her, looking worried. "How did you get in here, Mango?" she said drowsily. Then, gathering the blanket around her, she padded to the front door. Mango followed and, when she saw Delaney standing there, the tabby shot out through the door, across the front porch and up into her tree.

"My God, Hazel—I thought you were dead! Why haven't you been answering my calls?" Delaney burst into the hallway, her panic morphing into fury. "I've been trying to reach you for hours!"

Seeing the love and fear in her eyes made Hazel's knees give way as another wave of sobbing seized her. Delaney fell down beside her, wrapping her up in her arms and holding her until the tears began to subside.

"I heard what happened. For God's sake, Hazel. What were you thinking?"

A tangle of words tumbled out as she tried to explain. Delaney kept opening and closing her mouth, trying to get a word in edgewise, but it made her look like a swimmer bobbing up and down, gasping for breath, frightened by how quickly a storm could turn familiar waters into a raging river.

"Hazel, slow down!"

Delaney pushed Hazel off her shoulder, steered her back into the living room, and sat her down on her grandmother's worn leather couch. The one that smelled like pipe tobacco and felt like butter. Then she opened the liquor cabinet. "I need a drink."

Like her grandmother and mother before her, Hazel kept the crystal decanters in the cabinet filled. Delaney pulled out two lowball tumblers and gave them each a hefty pour of Irish Whiskey.

"Here, drink this."

Hazel took the glass from her and shot the golden liquid back, feeling it burn her throat, before Delaney could even take a seat.

"Hit me again."

Delaney took the empty and handed Hazel the full glass she had poured for herself. Then she sat down beside Hazel, who had settled back into the soft leather, cross-legged.

"Okay, let's start from the beginning." Delaney could only manage that matter-of-fact tone for a moment.

"What in the hell is going on? I mean with you and Sena. I haven't heard a peep from you since you two took off together looking like a couple of sex-starved high school kids at the Triple D. And then, next thing I know the whole town is talking about a big breakup in the middle of Main Street today." Delaney was equal parts worried and confused.

As calmly as she could, she told Delaney everything. All of it. The stories shared. The earth-shaking sex. The letting go. The moving forward. The dreams dared.

"Are you telling me that all of this has happened with a woman you basically just met?"

Hazel nodded, silent except for a sniffle.

Delaney took a long, slow breath. "Girlfriend, you need to get laid more often."

They looked over their glasses at each other and, after a long second, spontaneously burst into the kind of laughter that only love could ignite in the midst of sadness and pain.

"You really gave me a scare, Hazel. When you didn't answer my calls, after being totally out of touch for days, I didn't know what to think."

"I know, Delaney, I know. I'm so sorry."

Delaney didn't have to say it. Hazel knew they were both remembering that terrible night, right after Mom died, when she accidentally took too many sleeping pills. Accidentally. That's what Delaney told everyone while Hazel spent a few days on the psych ward in the hospital over in Sierra Vista. Nobody needed to know otherwise, except for Knox, of course. He slept in the family lounge every night Hazel spent there, just in case she needed him. Delaney canceled all of her salon appointments so she could take the day shifts. Hazel had never done anything like that again, never even been tempted. It was hard for her to imagine now that she had ever thought, for even a moment, that she was all alone.

"It's all right. You're forgiven." Delaney's smile was tender and honest. "Just don't do it again."

"Cross my heart."

They sat without talking, deep in thought. In the distance, Hazel could hear the early evening howls of a pack of coyotes.

"I really messed up, Delaney."

Delaney nodded. "What are you going to do?"

"I don't know. She won't answer my phone calls or my texts."

"You sent a text?" Delaney was shocked. "Who showed you how to do that?"

"I'm not stupid, Delaney. I just don't like it. It's so…impersonal. But I'm trying everything." She started to cry again. "I don't even know where she went or when she's coming back. *If* she's coming back."

"I don't know why I think this. Just a feeling. But I am positive she's coming back, Hazel. And you're going to have to fix things with her. But first you need to fix the mess you helped make in this town."

Hazel looked up and into her eyes. "I don't know what I would do without you, Delaney."

"Me, either."

While Delaney poured them each another whiskey, Hazel went to the front closet and pulled out a box. She grabbed a lighter from a kitchen drawer and headed out to the fireplace in the courtyard with Delaney close behind. Mango was perched on the hearth, waiting, like a priestess appointed to oversee a cleansing rite.

"All right, Mango, I know. This should have happened months ago."

The tabby appeared to nod her head, then leapt up onto the wall, knocking a large tile loose, and disappeared into the night.

The box held SOS flyers. Hazel brought them home after a meeting to hand out to neighbors, but never did. She realized now that she had been feeling uneasy about that group for a while. The homogenous faces. The angry tone among too many members.

Sirus sneaking around, having meetings and making plans behind her back. It all made the fact that she had done nothing to stop them sooner even worse.

She put the box inside the fireplace and lit it. Within minutes, the contents were ablaze.

As warm as it was outside, Hazel stared into the flames until nothing but a pile of ash remained. That's when she noticed that something appeared to be hidden beneath a tile Mango had kicked loose. She carefully removed the tile and discovered a small, tin box.

"What is that?" Delaney leaned forward, wide-eyed.

"I have no idea." Hazel gingerly brushed away what seemed like a century of dust. "But it has my great-grandmother's initials on it."

"Those are *your* initials," Delaney said breathlessly, eyebrows scrunched in confusion.

"Yes, they are. We have the same name, remember?"

Delaney nodded, pressing folded hands to her mouth, peering up at Hazel. "Open it."

The night was still, except for the chirping of crickets. The red heart of Scorpio beat in the cloudless sky above them. Hazel sat down with the box in her lap and carefully lifted the lid.

Delaney leaned closer, straining to see. "Are those...letters?"

They were. Dozens of them. All in neat, precise handwriting. A woman's hand. Each one beginning the same way.

My dearest H.

They were all signed the same way, too.

My heart is yours forever.

C.

Delaney covered her mouth with both hands, leaving only saucer-shaped eyes visible. "Oh, Hazel. Do you think...are these love letters from your great-grandfather?"

Hazel looked up and off into the distance, into a space and a time that no longer existed. "No. My great-grandfather's name was John. These letters are from someone whose name starts with C." Her words hung low and heavy, like ripe quince clinging to the scraggly branches above. Hazel had always wondered what made John spend everything they had to give his wife such an extravagant gift. Could it have been his last best effort to win her heart? A heart that belonged to someone else. A friend who was more than a friend.

Suddenly, the latch on the metal gate behind them clicked and the gate began to creak open slowly. The hair on Hazel's neck and arms stood up on end and she knew, even before she turned to see who was coming into the courtyard, that there was no one there.

"Do you...do you feel that?" Delaney's voice was shaking.

"Yes. I do."

They both looked toward the gently swirling energy that had settled in the middle of the courtyard.

"Do you...do you *see* that?" Delaney's eyes could have swallowed the moon.

Hazel kept her eyes focused, her voice steady. "Yes."

Delaney dropped her voice to something just above a whisper, as if the being before them could hear or would care. Which it might. "Is this what you saw that night after your mom died?"

Hazel nodded.

"Do you think it's your mom?"

"No," she said quietly. "I thought so before, but I don't know."

As they watched, entranced, the cloud of energy separated into two distinct strands of light, one emerald green, the other as orange as the desert sun, and they danced in the moonlight, dipping and skipping, encircling and embracing, gracefully twirling as though they had been doing it together for eons.

"Are you seeing this, Hazel?"

She smiled at how cute Delaney was when she was awestruck. "Yes, I'm seeing this."

Hazel had spent a lot of time wondering about what she had seen and felt that night after the funeral. The story Sena had told her, about the woman who visited her in the casita confirmed it. This was her great-grandmother's courtyard. Her fireplace. Her letters. Her story. This was her soulful, shimmering dance.

"I think my great-grandma's friend was much more than a friend," Hazel whispered.

"Do you mean you think...do you think this is your *grandmother?*"

Hazel cradled the tin box in her lap. "My great-grandmother, Hazel-the-first. And, yes. I think she's here with C—the woman who was the love of her life."

"Oh my God, Hazel."

They sat and watched the dance until finally the two strands met again in the center of the courtyard, wrapped themselves tightly around one another and became one.

Delaney clutched her heart with her hands, her face shimmering in the light. "What do you think it means, Hazel?"

She wasn't entirely sure, but she had a sense. She and Sena were meant to be together. In spite of everything driving them apart, starting with her own stupidity, they were being called to dance.

"I think it means that I have some work to do."

CHAPTER SEVENTEEN

HOMECOMING

Sena's family had no idea she was even back in the state. As ready as Sena was to make a new start, she hadn't been ready to see them.

The last time she was home, they were as happy as Sena was miserable. Her mother and aunties fluttered around the kitchen like the orange Queen butterflies found in Sonoran desert washes in springtime, descending to stir a pot of pozole or roll flour and lard dough balls into tortillas, and then flitting off again to find the next project.

"Sena!" Her aunts pinched her on the cheek. "When are you getting married? Aren't there any handsome men in California? You should see Señora Hernandez's youngest boy, now that he's all grown up. So handsome! And he has a very good job. Should we invite him over?"

"Sena! When are you coming home to stay? Your mom and dad miss you so much. And your brothers need you in the business. They need someone who understands all those computer things."

"Sena! Why aren't you helping us here in the kitchen? Come here and taste the soup. Do you think it needs more salt? More garlic?"

Her father didn't talk to her at all. He and her brothers were busy doing chores or sitting out under the giant cottonwood behind the house, shooting the breeze with uncles and her male cousins, or huddled in Dad's office talking business.

She wandered the property and through the house, alternating between exasperated eyerolls and silent sobs, simultaneously sad and irritated. No one asked a single question she actually wanted to answer the whole two days she was in town.

She hadn't been back since.

It was suffocating to be so wanted and so unseen.

So, yes. She was going home. But she wasn't flying into the embrace of her family. She was, instead, barreling down the road, across the San Pedro and its luscious woodlands, toward the ranch, because more than she had ever needed anything before, she needed Alegre, the only creature who had ever loved her unconditionally.

When her father gave the horse to her, for her sixteenth birthday, she made lists of possible names, wanting to choose exactly the right one for the magnificent, gray colt. For a few days, she settled on Puma, in honor of the mountain lion that had appeared in her visions from the time she was a small child until she was old enough to know better.

She also played with giving him a gender-bending name like Hypatia, after her hero, the first female mathematician, who was killed by a mob of Christian zealots in the early 400s. There was never a day in Sena's life when she didn't realize that being different always threatened somebody.

Her favorite name was Hombrecito. Little man. The playful nickname the ranch hands called her when she was a little girl and her father was out of earshot. But even that didn't seem quite right.

Sena's father stepped in a month after her birthday, when the colt was still nameless. She was in the stable, brushing his coat until it shined. It was the only time, after she turned thirteen, that she could remember him seeking her out for anything other than a lecture, which was why his words that day were so memorable.

"Sena, I have watched you with this colt every day for the past month. I see the way you rub your nose into his shoulder, breathing in the smell of prickly pear honey and fresh pine. I see the way you bend down to whisper your secrets in his ear. I see how happy you are to have a friend who loves you just as you are."

Her father turned to the colt, who was busy nuzzling Sena's hand. He put his rough right hand on the horse's forehead. A grateful blessing. A solemn christening. A benediction, both for the horse and for Sena.

"You will be called Alegre. Because you make my daughter happy."

Little did Dad know that the thing Sena wanted most of all was his attention and affection. But Alegre did make her happy. That would have to be enough.

It had been a couple of hours since she left Hazel in a puddle on the pavement in Owen Station and the phone had been blessedly silent. Sena had stopped trembling, but her heart was still raw when she came to the end of the long gravel road that led to the ranch. A large animal skull and a sign declaring "Abrigo Family Enterprises, Inc." hung above the large metal gate.

She stopped the car and took a deep breath.

Then, slowly, she made her way toward her homecoming.

Mom was wearing an apron, of course, because she had been cooking all day, like always. Sena came in through the kitchen door without knocking, as if she had just been out for a long ride.

"Oh my God! Sena! I'm not seeing a ghost, am I? Come in, come in. Let me look at you!" She threw her arms around Sena and then made her sit down.

"What can I get you to eat? You're hungry, no? You must be starving, you are so skinny. Let me get you some beans!" Mom always had a pot of them on the stove.

She didn't ask why Sena was there or why she looked like she'd been rung out or why in the hell she hadn't come home for the past six years or why sometimes she didn't even return her mother's phone calls. She just scooped some beans out of the pot on the stove, heated up two tortillas, put the plate down in front of Sena and kissed her on the forehead.

"I am so happy to see you, sweetheart."

Mom's love and tenderness were almost too much to bear. Sena turned around in her chair, wrapped her arms around her mother's waist, buried her face in her mother's bosom, and began to sob.

"Oh, Sena. What has happened to you? What is it?"

This was not how Sena planned for this to go. But Hazel—and that damn town—had done something to her. Gotten inside. Chiseled away at the shell around her heart. Blasted apart the wall she had always counted on to protect her. She was raw, exposed. And she could not find words to speak. So Mom just held her until the crying stopped.

Then, Sena did as she was told. She ate.

"I'm sorry I surprised you like this, Mom. I just...I mean, I wanted to...I mean, I didn't know where else to go..."

"Whatever is going on, Sena, I'm glad you came here. You can always come home, no matter what." The deep wrinkles in her mother's brow made Sena feel guilty.

Just then there was a noise at the kitchen door and Sena's brothers burst in.

"Whose fancy car is that outside?" Junior asked, heading right to the stove to grab some food, not even noticing Sena at the table. Their mother just pointed.

"Sena!" her brothers yelled in unison. "You're home! Wait a minute. What is going on? *Why* are you home? Are you all right? Why didn't you tell us you were coming? You don't look so good. Is it a man? Did he hurt you? Honest to God, Sena, I will kill him. I will find him and kill him and kill everyone he has ever cared about. How long are you going to be here? Do you need money? You look so skinny. You look so sad. What did he do, eh? Where is he? What is his address? Is he in California? What is his name? Who are his people? So help me God..."

Her brothers were talking over one another, their words tripping and tumbling out of them like coins spilling out of a slot machine. Sena didn't know whether to laugh or cry. As angry as it made her that they had all of their father's attention and favor, she never blamed them.

"Come here and give me a hug, you big goofballs."

Both Junior and Jesús towered over her, although she would forever think of them as her littles. They fell over themselves, scooping her up in their arms, and she let herself be embraced, relishing the soft chambray of their work shirts, their rough hands and their clumsy love.

When they put her down, they sat together at the big wooden table. "Okay, Sena, let's have it. What is going on?"

Her brothers' faces looked so similar to each other. Sun-baked skin, the same long nose she saw in the mirror every day, identical smiles, dimpled on the right side and slightly crooked on the left, making them look like they were both in on the same goofy joke, which they usually were. She saw her grandfather in them, too—his kindness and his strength, if not his wisdom.

Sena thought very carefully before she answered.

"I'm okay. I've had a very rough few months. I quit my job and I'm moving back to Arizona. I bought a house in Owen Station. I'm starting my own development company. My heart is broken but, believe me, *I do not need you to go beat up some man.*"

Her brothers looked puzzled, but Mom became very still as Sena's words began to sink in.

For almost every other creature in the Arizona desert, there was a kaleidoscopic burst of new life following a monsoon. The morning glories and poppies bloomed for a second time. The ocotillo sprouted inches overnight and waved, lush and green, across the hillsides. Monarchs emerged, coloring the landscape. Birds and beetles and even some mammals fired up for a second season of banging and breeding.

But Sena was exhausted.

Tired of being invisible. Tired of trying so hard to be worthy. Tired of being alone.

Mom's voice finally broke the silence that had imprisoned them all for so many long years.

"Did she hurt you, sweetheart?"

Her brothers looked up, startled, and Sena's eyes grew moist. She paused, looking deeply into her mother's eyes, and then finally nodded.

"And you?" Mom raised an eyebrow, as if she already knew the answer, not because she knew Sena but because she knew what it was to live and to love. "And you, Sena. Did *you* hurt *her*?"

Sena closed her eyes but couldn't block out the accusations she screamed into the street, ears shut to any explanations Hazel might offer, the squealing tires, the unanswered calls, the frantic, apologetic texts. She could not unsee Hazel, crumpled on the pavement, crippled with grief.

She nodded again, eyes still shut tight. "Yes, Mom. I hurt her, too."

"Can it be fixed?"

Sena took a deep breath, filling her lungs with the smell of her mother's kitchen, cumin and garlic and lime. When she opened her eyes, she exhaled, releasing her deepest fear.

"I don't know."

Then, a prayer.

"I hope so."

Mom looked at her across the table and Sena could see the depth in her eyes...fountains of joy and pools of sorrow...formed by a long life as a daughter, wife and mother...a woman navigating a constantly changing universe. "I don't know if you can hear this right now, Sena," her mother said steadily. "But take it from me... there is nothing so broken that it cannot be fixed."

When Sena began to cry, her mother came around the table. She was a full four inches shorter than Sena but, in that moment, she was a giant. She took Sena's hands and lifted her out of the chair and onto her feet.

"I wish I could wipe this sorrow away from you, Sena. I would give anything to be able to do that. But I do want you to hear me now. *You...are...enough.*"

Sena could hear her mother speaking, but the words fluttered in the air between them, unable to reach her, caught in a swirl of memories and secrets and disappointments and doubts.

"Sena, are you listening to me?"

Mom squeezed her hands, shaking them, as if trying to jostle open a path to Sena's heart. Sena refocused, straining to hear. Her mother was trying to tell her something.

"From the moment I felt you stir inside me, I have loved you. No more and no less than I love your brothers. You were my first.

You are my heart. There is nothing you could ever do, Sena... nothing you could ever be...and no one you could ever love...that would make me stop loving you."

Her mother reached up, pulled Sena's head down toward her, and kissed her on the forehead.

Sena was incredulous. Had she heard that right? Was Mom saying what she thought she was saying?

"Mom, why haven't you said these things to me before?" Sena asked, searching her mother's eyes.

Her mother dropped her head, closed her eyes, and took a deep breath. When she looked up at Sena again, the wrinkles on her brow, around her mouth, and under her eyes had deepened. When had Mom started looking so old? And how much of that was Sena's fault? How many nights had her mother lain awake, worrying about her daughter? Sena realized she was not the only one in that family whose heart had been bruised.

"I am sorry, Sena. Sorry that I have not been able to say these things to you before, in a way that you could hear. More sorry than I can express. But I see you, Sena. I believe in you. I am so proud of you. You are perfect. Just the way you are."

Sena was afraid to move, to believe, to feel, but she did not drop her eyes. Her mother would not let her.

"Sena, do you understand me? Do you?"

She slowly nodded and then leaned over and buried her face in her mother's shoulders. Silent sobs shook her body. Tightly, carefully, her mother cradled her like a baby bird with a broken wing.

Over her mother's shoulder and through her tears, Sena saw her brothers watching them. How long would it take for the shock of realization and understanding? How hard would it be for all the pieces to fall into place? Were they even capable of understanding what was happening? Then they looked at each other, and back at Sena. Without speaking a word, they jumped up from the table in unison. Their heavy boots crashed across the floor as they came to her, to wrap both her and Mom in their arms, like a protective cocoon.

It was all so unexpected. Wonderful. And confusing. *Love isn't real*. That's what she told Hazel that night outside The Triple D, before Hazel cracked open her heart. And Sena had every reason to believe those words were true. She had spent most of her life feeling invisible in her own family. Believing that everything she had accomplished—everything she had grown to be—was in spite of them. That she was on her own. But this felt real, too…the embrace of her family…the love that filled that circle.

She pulled away from them.

"I'm going for a ride. I love you all. But I need some time to process all of this."

No one looked surprised. Going out with Alegre was what she had always done when she needed time and space to think things through.

Her brothers stepped back, nodding. Mom took her hand and kissed it.

"Your father…"

"I know, Mom."

They had all felt his absence in the circle, Sena was sure of it. She would have to deal with him later.

The rain had stopped but it was steamy, as it usually was once the monsoons began, and the sun was already on its downward journey when Sena scooted out the kitchen door and headed up the gravel road to the stables. There wasn't a person in sight when she got there, and she was thankful to be able to greet Alegre alone.

A familiar snort, snort, snort in rapid succession followed by a high-pitched jiiiiii brought Sena back. She would recognize Alegre's voice anywhere.

She swung the stable door open to find Alegre looking at her over the top of his stall door, as if he had spent six years standing there, just waiting for her to come home. He shook his head up and down in silent greeting and took four steps back so she could come inside. No guilt. No shame. No questions. Sena put her arms around his neck and buried her face in the sweet smell of creosote and honey and pine. They rode together for hours.

Back in the stable, just as she was closing up for the night, her father appeared in the doorway.

"Hi, Sena."

"Dad."

She turned to face him. He looked older than the last time she was home. But his back was as straight as ever. His feet were firmly planted, hands on his hips, his chin jutting forward. Proud. Strong.

"Did Mom talk to you?" Sena's question had thorns. She was prepared to protect her heart against all possible attacks.

"Yes."

"So you know?"

"I think I have always known."

"Then, why?" She could not control the whine in her voice. It made him look away.

"Sena, you do not understand."

"Then tell me. Explain to me why, since I was a little girl, you have treated me like I was invisible?"

"Invisible? What are you talking about, Sena? You have always been the brightest light in the sky, outshining everything and everyone."

"Well, it's how you have made me feel. All I ever wanted was to be with you, to work and ride and hunt and play next to you. But nothing I ever did was good enough. I—" She pounded her chest. "I…was never enough." Sena's voice grew louder with each accusation until she was yelling. Alegre gave a loud snort from his stable. He wasn't happy, either.

"You gave me Alegre, but you did not *really* want me to be happy. You did not even see me."

She swung back around to face her father and it gave her twisted pleasure to see him wince, as if in physical pain.

Eyes downcast, he whispered, "Your happiness is all I have ever wanted, Sena."

She was ready for the kill. "Well, you have no idea how much pain you have caused. You can't even begin to imagine how alone I have always been…or how lonely."

After having carried these words within her for most of her life, she aimed them now with expert accuracy, knowing they would finish him off. Maybe her own pain would disappear if she could finally transfer it to him. But it didn't make her feel any better to see him in such agony.

Before he could see her tears, she turned and raced out of the stables, back down the road to the house.

"Sena!" her mother shouted when she threw open the back door and ran through the kitchen, to her old bedroom, where she slammed the door shut, threw herself on the bed, and let the sobbing overtake her.

She did not answer the soft knock a few minutes later but heard the door creak open and her father's boots cross the floor. He sat on the edge of the bed.

"Sena, I know this is hard to understand. But all I have ever tried to do is save you from pain. You have always been different. So smart. So driven. So…special. I could see the way other children treated you. I knew it would only get worse out there…" He gestured toward the window and beyond, to the world Sena had always wanted so badly to conquer.

"I could not bear the thought of that world rejecting you, hurting you."

"And so…*what?*" Sena flipped around and sat up to face him. "You decided *you* would hurt me, instead?"

His eyes were wounded but his voice was steady. "I did not mean to hurt you, Sena. I thought that, if you would allow yourself to be embraced by your mother and your aunties, that you would find your way onto a traditional path, where you would be safer."

"And what if I didn't *want* that path? What if it was impossible for me to take that path?"

"Then you were going to have to make your own way. There was no path for you here, Sena, no road carved by someone else before you, through the traditions and history of this place."

"You could have helped me."

Her father's shoulders slumped and his eyes dropped to the floor. "I'm sorry, Sena. But I did not know how."

Sena had never heard such a raw admission from her father or seen him look so vulnerable. He was the most powerful person she had ever known. He commanded every room, won every deal. He

was the person everyone else came to for advice because he knew...
everything.

"I did not know how..."

The words echoed as the air around them grew still. An orange
glow from the setting sun made the old medals and trophies that
lined her walls sparkle. The sound of dishes clattering in the kitchen
wafted in. From a distance, she could hear horses neighing and
snorting, and the laughter of ranch hands as they shared an evening
toast in the shade of the mesquite trees.

Sena's father took her chin in his hand, lifting her face up
toward his, and she could feel the calluses. When she looked into
his eyes, they were wet.

"Sena, I am so happy you're home."

Mom made a feast for dinner that night. Her brothers and their
wives were there. And the kids. Three more had joined the family
since Sena had last been home, two of them still in diapers. It was
chaos. Dish after dish was passed—stories were told—there was
laughter—and, of course, Bacanora. They wanted to know all about
Sena's plans in Owen Station. She wanted to know all the latest
news about the family and the business. Later, Jesús pulled out a
guitar and Mom sang. They all hugged her tightly, as the night was
ending. The little ones clung to her legs.

Love is the *only* thing that is real. That is what Hazel said that
night at The Triple D. She didn't say it was perfect. Or easy.

But this was real.

Her family had loved her the best way they knew how. She
could see that now.

Healing would take time but this was a start.

Maybe Mom was right about broken things.

CHAPTER EIGHTEEN

RECKONING

Hazel was feeling less steady than she did last night, with Delaney by her side, literally surrounded by her great-grandmother's energy. The windows on the old house were rattling, and outside, the wind howled, blasting tiny shards of rain mixed with Sonoran sand sideways across the patio.

She still hadn't heard from Sena and couldn't imagine where she'd gone. Keeping one ear open all night long, she waited and prayed to hear Sena's car pull up. But it didn't. She hoped to God everything was okay, that Sena was safe and that, wherever she was, she would somehow be able to find her way back to Owen Station... to give Hazel the chance to apologize and make things right between them.

But today wasn't about Hazel or her broken heart or anything *she* was feeling. Today was about how broken this town was. About the lies it had told itself, the damage that had been done, and the people who had been hurt. Today was for reckoning with the truth and beginning the long, slow process of making repairs.

After a cup of strong, black coffee and a slice of dry toast, she quickly did the few dishes in the sink and headed to her closet. On autopilot, she grabbed one of a dozen or so pencil skirts but changed her mind and pulled out a pair of jeans and the V-neck tee she bought at the Lilith Fair Revival in Chula Vista her junior year. Then she reached into the back of her closet and pulled out the red Doc Marten boots that had been collecting dust for more than a decade. She bought them right about the time they stomped up the runway in Paris but, by the time they became the emblem of antifashion fashion, she was learning how to give injections blind because she couldn't see through her tears. She was going to need a pair of ass kickers on her feet today.

Pausing to look in the mirror before she headed out to face the day, Hazel inspected her reflection, a little suspiciously at first, like it belonged to a stranger or someone she used to know. But when she ran her fingers through her hair, she felt a surge of something she hadn't felt for a very long time.

Courage.

Mango was sitting at the foot of the willow, watching as she got in the car. "Tell Mom I could use a little extra help today," she said, pulling the door closed. Then she paused, rolled down the window, and yelled. "Actually, Mango. On second thought, tell Mom I got this."

As if on cue, the cat bounded up the driveway, leapt onto the adobe wall and up onto the hillside behind it, and disappeared into the brush.

Hazel was headed to KBIS-FM, the inauspicious offices of Owen Station's only radio station, headquartered in the basement of the old town hall, a mostly empty building that probably should have been condemned. A few years back, when KBIS-FM ran out of money and got evicted from the building from where they had been broadcasting local news, high school sports, and the town's soundtrack for the past fifty-seven years, the town council voted unanimously to rent the basement to them for a dollar a month. That might be more than the space was worth.

"Morning, Walt." She squinted through the darkness to make sure it was, in fact, KBIS-FM's manager she saw. He and Dad had gone to school together. They weren't friends, but Walt came to the funeral. Said he thought Dad was a good guy. And Walt had always been a Hazel fan.

"Morning, Hazel. Everything okay? Don't usually see you down here." He paused thoughtfully. "Actually, don't get many visitors down here at all."

His skin was so pale, he looked like he didn't get out much, either.

"Yep, everything's okay," Hazel said. "But I have a PSA I'd like you to put on the air this morning. If you can. I mean, if it's not too much trouble."

Walt dug under the pile of country music records, empty pizza boxes, and old newspapers on his desk.

"Here's the form." He sounded bored, but there were protocols—which gave her an idea about how to handle Sirus. Walt handed her a clipboard with a crinkled, coffee-stained piece of paper attached. She filled it out and handed it back.

"It's pretty simple," she said. "I just want you to tell everyone that the Save Owen Station meeting scheduled for tonight at the library is canceled."

Walt scratched the three-day growth on his chin without looking up, appearing to be deep in thought. After what seemed like a long couple of minutes, he tilted his chin down and peered at her over the top of his yellow-tinted, plastic brown-framed aviator eyeglasses. They would have been retro cool on somebody younger. Walt just looked like he couldn't be bothered to buy a new pair since 1997.

"Are you sure you want to do that?"

She set her jaw and looked him square in the eye. "Never been more sure of anything."

He looked at her over his glasses for a long minute. "Okay, then, young lady." Then he got up, came around to the front of the desk, and stuck out his hand. "Let me be the first to thank you. The mayor and council have been talking behind closed doors and off the record about how to respond to those idiots. After those letters in the paper this weekend and that protest yesterday—well, everyone's kind of afraid of them, especially with Mr. Money Bags Sirus leading the pack—you know he's donated to all their campaigns. I'm glad somebody in this town has the guts to stand up to them."

Hazel hung her head. "I should have done it months ago, Walt."

That truth haunted her. How could she have been so blind to what was going on? She closed her eyes but all she could see was Sena's face, tortured by betrayal, right before she turned and ran away. So much damage had been done. Could it ever be repaired? Hazel didn't know. She would do everything in her power to earn Sena's trust back. But, whether or not she could make things right with Sena, today she was damn well going to start making things right in that town.

Walt shifted uncomfortable. "It could be dangerous, Hazel."

They both stood very still, looking at each other, as if they knew that, if they took one step forward, everything would change. From the other room, Hazel could hear the soft whir of the household fans Walt used to prevent the equipment from burning up. She knew there was a cot back there, too. That Walt had moved in and was living there because the station couldn't pay him enough to afford rent on his own place. There was so much about her town that Hazel hadn't wanted to see before. As much as she loved its history, that glory was past. The mines had been closed for fifty years. Owenites were resilient, but life was tough. Walt wasn't the only one just scraping by. Sena could see something Hazel couldn't. Possibility. Opportunity. A future. Knox saw that. Hazel felt like an idiot for not seeing it, too.

Finally, Walt let out a sigh. "Are you sure you're ready?"

R.E.A.D.Y. Prepared. Equipped. Primed. READY.

She closed her eyes and took a long, slow, deep breath. No, she wasn't ready. But she was going to do this anyway.

"Yes, Walt. I'm sure."

"Okay, then." He put his hand on her shoulder. "Be careful out there, Hazel."

His words echoed in her ears as she headed back up the stairs and out onto the street.

It wasn't long before the library phone started ringing.

"Owen Station Public Library. How may I help you?"

"Here's how you can help me. Go to hell."

Click.

"Owen Station Public Library. How may I—"

"You're going to pay for this, little lady."

Click.

"Owen Station Public Library. How may—"

"You know we're just going to meet somewhere else, right?" She recognized the snarling voice, exploding with rage. "You can't actually cancel our meeting."

"Hi, Sirus. Yes, I realize that. But I can prevent you from meeting here tonight."

"It's public property!" he yelled. "My tax dollars pay for that building—and pay your salary, you little bitch."

"Sirus, I will not allow you to speak to me that way." She was shaking but her voice was calm.

"I'll talk to you however I want. You have no right to do this."

"It's done," she said with a finality that most people wouldn't have argued with.

Sirus wasn't most people.

"That library is a public building. You can't restrict our First Amendment rights just because you don't like what we're saying."

"No, I can't do that, Sirus. I know the law as well as anyone. But I don't have to allow you or anyone to meet here after hours. The library closes at three p.m. today, now that our budget has been cut again. There is no one here to staff it at night."

"You've been doing it," he barked. "You've been doing it for *months.*"

He was right. What in the world had she been thinking?

It took effort to stay focused. "You're correct, Sirus. But I did that on my own time, on my own dime. It was wrong. I won't do it again."

"Okay, fine." But he wasn't about to give up that easily. "We'll just move our meeting to noon today. People can come during their lunch time."

She took a deep breath. Now things were going to get even trickier. "That won't be possible today, Sirus."

"Why not?" he snapped back.

Another breath. "You do not have a meeting room request form for today on file."

He exploded. "Meeting request form? What in the hell is going on, Hazel?"

She flinched, even though he was all the way across town. But she did not back down.

"I will be happy to send you our new form, Sirus. It includes our new policies, which cover user behavior, among other things. You'll need to leave your guns at home, for starters. And you will not be allowed to intimidate or disrespect other library patrons or staff members."

"There's only one staff member." His voice dropped an octave and became slow and threatening. "Which means, you're alone in there all day, every day, aren't you?"

Her heart leapt into her throat and she gasped, in spite of herself.

He made a low chortling sound. "You and that girlfriend of yours aren't afraid of us, are you, sweetheart?"

She was terrified but would not give him the satisfaction of showing it. She just needed to get him off the phone. Now.

Conjuring up her most officious tone, she brought it to a close. "I'll put this form in the mail tomorrow. Mail it back or drop it off once you have it filled in. The approval process takes ten business days. Per our new policy."

"Your. New. Policy. My. Ass." Sirus spit the words through the phone. "You're going to regret this."

Click.

With shaking hands, she put down the phone and leaned against the cool wood of the worn counter to steady herself. After a few deep breaths, she realized she needed to figure out the next steps. This was all happening faster than she had anticipated.

The County had insisted on digitizing the card catalog—although she still preferred to use the old system—and had given her a desktop computer. It sat under a cover in her office, where she used it about three or four times a month. She fired it up and went to the American Library Association's website. A template she found there helped her create Owen Station Public Library's first ever written policy.

"Welcome to the future." Her voice startled the empty room to attention. It had been a long time since anything new happened here; the air felt suddenly different, cleaner, alive.

One thing Sirus was right about, Hazel couldn't legally or ethically prevent his group from meeting at the library just because she didn't like the things they stood for. That didn't mean she was powerless, though. Far from it.

She grabbed a notebook and a pen and headed to the stacks upstairs. In the 300 section, she found what she was looking for. She had heard the author—a law professor—speak when she was in college. He thanked librarians for being defenders of free speech. And then he talked about his father, who had survived a concentration camp. That's why the professor was opposed to censorship of any kind—he said it's always the marginalized who have the most to lose when government has the power to silence voices they don't like. He said there are two things that need to be done, instead. Support those who are the targets of hate. And education to change hearts and minds.

Hazel tucked the book under her arm, headed back down to her favorite corner, opened her notebook, and started writing. At the top of the page, she wrote the first draft of a new mission statement for Owen Station's library.

Our library strives to be an engine of educa...

She crossed that out and started again.

Our library is *an engine of education, a sponsor of healthy public discourse, a place where strangers meet and prejudices are challenged, where ignorance is banished by fact, and where minds and hearts are expanded and changed.*

She read it out loud to her little friend. "What do you think, George? A little wordy, maybe. But not a bad start."

Then she began filling her notebook with scribbles and scraps of possibilities. Lecture series. Workshops. Community art projects. Special displays on queer, immigrant, Black, Chicano, Indigenous authors. Poetry contests. Spanish language classes. A self-publishing hub and writing circles to empower Owenites to tell their own stories. A community advisory board with members representing all the beautiful diversity of Owen Station, asking those with lived experience to lead.

"George, my banana-loving friend, we might even need to go fully digital."

She looked up to see the cover of *Curious George Votes* staring back at her. The little monkey was dropping his ballot into a box.

"Let me guess. You vote yes."

Hazel stared off into the late morning sunlight filtering through the library's large leaded glass windows. Then she flipped her notebook open and watched as the pen she was holding started moving across the paper, almost of its own accord.

You can't change the present if you spend all your time in the past.

Hazel closed her eyes, letting the whole truth sink in.

All these years she had been so afraid of what she might lose, she buried herself in the past. And then she got stuck there. Her friends were right. Her house was filled with antiques. And a lot of old stuff that was just junk, too, if she was being honest. She drove an antique car. She wore antique jewelry. She spent her working hours in an historical building and her off hours trying to make sure no one could build anything new. She treasured her memories of the past at the expense of making new ones. And she was so sure she was right about it all that she blew the one, best chance she had of finding love. But she now could see that it wasn't just herself she was hurting. She had hurt Sena. She had hurt this town.

The chair almost toppled backward as she abruptly got up on her feet. "I'm a public servant, dammit!" She was talking to George and to the ghosts but mostly to herself. "I have a responsibility. And I've totally blown it. I let this library become an empty, irrelevant dinosaur on my watch and I've allowed what is happening in this town now to incubate right under my nose. My silence, my inaction, my naiveté has caused so much harm. This isn't just Sirus's fault. It's mine."

She trailed off as she dropped back down into the chair to cover her face with her hands, trembling with shame and sorrow. That's when the sound of honking horns and angry voices first penetrated the library's thick front door.

CHAPTER NINETEEN

PUMA

It had stormed overnight, making it difficult for Sena to sleep. Also, she could not stop thinking about Hazel. Every time she pictured her standing in the middle of that angry crowd, she tasted metal like the edge of a dull blade.

But, then, she felt the warmth of Hazel's body against her, as Antares glowed above them. A beating red heart. Pulsing. Too powerful to ignore.

Had it all just been an illusion?

Sena didn't know. But she did know this: what was happening inside her, to her heart...that was real.

She was so tired of hiding. Behind the clothes, the car, the high-powered credentials. Living life like it was a game to be won. Always needing to be on top. Invincible.

Well, she wasn't invincible, by God. She was a real, flesh and blood human being. Whose heart could be broken. Hazel broke it yesterday.

But, if it hadn't been for Hazel, she would never have been able to even acknowledge that. With Hazel, Sena had allowed herself to be opened. Literally.

A flush of hot energy flowed through her body as she thought about it. But it wasn't just the sex. With Hazel, Sena had been... vulnerable...honest...real.

There had to be something more to the story. Hazel had tried to explain. But Sena didn't want to hear it then. Through the noise of her own pain, she couldn't hear it.

Nothing is so broken it cannot be fixed.

How badly Sena wanted to believe her mother's words were true.

The sound of clanking pots and pans drifted through the house and into Sena's bedroom. Her mom was bustling around the kitchen before the sun was even up. Sena pulled the colorful, handwoven blanket up over her head and, exhausted from a night of tossing and turning, managed to fall back asleep.

It was after nine before she got up, pulled on her clothes, and wandered out to see what wonderful things her mother had cooking on the stove.

She was surprised to see that breakfast wasn't on the table. Instead, her mother had filled a thermos with coffee and wrapped up some pan dulce, Sena's favorite pastries, to go.

"What's this?" Usually, her mother would be doing everything in her power to get her to stay.

Her mother smiled through pursed lips. Her don't-mess-with-me-I-know-best look. Sena recognized it right away.

"Sena, you have things to do today. Broken things to fix—"

Sena tried to interrupt. "Mom! Those things can wait. I want to spend more time with you and—"

"No, no, no," her mother said, shaking her head. "I want to spend time with you, too. And we will. But this cannot wait. Your heart is calling you, Sena. You must follow it."

Tears formed behind Sena's eyes—this was starting to be a thing—and she put her hands together, like she was praying. "I love you, Mom."

Her mother threw back her head with a cackle. If she had busted a move and started singing a Beyoncé song, it could not have been more surprising. It felt so good to hear laughter. It made Sena feel light, hopeful.

"I love you more, Sena. Now, be quiet as you collect your things. Your father is still sleeping. He was at the office until very late and then up half the night, making sure the horses were all okay during the storm. I will tell him you said good-bye."

"Tell him I love him, please."

"Of course. He already knows that sweetheart."

"I won't stay away so long this time."

"I hope not." A sly grin crossed her face. "Maybe next time, you'll bring someone special for us to meet."

Sena threw her arms around her mother and squeezed her tight.

It was midmorning by the time she got in the car but, still, she had the road mostly to herself. Her mother's to-go package and a station playing Mexican folk ballads with a polka beat kept her company for the ninety-minute drive.

Jessica, her roommate at USC, would be screaming to turn it off if she were in the car with her. Which she wouldn't be. Which was just fine.

Jessica Johnson. Of *those* Johnsons. Sena hadn't thought about her in ages.

"What a privileged little bitch." Her voice sliced the air, surprising her, and she guffawed at the sound of it. Guess she still had a few things bottled up. But it was true. Jessica was a bitch.

Sena's abuelo had shared his love of Norteño with her. It blended Mexican revolution folk music with the music of twentieth century immigrants from Eastern Europe. He told her they came south and west by wagon and by train, looking for opportunity and work, bringing their accordions and dances with them. Together, these peoples forged a new soundtrack for the land they shared, here in this in-between place called the Borderlands.

Who in the hell do the descendants of those immigrants think they are, anyway? What right does Sirus or any of them have to lay claim to anything on this land?

She was just outside of Owen Station when the mountain lion appeared. Her headlights flipped on as she entered the tunnel that led to town, and there he was, standing as still as a statue in the middle of the road. She slammed on the brakes, tires squealing, and skidded to a stop.

The animal didn't move. He just stood there.

Looking. Right. At. Her.

They stared at each other for what felt like several minutes. Sena couldn't feel her feet or hands. She was paralyzed, face-to-face with Puma, who had visited her as a little girl. The cat she thought was a figment of her imagination. She didn't even dare blink.

"What do you want from me?" Sena's voice was shaky but clear.

Her grandfather was the only person she had ever told about her visions. He died while she was away at USC. But she heard his voice now, as clearly as if he had been sitting beside her. "Sena, when Puma visits you, pay attention."

She stared at the cat in the middle of the road, who stared back at her. "Well, what do you have to say to me, Señor Puma? What do you want me to do?"

Again, she heard her grandfather's voice. "You are powerful, Sena, and you are free. Do not be afraid, even of love, even in the face of danger."

The big cat took one last long look at her and then leapt right over the top of her car. And he was gone.

Sena exhaled the breath she had been holding since her car skidded to a stop. It took a long several minutes before she could put her foot back on the gas and aim herself toward Owen Station. It had been foolish to reject the wisdom of her elders.

She would not be so foolish again.

The town was quieter than usual when she pulled in, as if everyone had gotten a memo to stay home or behind closed doors. She wanted to head right to the library, to get this over with, but wasn't sure what she was going to say yet.

She knew that she should be thinking, "What if it goes well? What is the best thing that could happen?"

Instead, she was thinking, "What if it doesn't? What if I get there and Hazel is angry, defends her involvement with that horrible group, says she made a mistake to get involved with me and doesn't want to see me again?"

Shaking her head to chase off the voices competing for attention, she decided that what she really needed right in that moment was a dose of Knox. Maybe he had talked with Hazel. Maybe he had some advice, insight. At the very least, she could have a great cup of coffee while she thought it over. And she could just walk right across the street to the library, whenever she was ready.

If she was ever ready.

Knox didn't shout out his usual greeting when she walked in. He was staring down at the long copper counter, wiping circles on it with his towel. Jorge and Miguel, from next door, sat hunched over on their stools across from him.

"Looks like somebody died." Sena eased onto the stool next to Jorge. "What's going on?"

"Oh, sorry," Knox said absently. "Hi, Sena. What can I get you?"

"Seriously, Knox. You all look terrible."

"Hmmm. Well, I was just thinking about what a really special place this has been." He spoke so quietly, still wiping the same six inches of counter, she wasn't sure she heard him right. Then he looked off into the distance, or maybe into the past. "Did you know Hazel helped me pick out and refurbish every stick of furniture?"

"What do you mean 'has been,'" Sena asked roughly, trying to shake him out of his stupor, "like it *isn't* any more?"

"I'm closing at the end of this month, Sena. Banter & Brew is over."

Miguel stirred slightly but didn't change position. He was still leaning on the counter, his cheek resting on his fist. "We're done, too. Shutting down. Moving back to Hermosillo, I think. I dunno. It's all happening so fast…"

Sena spun around on her stool, trying to look at all three of them at the same time. "What? Wait! Why? Why on earth would you close your stores?"

Knox squeezed his eyes closed, every muscle in his face taut, jaw clenched, voice sharp and jagged, like broken glass, like shattered illusions.

"Our landlord won't renew our leases."

"You can't close! There's got to be a way to make a deal, to make this work."

Sena had learned this from her dad. There was always a way.

Knox fixed his green eyes on her, resolute, stoic, hard. "There is no reasoning with him, Sena. It's done."

"I just can't accept that, Knox. There is always something."

"Sena." He spoke her name like a stone and it hit the counter with a thud, startling her into silence.

"Oh my God, Knox." She dropped her head into her hands. "This is all my fault."

"This is nobody's fault, Sena," Knox said sternly, "except for Sirus. It certainly isn't yours."

The noise of honking horns and yelling reached them just as she was about to object.

"What the hell is that?"

Knox reached across the counter to grab Sena's hand. "Don't worry. I'll see what's going on."

He shot across the shop and opened the door wide enough that they could all see a crowd forming in front of the library. Jorge and Miguel jumped off their stools, rushing to his side.

"What is it, Knox?" Sena cried. "What's going on?" She was scared to go see for herself.

Knox turned and looked at her. "A lot has happened in the last twenty-four hours. Hazel canceled the SOS meeting that was scheduled for tonight at the library. It was all over the radio this morning and everyone has been talking about it. Chief Garcia was in here earlier. She was worried there might be trouble. It looks like she was right."

"Oh my God. *Hazel!*" Sena jumped off the stool and ran toward the door, but Knox and Jorge each grabbed an arm and pulled her back.

"Sena," Jorge said, "stop and think. Look at that crowd. It's dangerous out there."

Struggling to get free, Sena shouted, "I don't care. Let me go! We can't just stand here and do nothing."

"Okay, okay. But calm down...please." Deep creases had formed in Knox's brow and he was working the muscles in his jaw. His voice was stern. "Whatever we do next, we'll do it together."

Sena stopped straining and the two men released her. Knox leaned over and kissed her lightly on the cheek. She squeezed his hand. Together, with Miguel and Jorge following close behind them, they stepped outside just as Hazel came through the library's front doors.

Chapter Twenty

Haunted

When Hazel pushed open the heavy wooden door, she saw a sea of growling faces on the library's steep front steps, spilling out onto Main Street.

"We're here for the meeting," Doc Adams barked. Her big, rough hands were clenched. She had pulled her graying hair back into a tight ponytail, making her weathered face look hard as rock.

Sirus was standing next to her. His hands were on his hips, exposing a holstered sidearm. Hazel ignored him.

"Doc, I'm disappointed in you." That was all she could find to say.

Hazel looked around like she had stepped over the threshold into a parallel dimension, one where everything was familiar—the buildings, the street signs, the cars, the faces—but nothing was the same. She tugged hard on her ear.

Okay, that hurts. Good.

She closed and opened her eyes. Twice. Clearly, she was awake.

Maybe I'm having a stroke? Is this what it feels like?

She held her hand in front of her face, examined her palm, and made a fist. It worked.

No, not a stroke.

She looked up. The air was heavy and the clouds above looked as hostile as the crowd. The temperature was unbearable. Had to be at least 103. Another storm was brewing.

Over the sound of the mob, a siren blared. Hopefully, that meant Chief Garcia was on her way.

Also, someone was calling her name.

"Hazel! Hazel, I'm coming!" Dressed in a black clerical shirt, even though it was hotter than hell, Pastor Bexley was elbowing his way through the crowd, making himself as small as he could, squeezing sideways where people wouldn't or couldn't move aside. Hazel watched him curiously. He looked like a collared lizard darting through sagebrush as he made his way to the top of the stairs.

Out of breath, he took Hazel's hand. "Are you okay?"

His sandy brown eyes were both tender and terrified, and his dimpled chin trembled, as though he was trying not to cry. "Hazel, answer me. Are you okay?"

Her voice moved through a thick fog, muffled. "Yes, yes. I'm okay."

"I got here as quickly as I could. As soon as I heard they were coming." His eyes darted toward the crowd.

She scrunched up her face. "But, but, why are you…what are you…"

She couldn't comprehend any of it. The anger. The reason for this crowd at her door. Neighbors who had become strangers. Why this minister was standing there, holding her hand.

He talked quickly. "A lot of these people are members of my congregation, Hazel. I'm ashamed to admit it, but it's true. I've heard the grumbling, even been invited to the meetings, seen the numbers grow, felt the temperature rise. I know the TV shows they're watching, the talk radio they're listening to. I've seen it all happening in slow motion. And I've done…"

His eyes dropped to the ground.

"Nothing, Hazel. I've done *nothing.* Just kept preaching love and peace and telling Bible stories, hoping they'd make the connections on their own, not wanting to believe that the people I love and serve could turn on others like this."

When he looked back at Hazel, his eyes were moist. "Jesus taught us to welcome the stranger, Hazel. That's the number one thing. To love our neighbor as ourselves…"

He was definitely going to start crying. What good did he think he would do there? What could any of them have done?

Suddenly, Bexley let go of Hazel's hand. He stood up straight, taller than he actually was, turned to the crowd and stretched out his hands and arms, a way to get their attention, a sign of authority, an ancient blessing.

"Friends," he called out. "Friends, listen to me!"

Those toward the front of the crowd began to quiet. Out of respect? Curiosity? Probably a little of both.

Across the street, Knox was standing outside of Banter & Brew with Jorge and Miguel. And Sena.

Sena was there.

Hot tears filled Hazel's eyes and she realized she was having trouble breathing. Sena looked so small all the way over there. Pressed up against the building, stuck at the back of the crowd. She looked confused and frightened. Hazel wanted to yell for her, tell her to run away, to go someplace safe, someplace where she wouldn't have to see what was happening, where she wouldn't have to hear the horrible things people were shouting. She wanted to scream at Knox to take Sena home, to protect her. But the crowd was so loud and they were so far away and Hazel's voice wasn't working. She realized her face was wet and she rubbed away the tears.

The siren stopped and she wondered if Chief Garcia would also get trapped back there somewhere. What could she do anyway? There were so many people. And they all looked so angry. She knew most of them, but she didn't know any of them.

Pastor Bexley called out again with outstretched arms. He waited until even the ugly signs and flags that had been wildly waving were still before he began the sermon of his life.

"Friends, I want to warn you. Some of the things I am about to say will be very disturbing. If you have been a victim of violence, you may want to prepare yourself. I am sorry that my words may reopen old wounds. But it is important for the truth to be told, especially for those of us who have too long avoided or ignored it."

He took a breath.

"In the year of our Lord 1882, not far from this very spot, a man was hung by an angry mob."

He paused dramatically. Or maybe just because he was terrified. Hazel could see the sweat pooling on the shirt beneath his arms and on his back. But when he continued, his voice was strong.

"That was a time in our history when Owen Station was filled with people who had come from somewhere else. European immigrants and children of immigrants, women and men who were trying to escape poverty and persecution. But the freedom and prosperity they found here came at the expense of others. Indigenous tribes were murdered, their sacred grounds stolen and stripped for minerals to feed the needs of a growing nation. Mexicans, who had lived here long before any borders were drawn, were prevented from working underground because those higher paying jobs went to whites. Chinese immigrants, who helped build our railroad, were not allowed in town after dark. Former slaves, who came looking for opportunity and happiness, were given only the hardest jobs no one else was willing to do."

Bexley paused again. His hands were shaking.

"On that day in 1882, three mine investors got off the train. They came from back East to watch their money at work. Instead, they saw a man swinging from a tree. Believing that education and knowledge is the key to peace and prosperity, wanting a different and better future for our town, they built this magnificent library."

As the young man spoke, the sky darkened and the air grew even heavier with the threat of storm. Droplets began to bounce on the pavement and upturned faces, but no one moved. Time had frozen.

"I know some of you are worried about the direction our town is going. You miss the days when we all knew each other, looked out for each other's children, danced at each other's weddings, brought casseroles to lift each other's spirits after a funeral. But, my dear friends, I am here to tell you this painful truth: that community you are missing was never anything more than a hopeful and fanciful dream. There have always been those among us whose lives have not mattered, whose voices were not heard, whose deaths and disappointments we did not mourn, whose land and labor we stole to enrich ourselves. Everyone talks about how Owen Station is filled with ghosts. And maybe it is. But the thing that haunts us most is our unacknowledged, racist past."

His voice reached a crescendo.

"And I want you to hear me clearly: we are all—*every single one of us*—less than we could be and were meant to be because of it."

The powerful scent of creosote swept down the street and everyone could hear the rain rushing toward them. Bexley did not stop.

"But today, my friends, can be a new day. Standing here, in the shadow of our darkest history, on the steps of our brightest hope, I beg you to join me in accepting who we have been and committing ourselves to becoming who we want—and who I believe we have been created—to be."

No one moved, even when the preacher stopped talking and lowered his arms, even though they were all about to be baptized.

A bolt of lightning streaked across the sky to a deafening crack of thunder and Hazel's hair stood on end. Someone screamed, "Fire!" People in the crowd started running, although some were standing in the street pointing at the library. A second loud crack made everyone duck. Hazel thought it was just another lightning strike…until Pastor Bexley and Doc Adams, were kneeling next to her.

Something was burning. Her arm. Oh God, it felt like it was on fire.

"Is that blood, Doc?" Her voice was floating somewhere above her body.

"Yes, that's blood, Hazel. I'm so sorry. I'm so sorry about everything. Don't worry. It'll be okay."

There was so much blood.

Hazel watched, in a fog, as Doc stripped the black shirt right off of Bexley, whose hands were shaking too hard to unbutton it. She wrapped it around Hazel's arm and held it, pressing down hard.

Bexley went back to rocking back and forth on his knees, head bowed, hands clasped together, as pale as his white undershirt, lips moving. She couldn't hear what he was saying because the rain was so loud. SO LOUD. Pounding the stairs, the railing, the roof, the street. And someone was yelling. "Get an ambulance to the library right now, dammit! And send the fire trucks—now!"

"What happened, Doc?" Hazel turned her head to look into the Doc's eyes. Everything was starting to spin, even though she was pretty sure nothing was moving. Doc didn't answer. Instead, she held up three fingers. Or maybe four.

"How many fingers do you see, Hazel?"

The fog that trapped her voice was getting thicker. Hazel closed her eyes.

"Hazel! Hazel, open your eyes. Look at me." Doc sounded angry. Why was everyone always so angry?

Someone picked up her other hand, on the other arm, the one Doc wasn't trying to crush. It was hard but she turned her head in that direction and opened one eye. The other one was happier closed.

"Hazel! Oh my God, Hazel." Sena covered her hand with kisses.

She looked so worried. And her hair was all wet, it was plastered to her head. That was funny. She looked funny. But worried. Why was she so worried?

"It's okay, Sena," Hazel slurred. "I don't feel a thing." That was true, too. She felt fine. Better than fine. She was floating on a cloud. And now Sena was there with her. And Knox, too.

"Hi, Knox," she said. "How's it going? Oh, hi, Jorge. Hi, Miguel." They all looked like they took a long shower together. Now they were bending over, looking at her like she was the drain at the bottom of the shower where the water was swirling away.

No one was laughing. Something must have gone terribly wrong.

"Sena, Doc won't tell me anything. What happened? Why are you crying? I'm sorry I made you cry, Sena. Where did you go, anyway? I was so worried about you when you didn't come home. Can you ever forgive me?"

Sena just kept kissing her hand and then started stroking her forehead. "It's okay, Hazel. Everything is going to be okay. The ambulance just got here."

"Ambulance?" That was big news. Hazel tried to shake her head and forced both eyes open to try to see through the fog. "Why is there an ambulance? Who got hurt? Are you hurt, Sena? I didn't mean to hurt you."

"I know you didn't, Hazel. I'm sorry I ever doubted you. I'm sorry I ran off and didn't listen to you. I love you, Hazel. I love you so much. It's all going to be okay. Hush now. Try to stay calm."

"Oh, Sena. You *do* believe in lub! I lub you, too. I lub you so mush."

Suddenly, everyone except Sena got up and stepped away in unison.

What's that called? Synchronized swimming?

It was like that only they weren't swimming. They were floating. They were all floating away. They were making room for two mermen who wanted to pick her up.

"Please, ma'am." One of the mermen, the one with wet blond hair who looked a little like Jimmy, wanted Sena to move out of the way, too. But Sena wouldn't move. She wanted to keep holding Hazel's hand.

"Ma'am. *Please.*"

He didn't have to be so gruff. Jimmy. His name was Jimmy. Jimmy was there the night Mom died. Jimmy took Mom away and then Mom was...dead. Mom was dead, dead, dead!

"Sena! Please don't leave me." Hazel reached wildly for Sena's hand as the other merman grabbed her legs and the one who looked like Jimmy reached under her torso to lift her up. "What are you doing? Where are you taking me? I don't want to be dead! Please don't take me!"

"Hazel, I'm right here." Sena was shouting. She was so loud Hazel could hear her over the water that was splashing everywhere. "They're here to help you, Hazel. Stop fighting them. Please! I'm coming with you. I promise, I'll be right next to you the whole time. For as long as you'll have me. Forever and always."

Well, she certainly didn't want to fight anymore. One fight with Sena was enough for a lifetime. And Sena told the truth. Sena was sitting right next to her when they put her in that big noisy ice cream van and pulled the doors closed. She was holding Hazel's hand and brushing the hair off her face and kissing her forehead.

Then everything went black.

CHAPTER TWENTY-ONE

FAMILY

S ena was working hard to control her rage.
     Hazel didn't die.
That's all that matters.
She's okay.
Everything's going to be okay.
The bullet went right through Hazel's forearm without hitting an artery. The docs said that, if you were going to get shot, that's how you wanted it to happen. But there was tissue damage and the bone was nicked.

Sena had spent tortuous hours in that waiting room, with Knox, Delaney, and Lace, waiting to hear from the surgeon. It was almost as bad as waiting for the paramedics while Hazel was sprawled out, bleeding all over the place. Almost.

But she's okay and she's finally going home.

Now Sena wanted to kill her.

"Hazel, what were you thinking? What would make you try to take on that crowd by yourself?"

"I wasn't alone." Hazel's smile was lopsided. She'd been awake all morning, as doctors and nurses paraded in and out of her room, but she was fading. "You were there and Knox and Pastor Bexley…and Jorge and Mango…and my mom…and Hazel-the-first and her beautiful girlfriend and…" her singsongy voice trailed off and she fell asleep.

"Looks like the pain killers are still making her a little loopy." Knox walked in carrying another round of flowers and balloons. Townspeople had been sending them by the dozens for days.

When he deposited them on a table, he reached over and tenderly brushed Hazel's cheek. "What's the latest news about our patient here? Still getting discharged today, I hope? Everybody's eager to see her."

"Yep. As soon as she wakes up. Her doctor stopped by early and gave her the all clear. A nurse just dropped off the paperwork. She made the mistake of saying again how lucky Hazel is. Seriously? She got *shot*. That's not exactly how I define lucky."

They both stood for a moment, silent sentinels on either side of Hazel's bed. When that gun went off, everybody else thought it was just another crack of lightning. But their eyes were on Hazel. They saw her hit the ground. They raced to her side, saw the blood, prayed for her to be okay.

"Believe me," Sena said, "the staff here won't say that again while I'm in earshot."

Knox reached across the bed and took Sena's hand. "I know she did it for you. Canceled that meeting. Challenged Sirus. Brought this whole thing to a head. I've never seen her more in love than she is with you." He let go and looked down at Hazel.

"But I think she did it mostly for all the rest of us. To wake us up."

He looked up at Sena, his expression both serious and sad. "We all see, now, how much work we need to do."

Sena nodded. She knew exactly how much work needed to be done by the people of Owen Station. Yes, Sirus was a bad guy. But too many people either lined up behind him or didn't move fast enough to stop him, because they owed him something, or because they were naïve and didn't want to believe something so ugly could exist in their town, or because they agreed with him. Owen Station needed a reckoning. She hated that Hazel had to get hurt for that to happen.

But it did seem to be happening.

The monsoons had cooled things off and something new was definitely in the air. Cleanup efforts at the library started immediately after the fire and hadn't stopped. Bexley and his congregants had organized it.

"How are things going at the library?" She hadn't left Hazel's bedside, just as she promised, so she was eager for news.

"Well, fortunately, our new assistant fire chief has figured out what happened. Allison and a couple of her firefighters were on the air with Walt this morning. Seems a current from the lightning strike got in through the phone box—because of course Hazel still had a land line. It jumped from there to the copper water pipes as it tried to find a clear path to ground. The whole thing would've burned to the ground if Allison and her guys hadn't gotten there so quickly—"

"And there wasn't so much rain," Sena added.

"Yeah, that, too. But the damage inside the library is pretty bad. Hazel is not going to be happy. All twelve of the vintage file cabinets that held the old card catalog were obliterated. They were her pride and joy. All that's left is the brass hardware. The huge mahogany tables, which have been in the research room for decades, are gone, too. I can still remember sitting at them myself, studying for exams, flirting with girls. I think I probably flirted with Hazel at one of those tables. You know, before we knew." He winked at Sena. "The fire never made it to the stacks, thank God, but everything on every floor is covered with ash. And everything smells like smoke."

Sena crossed her arms. "I heard Doc Adams is working on getting the library cleaned out."

"That's right. And I don't blame you for sounding skeptical after everything that happened. Doc's not exactly my favorite person right now, either. But she organized a group of ranchers to scoop out what couldn't be saved. They're filling up their pickups and hauling it all out to the dump on the edge of town. She's been telling everyone who will listen how wrong she was to go along with Sirus—they all were."

Sena wasn't sure she would ever trust that woman to go anywhere near Hazel again, even after she jumped in with emergency care at the library that day. It was going to take a while to heal the wounds that couldn't be seen.

"How are my Y ladies doing?" Sena was so proud of them. She'd connected them with Jorge and Miguel to organize food for all the volunteers.

"They've fallen head over heels for 'the boys,' as they're calling them, and they're using the tasting room as a staging location to serve lunch every day to whoever's on work detail. It's like a little love fest next door to my place."

So, side by side, long-time residents of Owen Station and the most recent newcomers were working together to fix what had been broken. Sena allowed herself to feel a little hopeful. The work ahead was likely to be more marathon than sprint.

Hazel's eyes were bright when she finally woke up again. "Sena, you're still here."

"Of course I am." Sena leaned over to kiss her. "Where else would I be."

Hazel grabbed Sena's hand. "We have a lot to talk about don't we? I want to talk—and listen—and learn. I want to do better—be better."

"We have plenty of time for that, Hazel. Right now the only thing that matters is you getting better."

Hazel turned toward Knox. She wanted details, which came as no surprise. "Knox! I'm glad you're here. I don't remember anything after Pastor Bexley's speech. Sena doesn't want to tell me about it."

"Of course I don't. I don't even want to think about it. I don't know why you do."

"Because she's Hazel." He turned to the happy patient and his face cracked into a grin.

"You're going to love this." He paused dramatically. "The bullet came from an antique Bisley 1895."

"The last model to carry the Colt Frontier designation? Are you kidding me? The six-shooter the Old West made famous? The one that starred at the O.K. Corral?"

Sena and Knox looked at each other across the bed. His eyes twinkled. "Only Hazel would be delighted by the gun that shot her."

"The struggle is real." Sena was not amused.

"But where in the world did it come from?" Hazel's curiosity was insatiable. "Who had it?"

"If you can believe this, Hazel, it was Angus Murphy. You know he's ninety-six now. The family moved his collection of guns out of the house long ago, worried about keeping him—and everybody else—safe. But he wouldn't be parted from his Bisley. It's been in the family for generations."

A cloud crossed Knox's face. The rest of the story, which Sena already knew, was worse.

"The family didn't know he had a box of ammo hidden in the back of his closet. When Angus heard about the protest, he said he did what he always does before leaving the house. He strapped on his holster and his loaded sidearm."

Knox stopped, his gaze wandering to some point off in the distance, jaw twitching. Sena knew exactly what he was seeing. That day on the library steps he swore he'd kill the person who did this to Hazel.

"And then what happened?"

Knox cleared his throat. "Well, it's not even clear that Angus knew what the protest was about, Hazel. You know, he's hard of hearing, so when he got to the library, he went up as close as he could get to the base of the stairs. When Chief Garcia interviewed him, back at the police station, he told her how impressed he was by that nice young preacher. By the time Bexley finished, Angus thought the protest was in *support* of welcoming newcomers to town, not the opposite."

He paused while Hazel absorbed it all.

"Elena is mortified by everything that happened, Hazel." Sena said.

Elena Murphy, Angus's granddaughter, was an artist, but had just moved back to Owen Station to help out with the business side of the family's mortuary and funeral home business. Sena had already tapped her for the committee that would be building out Owen Station's ecosystem for young women entrepreneurs.

"I know Elena. I bet she is."

"Angus wasn't aiming at you, Hazel," Knox added softly. "And he certainly didn't mean to hurt you. He just got startled and confused when he heard the crack of lightning and everyone around him dove for cover. He pulled out his weapon to stop the shooter he thought was on the loose. No one was more unprepared than he was when it went off in his hand. Chief Garcia, who had been scanning the crowd for any sign of trouble, saw Angus too late to stop him from firing the first time."

"Dana made damn sure he didn't fire again, though," Sena said.

Knox's mouth clicked shut and four eyes snapped in her direction. She dropped her head, looking away, but only for a moment. "You know what," she sniffed, straightening her shoulders, "I'm sorry not sorry, you two. I'm just so angry about all of this. I grew up hunting, learned to use a gun on my family's ranch, and frankly I'm a way better shot than either of my brothers. But the macho fascination with guns in this state repulses me. I just don't understand why someone needs to strap one on to go to the grocery store…or the library."

"She's not wrong, Hazel. We could have lost you."

"Knox, you could plant Sonoran wheat in those furrows on your forehead." Hazel wasn't exactly smiling, but she clearly wanted to lighten the mood. She looked up at Sena. "Please tell me Chief Dana didn't arrest him."

"Of course she did, Hazel. He *shot* you." Sena jutted her chin in the air, daring them to argue with her. "He's been charged with aggravated assault, a felony. The judge let him go home on bail, but he's going to have to answer for what he's done."

Hazel grimaced. "It sounds like it was an accident."

"That doesn't matter."

"Come here," Hazel said with a grin, pulling Sena close enough to plant a kiss. "You're very sexy when you're protective."

"You two are adorable. And I'll take that as my cue." Knox gave Hazel a peck on the forehead. "I'm so glad you're okay. Sena is taking care of your ride home today. I'll check in on you later."

When the door clicked shut, Hazel gave Sena a goofy wink. "Alone at last!"

That made Sena more tingly than she probably ought to have felt, given that her girlfriend had her arm in a sling because she just got shot.

"You shouldn't tease me like that, Hazel. You have that rumpled, I-just-spent-six-days in a hospital bed look that is so irresistible. I can't be blamed for anything that happens if we're left alone for too long."

Hazel chuckled as she stepped out of bed to pull on the clean clothes Delaney brought from home. When she looked wobbly, Sena steadied her. That nurse said she should expect to be a little dizzy for a while.

Hazel carefully lowered herself into the wheelchair for her grand exit. She had no idea how grand it would be.

"What about all the flowers?" She tipped her head backward to look at Sena, who was pushing her down the hallway toward the front door.

"Don't worry about it. We'll have lots of help getting them home."

"What do you mean?"

Two nurses jumped in front of them just then and swung open the big double glass doors with a flourish as the parking lot erupted in cheers. Horns were honking and a large pickup truck began blasting Katy Perry's victory anthem "Roar" as a dance party broke out right there in front of Owen Station Community Hospital. Mexican, American, and Rainbow flags were flying everywhere and people held signs shouting "Love Is Love" and "No Human Is Illegal!" Sena's little brothers, wearing their go-to-town boots, crisp white button-downs, and white Stetson hats to match, jumped out of a white F-350.

"Oh my God, Sena, are these knights in shining armor your brothers?"

Sena thought her heart might burst with joy.

Jesús scooped Hazel up like she was a kitten and gently placed her in the back seat. Sena hopped in beside her as a small army of volunteers filled the bed of the truck with flower pots, and vases and boxes of gifts that had been filling Hazel's hospital room.

"Time for a parade," Junior shouted as he stepped on the gas.

The whole honking, cheering, flag-waving town followed them, winding through the streets, beside the copper-colored hills, toward the historic district. When they got near Main Street, they could see the street had been set up for a festival. Colored lights and streamers had been hung and mariachis were playing. They smelled the food before they could see it.

"Sena, what in the world is happening? Did you have something to do with all of this?"

"Maybe," Sena said, smiling. "Everyone is so happy you are okay. Especially me."

"Well, I'm glad I'm okay, too. But this is embarrassing. I haven't done *anything* to deserve this."

"That's not true, Hazel. I know what you risked to do the right thing. My God. When I think that I could have *lost* you…"

Sena reached out and gently brought Hazel's hand to her lips for a kiss. "But to be honest, all of this is about more than you. Everybody's really trying to come together after what happened. They've been working nonstop to clean up after the fire. There have been serious conversations started about the history of this town. The mayor, to his credit, is helping make that happen. There are a whole lot of hard truths to be told and heard, wrongs that need to be righted, and it won't be easy or quick. But things are moving in a good direction. And today everyone just wants to—"

"Dance!" Jesús had already hopped out of the truck and was opening the door to pick Hazel up again. She put her hands out to stop him, laughing.

"I'm not sure I'm up to dancing quite yet, but I can walk, Jesús. Just help me climb down. This truck is a monster."

Sena scooted around to help and let Hazel take her arm as they began making their way up Main Street, which was already filling up with people. They waved to Pastor Bexley and Delaney, who were hurrying up the sidewalk toward them, holding hands.

"Okay, I haven't been in the hospital that long. When did *this* happen?" Hazel asked as Delaney gave her a big hug.

"Oh, honey, have I got stories to tell!"

Hazel turned to the pastor. "I don't even know what to say, Pastor Bex—"

"Please, Hazel. Call me Derrick."

"Okay, Derrick. I don't know what to say. You were amazing."

He hung his head. "I'm not amazing, Hazel. I'm ashamed. It took me way too long to call out what was happening. If I had done it sooner, maybe all this wouldn't have…maybe you wouldn't have been…maybe we…"

"Yes, you're right." Hazel's smile faded. "You should have stood up sooner. So should I."

Hazel turned to face Sena. Her jaw was set, her blue eyes clear. All around them, people ate and talked and laughed. Music played. But Sena didn't see anything else. And the only sound she heard was Hazel's voice.

"I know we have a lot to talk about and I have so much to learn. But I also know that I failed you—and I failed this town—when I refused to see what was really happening here, and took so long to do something about it. I'm sorry, Sena."

Sena hadn't realized how much she need to hear those words.

Hazel turned back to Bexley. "A lot of us should have stood up sooner, Derrick. We didn't. And we have to answer for that. But it won't help for us to get lost in guilt and shame. We have work to do. I need a day or two, but I'll be ready. I'm looking forward to working together with you on this."

"Me, too."

Derrick shot Hazel a grateful smile and then Delaney pulled him by the hand. "Let's go get some of those tamales. They smell orgasmic."

"You have no idea," Sena said, smiling, as she watched the couple turn and head up the street.

Then she leaned over and gave Hazel a gentle kiss. "I love you, you know."

"I love you, too, Sena. More than I can say."

"Okay, then! Junior and Jesús. We need some tamales. Lead the way!"

Her brothers gently pushed through the crowd, making a path so that no one accidentally bumped into Hazel. She was clearly in more pain than she was letting on. "We've got a table already reserved for you, Hazel, and a place where you can sit and rest."

They passed a dozen booths up and down the street. Sena waved at Tessa, who was sharing samples of her favorite wines in a booth right next to Lace, who was giving out free condoms. She was demonstrating how to use a dental dam to an older couple, a tall woman and one with a mess of purplish hair.

Hazel cried out in a surprising burst of energy. "Hey, Manda! Alex! Hi!" Both women waved wildly back.

Jorge and Miguel were offering tastings outside their shop and there was a line half a block long, already. The mayor and town council were in a listening tent, taking suggestions about how to make local government more inclusive. Owenites of all kinds were adding their own words and drawings to help tell the history of this quirky little town on a giant canvas the museum had set up in the park.

The food tables were at the top of the street. Sena's brothers led them to the one with the longest line and spun around to the back of the table.

"Mom!" They both shouted as Junior picked her up and spun her around. She was wearing an apron of course and holding a giant spoon, which she used to whack both the boys.

"Mom, stop! We're here for some of your tamales and beans!"

Her laughter was like the sound of birds splashing in the flowing water of the Santa Cruz after the monsoons have come.

"Put me down, you silly boys!"

Sena gently steered Hazel around the table to meet her mother, who slowly put down her spoon and wiped her hands on her apron. Somehow she managed to enfold Hazel in a warm embrace carefully, without touching her injured arm, and held her tight. When she finally let go, there were tears in her eyes.

"Sweet girl. This daughter of mine is softer than she looks. Take good care of her heart, okay?"

Hazel nodded solemnly. "I will."

Sena's father arrived, carrying more trays of food.

"Dad, this is Hazel," she said formally. "Hazel, this is my dad."

He set down the load. Then he put one hand on Sena's shoulder, and one hand on Hazel's, so that he could see them both side by side. He looked deep into Hazel's eyes, first. Then he looked at Sena.

"Alegre." The word hung in the air, a statement of fact, a prayer of thanksgiving, a blessing. "You look happy, Sena."

"I am, Dad."

"Well, then, I just have one thing to say to you, Hazel." A smile the size of Sena's heart stretched across his face.

"Welcome to the family."

EPILOGUE

SIX MONTHS LATER

Hazel's physical therapist said she'd never had a patient who worked harder, and Hazel was back to normal in no time. Repairs to the library, however, took what seemed like forever, in spite of countless volunteer hours.

Hazel made sure repairs to the structure met historical guidelines—Owen Station's library was on the National Register of Historic Places, after all. But she also wrote grants and raised private dollars to introduce new services, integrate new technology, and make infrastructure upgrades to reduce the library's carbon footprint.

The town was excited for the Grand Re-opening, which was scheduled for right after the first of the year. But first, the building had to pass a series of final inspections. When Assistant Fire Chief Allison Jones stopped in to do the final fire safety check, Hazel was there with Sena, Lace and Tessa.

"You seem to have healed up nicely, Hazel," the chief said.

"Well, happiness is the best medicine, right, Chief? And I've never seen her happier." Lace grinned and gave Sena a friendly punch in the arm. "Love'll do that to you."

"She's not the only happy one in this picture." Sena grinned back as she put her arm around Hazel.

"I see that." The chief looked at Sena. "Things are going well for you, too, I take it?"

"They are great, actually. Things are moving a little more slowly than I'd like with the old downtown development…"

"That's because you have a committee for everything, Sena." Hazel smiled.

"And *that* is why it's all going to be so successful," Tessa added.

Sena nodded. "That's what I'm hoping. In the meantime, I'm having so much fun working with Knox to transform the Goldstar building, where Banter & Brew is located. Before Sirus left town…"

"Good riddance." Lace and Tessa said in unison. They looked at each other and then at the group.

"We do that all the time," they both said at the same time. Then they started laughing.

Lace swore there was nothing but friendship between them, but Hazel and Knox had a secret bet going. Hazel wanted all of her friends to be as happy as she was.

"As I was saying," Sena continued, "the old bastard made an offer Knox and I couldn't refuse on the Goldstar. We bought it together and we're turning it into an incubator for small businesses."

Hazel jumped in. "And I'm working on building a digital collection of workshops on how to start and grow a small business to support the entrepreneurs who will be moving in. I've asked Lace and Tessa to put the first few together and we'll record them here at the library."

"Any chance you'll be offering a workshop on using social media for your business?" Chief Jones asked.

Hazel nodded. "Have you got a new business we don't know about?"

The chief smiled conspiratorially. "Well, not exactly. But maybe you've heard that I've started a new band? All women—all first-responders."

"I did hear that! Tell us about it."

"I'm on lead vocals and guitar." She smiled sheepishly. "And Chief Garcia is on drums and percussion. The rest of the band is still coming together, but we are having so much fun. It's like living out a teenage fantasy. We're calling ourselves the Fireballs. But we need help with branding and marketing."

"You got it!" Lace and Tessa said at the same time.

They were ridiculously adorable.

Everyone was excited and peppered the chief with questions. Before she left, Tessa had the band booked for the next Bud Break Bash—the big festival she hosted out at the vineyard every year.

Hazel had never felt more alive.

The next day she was at home in the kitchen, sitting cross-legged on the floor, surrounded by half-filled boxes, when Sena popped in the back door.

"From the looks of it, I'm hoping you've decided to move in with me, after all."

"Not everyone moves as fast as you do, my dear." Hazel turned her face up to let Sena plant a kiss on her smiling lips. "But you better believe that when I do, I'm bringing all the things. You'll have to add on an extra room just for my collection of forty-fives."

"Forty-fives? Oh, right, those are…what are those things called again…little tiny records?"

Hazel stuck her tongue out and laughed.

"Seriously, though, how's it going? What's it feel like to go through all of these family heirlooms?"

"And junk. Let's be honest. A lot of it is junk."

"And junk," Sena agreed cheerily. "I bet it's bringing back a lot of memories."

"Yes, lots of memories." Hazel rolled her eyes. "Take this, for example." She lifted a scratched up frying pan with a broken handle out of the box in front of her. "I think my grandma used S&H stamps to buy this whole set of pans at the grocery store the year she got married, along with these ugly plastic dishes."

"S&H *what*, now?"

"*Stamps*. They were used for like a hundred years, until the 1980s, like a reward program, for buying things. Anyway, my memory of these pans and dishes is how nobody ever used them. But they were all crammed into the cabinets, which made it impossible to find what you were actually looking for. I can't tell you what a great metaphor that is for my family—and my life. Stuffed so full of old crap, you can't do the things you want to do in the present."

She pushed her glasses up on her nose and ran her fingers through her hair. "I come by my crazy honestly, Sena."

Sena reached down and tugged Hazel's ear. "Ha. We all do, my love. We all do."

"Oh!" Hazel leapt up off the floor, nearly knocking Sena backward over a box marked *Random*. "I almost forgot. Look what I found this morning!"

She reached behind Sena for a professionally matted photograph that was sitting on the counter, and held it up for both of them to see. The name HORACE MCGEE—the photographer—was etched into the corner, along with the words NOGALES, ARIZONA. It was yellowed around three edges.

"See the purple-brownish hue?" Hazel's words tumbled out. "I'm pretty sure this is an albumen print, probably from the late 1800s. Albumen prints eventually replaced salt prints, which were popular at the time. They actually coated the paper with egg whites in the development process so that—"

Sena put a firm finger on Hazel's chin and brought her face around so that Hazel had to look at *her*—although she did manage to keep a single eye on the photo. Sena pressed the other finger against her own lips, a smile dancing at the corners of her mouth, sending a clear message.

"Hazel. Forget the history lesson, for a minute, will you please? Who *is* this in the picture? She looks Mexican."

A tall young woman with a large basket of flowers at her feet stared out of the picture at them, a long ribbon draped around her shoulders, something that looked like a tightly scrolled diploma in her hand, a large bow atop her head—and a silver brooch with a pearl inset at her neck.

Hazel leaned against Sena's shoulder and they both stood staring at the face in the photo, expectation swirling in the air.

"That brooch…who *is* this?" Sena asked this time in a whisper.

"Well, I wasn't sure at first. I found it in a shoebox, next to a bunch of other shoeboxes, all filled with old photos, in the back of the hall closet. It looks like a high school graduation picture, which would have been a little unusual for a girl from Nogales in those days, unless her family was well-off. She doesn't look like any relative I've ever seen. But I noticed the brooch right away, of course, and then I saw…" She slowly turned the matted photo over.

"*Celestina.*" The name swooshed across and seemed to linger on Sena's tongue.

"Celestina," Hazel repeated decisively.

Sena turned toward Hazel, questions and wonderment dancing in her wide eyes. Hazel had shared her great-grandmother's letters with Sena. They sat reading them together for hours one rainy Saturday as Hazel recuperated.

"Do you think this is *C*…from Hazel-the-first's letters?"

Hazel didn't make guesses. If historical facts couldn't be proven with multiple pieces of evidence, they weren't facts. Somehow, though, this didn't feel like a guess. She nodded. "Yes, I think we can say with certainty that this is my great-grandmother's friend, and based on those letters, her lover. The mysterious *C.*"

Sena put her arm around Hazel's shoulders and squeezed tight, sending tingles straight down her spine, through her groin, and down to her knees. "I'm going to have this photo framed and hung in my hallway." Hazel tipped her chin up and gave Sena a soft kiss on the cheek. "As far as I'm concerned," she breathed into Sena's ear, "she's family."

Sena's lips found hers and Hazel let herself be devoured as Sena sucked and probed, searching for her tongue. One hand reached for Hazel's breast as the other slid down Hazel's back to her ass…

"Wait!" Hazel came up for air, still holding the matted photo. Sena's flushed cheeks and startled expression made her feel a little bad. But… "Speaking of family, I have another surprise for you."

She grabbed Sena's hand and quickly led her into the second bedroom, which she had converted into an office—with a brand new computer—before Sena recovered enough to resist.

"This better be good," Sena said, chuckling. But her laughter turned into a squeal when she spotted the box in the corner of the room and heard the sound of…

"Kittens! Oh my gosh, Hazel. Where did these adorable little things come from?"

Sena was on her knees in seconds, gently caressing the two tiny, furry creatures, who looked about ten weeks old. They were loving every second of it, playfully clambering over each other, emitting the sweetest little meows.

"Last night as I was getting ready for bed, I heard scratching at the back door. I thought maybe it was Mango, coming home." The cat had been missing since Sena brought Hazel home from the hospital. "I got there as quickly as I could, but when I opened the door, there was no sign of her. Nothing. In fact, I thought maybe I just imagined it. Then, as I was turning around to come back in the house, I heard these little guys very softly meowing. They were tucked safely into a corner, right by the fireplace, all snuggled up together."

"Oh my God. Where do you think they came from?"

"Well, I don't know, obviously. But I think it must have been Mango. I mean, look at this one." Hazel picked up the little orange tabby. "It looks just like her."

Sena stood up and gave Hazel a kiss. "Do they have names? What are you going to call them?"

"I haven't decided yet. I'm thinking I'll call the orange tabby Vintage and this little gray and white striped one Vogue."

"Vintage and Vogue." Sena turned to Hazel with a smile the size of Gold Gulch. "I love it."

Windows were open throughout the house, letting in the crisp mountain air. "Come see what else I've done." Hazel led Sena from the office down the hall. The heavy Chippendale dining set was gone, replaced by a fun mid-century modern table and chairs—the table was glossy white and the matching white chairs had purple cushions. It would have made Mom happy.

"I hated that old dining set. Hazel-the-first hated it. And now that I've put the pieces together, it feels like a tragic reminder that there is no substitute for true love. So I sold it to that couple from Scottsdale who stayed here over Thanksgiving. Remember them? They fell in love with it. I would have taken half as much as they paid me. I had no idea it was worth so much, Sena—you should have told me! I made enough money on that sale to buy a bunch of new things *and* make a donation to the women's shelter you started."

"I love it, Hazel. You look more and more like yourself every day. And what you're doing with this house is beautiful."

Hazel laughed. "Yeah, based on my design sensibility, it looks like maybe I've made it all the way to the middle of the twentieth century."

"It looks good on you, Hazel. Also, mid-century modern is very much in vogue right now. If you're not careful, people will start calling you a trendsetter."

"Funny. If you believe that, I've got a 1914 Underwood to sell you."

"I'm not interested in an Underwood, whatever the heck that is. But I am interested in removing your underwear. How about you show me what you've done in the bedroom."

Hazel beamed with delight and took Sena by the hand, leading her back down the hallway.

"This is new." Sena gasped as Hazel opened the door to her bedroom with a dramatic flourish. "I like."

Hazel had relocated the handmade coverlet to the casita and replaced it with a luscious down comforter, gray linen sheets, and eggplant colored throw pillows. And the wedding photos had all been moved to another room. Hazel loved her family and she would carry them with her forever. But she was ready to live her own life, on her own terms.

"You've been busy." Sena seemed genuinely impressed with how much Hazel had accomplished and how quickly. "I'm learning that, when you want something, you can move really fast to get it done."

"Really? You're just learning that now? How long, exactly, did it take between the time you sauntered into Banter & Brew, in your fancy red-soled shoes, and I was stripping your clothes off in my casita?"

"Wait a minute! That was me stripping your clothes off!"

"Okay, okay. I guess it was all very mutual. But, for real. I wanted you the moment I saw you, Sena. I have never wanted anything or anyone more. I am so thankful for this. For you."

"I feel the same way, Hazel. Never in my wildest dreams did I think I would find this in Owen Station."

"Did you ever dream you'd find a redhead? Anywhere?"

"Not in a million years." Sena's laughter was as sweet as star jasmine in the springtime air.

"I'm thankful you have such an open mind."

"Oh, I'm open, alright. And wet."

Sena pulled her down on the bed and covered her with kisses.

Hazel wasn't stuck in the past anymore. She wasn't in a hurry to get to the future, either.

She was right here. Right now.

And there was no place she'd rather be.

About the Authors

Writing duo Kelly and Tana Fireside love traveling, cooking great food, and making music around a campfire. They've been best friends for more than twenty-five years and are still madly in love after sixteen years of marriage. It took them a long time to find their way to each other, and now they're never letting go. After working for many years in public and community service, they are writing stories to help spark a revolutionary love of self and others. They split their time between Sonora, Mexico, and traveling across North America in Howie (their House On Wheels) with a frisky pup named Gabby and her best friend, Chip the cat.

Books Available from Bold Strokes Books

A Degree to Die For by Karis Walsh. A murder at the University of Washington's Classics Department brings Professor Antigone Weston and Sergeant Adriana Kent together—first as opposing forces, and then allies as they fight together to protect their campus from a killer. (978-1-63679-365-8)

A Talent Within by Suzanne Lenoir. Evelyne, born into nobility, and Annika, a peasant girl with a deadly secret, struggle to change their destinies in Valmora, a medieval world controlled by religion, magic, and men. (978-1-63679-423-5)

Finders Keepers by Radclyffe. Roman Ashcroft's past, it seems, is not so easily forgotten when fate brings her and Tally Dewilde together—along with an attraction neither welcomes. (978-1-63679-428-0)

Homeland by Kristin Keppler and Allisa Bahney. Dani and Kate have finally found themselves on the same side of the war, but a new threat from the inside jeopardizes the future of the wasteland. (978-1-63679-405-1)

Just One Dance by Jenny Frame. Will Taylor Spark and her new business to make dating special—the Regency Romance Club—bring sparkle back to Jaq Bailey's lonely world? (978-1-63679-457-0)

On My Way There by Jaycie Morrison. As Max traverses the open road, her journey of impossible love, loss, and courage mirrors her voyage of self-discovery leading to the ultimate question: If she can't have the woman of her dreams, will the woman of real life be enough? (978-1-63679-392-4)

Transitioning Home by Heather K O'Malley. An injured soldier realizes they need to transition to really heal. (978-1-63679-424-2)

Truly Enough by JJ Hale. Chasing the spark of creativity may ignite a burning romance or send a friendship up in flames. (978-1-63679-442-6)

Vintage and Vogue by Kelly and Tana Fireside. When tech whiz Sena Abrigo marches into small-town Owen Station, she turns librarian Hazel Butler's life upside down in the most wonderful of ways, setting off an explosive series of events, threatening their chance at love…and their very lives. (978-1-63679-448-8)

Broken Fences by Jo Hemmingwood. Former army sergeant Seneca Twist has difficulty adjusting to civilian life until she meets psychologist Robyn Mason and has a place to call home. (978-1-63679-414-3)

Never Kiss a Cowgirl by Ali Vali. Asher Evans dreams of winning the National Finals Rodeo in Vegas, and Reagan Wilson wants no part of something that brings back the memory of what killed her father. (978-1-63679-106-7)

Pantheon Girls by Jean Copeland. Cassie Burke never anticipated the detour life was about to take when a meeting with a prospective client reunites her with a past love and reignites the star-crossed passion they shared twenty years earlier. (978-1-63679-337-5)

Roux for Two by Aurora Rey. For TV chef Chelsea Boudreaux and hometown boy Bryce Cormier, love proves as tricky as making a good pot of gumbo. (978-1-63679-376-4)

Starting Over by Nance Sparks. Jennifer has no idea if she can mend Sam's broken soul after the sudden loss of her wife, but it's never too late for starting over. (978-1-63679-409-9)

The Accidental Bride by Jane Walsh. Spinsters Miss Grace Linfield and Miss Thea Martin travel to Gretna Green to prevent a wedding, only to discover a scandalous passion—for each other. (978-1-63679-345-0)

Three Wishes by Anne Shade. A magic lamp, a beautiful Jinni, and a cursed princess make for one unbelievable story. (978-1-63679-349-8)

Undiscovered Treasures by MJ Williamz. For Cyl and her friends Luna and Martinique, life's best treasures often appear when you're not looking. (978-1-63679-449-5)

Curse of the Gorgon by Tanai Walker. Cass will do anything to ensure Elle's safety, but is she willing to embrace the curse of the Gorgon? (978-1-63679-395-5)

Dance with Me by Georgia Beers. Scottie Templeton mixes it up on and off the dance floor with sexy salsa instructor Marisa Reyes. But can Scottie get past Marisa's connection to her ex? (978-1-63679-359-7)

Gin and Bear It by Joy Argento. Opposites really can attract, and as Kelly and Logan work together to create a loving home for rescue cat Bear, they just might find one for themselves as well. (978-1-63679-351-1)

Harvest Dreams by Jacqueline Fein-Zachary. Planting the vineyard of their dreams, Kate Bauer and Sydney Barrett must resist their attraction while battling nature and their families, who oppose both the venture and their relationship. (978-1-63679-380-1)

The No Kiss Contract by Nan Campbell. Workaholic Davy believes she can get the top spot at her firm if the senior partners think she's settling down and about to start a family, but she needs the delightful yet dubious Anna to help by pretending to be her fiancée. (978-1-63679-372-6)

Outside the Lines by Melissa Sky. If you had the chance to live forever, would you take it? Amara Rodriguez did, and it sets her on a journey to find her missing mother and unravel the mystery of her own heart. (978-1-63679-403-7)

The Value of Sylver and Gold by Michelle Larkin. When word gets out that former Boston homicide detective Reid Sylver can talk to the dead, the FBI solicits her help on a serial murder case, prompting Reid to assemble forces once again with Detective London Gold. (978-1-63679-093-0)

When It Feels Right by Tagan Shepard. Freshly out of the closet Marlene hasn't been lucky in love, but when it comes to her quirky new roommate Abby, everything just feels right. (978-1-63679-367-2)

Lucky in Lace by Melissa Brayden. Straitlaced stationery store owner Juliette Jennings's predictable life unravels when a sexy lingerie shop and its alluring owner move in next door. (978-1-63679-434-1)

Made for Her by Carsen Taite. Neal Walsh is a newly made member of the Mancuso crime family, but will her undeniable attraction to Anastasia Petrov, the wife of her boss's sworn enemy, be the ultimate test of her loyalty? (978-1-63679-265-1)

Off the Menu by Alaina Erdell. Reality TV sensation Restaurant Redo and its gorgeous host Erin Rasmussen will arrive to film in chef Taylor Mobley's kitchen. As the cameras roll, will they make the jump from enemies to lovers? (978-1-63679-295-8)

Pack of Her Own by Elena Abbott. When things heat up in a small town, steamy secrets are revealed between Alpha werewolf Wren Carne and her human mate, Natalie Donovan. (978-1-63679-370-2)

Return to McCall by Patricia Evans. Lily isn't looking for romance—not until she meets Alex, the gorgeous Cuban dance instructor at La Haven, a newly opened lesbian retreat. (978-1-63679-386-3)

So It Went Like This by C. Spencer. A candid and deeply personal exploration of fate, chosen family, and the vulnerability intrinsic in life's uncertainties. (978-1-63555-971-2)

Stolen Kiss by Spencer Greene. Anna and Louise share a stolen kiss, only to discover that Louise is dating Anna's brother. Surely, one kiss can't change everything...Can it? (978-1-63679-364-1)

The Fall Line by Kelly Wacker. When Jordan Burroughs arrives in the Deep South to paint a local endangered aquatic flower, she doesn't expect to become friends with a mischievous gin-drinking ghost who complicates her budding romance and leads her to an awful discovery and danger. (978-1-63679-205-7)

To Meet Again by Kadyan. When the stark reality of WWII separates cabaret singer Evelyn and Australian doctor Joan in Singapore, they must overcome all odds to find one another again. (978-1-63679-398-6)